Tinsel, Trials, & Traitors

Mary Seifert

Books by Mary Seifert

Maverick, Movies, & Murder
Rescue, Rogues, & Renegade
Tinsel, Trials, & Traitors

Visit Mary's website and get a free recipe collection!
Scan the QR code

Tinsel, Trials, & Traitors

Katie & Maverick Cozy Mysteries, Book 3

Mary Seifert

Secret Staircase Books

Tinsel, Trials, & Traitors
Published by Secret Staircase Books, an imprint of
Columbine Publishing Group, LLC
PO Box 416, Angel Fire, NM 87710

Book layout and design by Secret Staircase Books
Cover images © Robertas Pezas, Kathryn Thomas, Bestvc, Patrick
Marcel Pelz, Smileus, Subbotina

First trade paperback edition: August, 2022
First e-book edition: August, 2022
* * *

Publisher's Cataloging-in-Publication Data
Seifert, Mary
Tinsel, Trials, & Traitors / by Mary Seifert.
p. cm.
ISBN 978-1649141002 (paperback)
ISBN 978-1649141019 (e-book)

1. Katie Wilk (Fictitious character). 2. Minnesota—Fiction. 3.
Amateur sleuths—Fiction. 4. Women sleuths—Fiction. 5. Dogs in
fiction. I. Title

Katie & Maverick Cozy Mystery Series : Book 3.
Siefert, Mary, Katie & Maverick cozy mysteries.

BISAC : FICTION / Mystery & Detective.

813/.54

In honor of all the attorneys in our family…

ACKNOWLEDGEMENTS

I am lucky to have found a home for the stories of Katie Wilk and Maverick and want to extend my unending gratitude to Stephanie Dewey and Lee Ellison for their help making this extraordinary experience a reality. Thank you to those dear to my heart who have provided encouragement, answers, unfailing support, and advice along the way: my family—John, Kindra, Adam, Charles, Danica, Mitch, Thomas, Jack, and Leo—I couldn't have done it without you; my readers and cheerleaders Colleen Okland, Jenifer Leitch, Evy Hatjistilianos, Brigid Fitzgerald, Jacinta Carlson, and Mary Gruber; my book buddies— Sandra Unger, Dr. Joan Christianson, Dr. Amy Ellingson, Eve Blomquist, and Maria Hughes; tech support from John Piotrowski and Tucker Piotrowski, to the beta readers I have yet to meet and thank, and anyone else I may have forgotten—you know who you are.

I am grateful to all who take time to read.

"I know that he often said that music is a better weapon
for stopping disorder than anything on earth."
—*John S. Carr (said of Wallace Hartley)*

"The first thing we do, let's kill all the lawyers."
—*William Shakespeare*

CHAPTER ONE

A relaxing walk normally cleared my head and gave me time to refresh at the end of a long week teaching high school math, but my sixty-five-pound Labrador retriever had other ideas.

"Maverick, please," I said through clenched teeth. He pulled me from one odiferous plant to another and the leash squeezed my fingers. My shoulder ached, but he wouldn't slow down.

The walk was good exercise and also satisfied the conditions of our training assignment. As a brand-new probationary team belonging to our local search-and-rescue crew, the coordinator expected Maverick and me to practice—seeking, finding, sniffing, communicating, and signaling. Maverick had the sniffing down pat—tree trunks, fire hydrants, tufts of grass, garbage cans, and unsuspecting crotches. However, he knew the residential blocks around our apartment rather too well, so I expanded our training ground to include the commercial blocks outside of our familiar home-base perimeter, providing different scents which he took every opportunity to investigate. You never knew when or where someone might need finding.

Maverick had inherited a predisposition for locating people and in our first three months in Columbia, Minnesota, he'd found more than I'd bargained for, including four superior friends, one grand landlady, four lost children, and three dead bodies.

He also could find every savory treat within a three-mile radius and we probably needed to change our training route again.

Maverick dragged me toward the neon beacon flashing the word "open," and the rich, warm coffee scent finished reeling me in. I tugged a black stainless-steel thermal cup from my backpack and ordered a chai tea. While I waited, the yogurt-dipped biscuit the barista offered Maverick disappeared in a spray of slobber.

"What's up, Kindra? No smart comebacks today?" I asked.

Kindra, a student in one of my math classes, always found it hilarious that I walked through the drive-up window. However, I tipped well enough so she never took the teasing too far.

She leaned out on her elbows and filled the take-out window. She shook her head, and staring at Maverick, said, "Who's that old lady with ya, handsome? Is that you, Ms. Wilk?"

Okay, she was back, but I searched her face. "Are you

still bothered by what happened yesterday?"

She chuckled. "That's right. You missed the fight." She looked down at her hands. "No, it's not that. It's my little sister." She looked up and forced a smile. "She isn't getting along all that well at her school so she's coming back to Columbia." I cocked my head in a question and she added, "Nothing bad. I just hope everything goes better for her here."

My eyebrows raised. We usually didn't exchange so many words.

"I mean with more than just me and my mom." Kindra sighed. "Patricia has a bit of a chip on her shoulder. I can't blame her though. I would too. She lost her hearing a few years ago and we thought it might come back, but it doesn't look like it will. Mom thought this school would be a good fit for her. She reads lips well, but I wanted to do something special for her." She grinned. "I'm learning to sign."

"Can you teach me to ask for my tea?"

Kindra brightened and flashed her hands. I thought I copied her actions well, but she giggled. She repeated her movements more slowly. Finally satisfied with my imitation, she handed me my cup, and touched the tips of her fingers to her lips and dropped her hand. She mouthed the words, "Thank you," as a car pulled into the drive-through and tooted its horn. Maverick and I stepped out of the way.

The coffee shop sat juxtaposed in a block of office buildings housing accountants, lawyers, dentists, and bankers next to the steel-sided warehouses in the industrial park, and provided the perfect location for lunches or break-times. I sat and tapped a rhythm on the glass-topped table under a red-and-yellow umbrella. I sipped my chai, and sadly noted the clouds gathering and the temperature plummeting. Maverick lazed under the table, and I cherished the canine legacy my husband left me after his death.

I slurped the last of my tea and stowed my cup, and Maverick and I started down the sidewalk toward Main Street. With only one block to go, Maverick halted in front of a fenced-in storage facility. No manner of cueing, coaxing, or bribery elicited a move on his part until the mesh gate growled open, and a dark sedan with tinted windows spun onto the street. Before the gate rolled closed, Maverick raced inside.

"Wait, Maverick," I begged. "Stop, Maverick. Stop." I deeply regretted wrapping the leash around my wrist and tripped along behind him.

He bolted to the opposite end of the facility as the access snapped closed and trapped us inside a nine-foot-high barricade. Maverick jerked me along until he reached the unit farthest from the entrance. He sat in front of the door and howled.

"Maverick."

Maverick pulled the leash taut.

I reached for my cellphone and remembered I'd plugged it into the charger before our walk.

"Quiet, Maverick," I said in a forced whisper. Then, I rethought my request. His howling might be a good idea, but as soon as I'd accepted that it might attract help, he ceased his baying and began pawing at the door.

His scratches marred the wood frame, and I strained at the leash. Maverick pulled back in response, clearly the stronger of the two of us.

"Maverick, no." Sweat dribbled down my back. We needed to work on our communication skills.

He stopped pawing and plopped down as two police cars squealed onto the entrance ramp with flashing lights and wailing sirens. After pulling in front of the keypad, one driver punched a code into the security lockbox. The door slid back and both cars bounced onto the lot straight at us.

I smiled so hard my cheeks hurt until the cars came to a halt and the doors on both sides of the cars flapped open like pairs of wings. The flock of officers took a protected stance and drew their weapons with a bead on me.

I unwound the leash, raised my hands, and squelched my smile.

Maverick howled again.

Temporary Police Chief Ronnie Christianson frowned and shook his head as he holstered his weapon and waved off the other patrolmen. The officers of one car dropped inside and slammed their doors. The car spun around, and only stopped long enough to enter a code in the lockbox before speeding out of the yard.

"You set off the silent alarms, Katie."

His partner fiddled with the lockbox and the *silent alarms* screamed. He gave an apologetic look and continued to experiment.

"What are you doing here?" At least that is what I thought Ronnie said over the now deafening blare. I'd met Ronnie on more than one occasion. None of them had been social calls.

I gulped. "Maverick and I were walking." I tried to figure out why I was here too. The sound of the siren changed to an annoying series of beeps. Ronnie's left eyebrow rose.

I read his lips. "How'd you get in here?" Using the international symbol for cut, he pantomimed a slice across his throat for his partner to silence the siren and waited.

I knelt to calm Maverick, and he stopped yowling. When the siren was just an echo in my head, I finished my answer. "Maverick managed to sneak in before the gate closed and he dragged me with him." My mouth was dry and I swallowed hard.

His partner set a laptop on the hood of their car, giving me the evil eye. Ronnie peered over his shoulder, shaking his head. Maverick turned back toward the door and barked. I wished I understood canine-speak.

"Please, Maverick." I tugged him away from the door. His barking stopped. I knelt next to him and scratched behind his ears. "It's been a long day."

Ronnie hitched up his trousers and tried to hold back a snicker. "We've spent the last six hours in traffic court. It's been a long day for us too."

As he neared us, he put out his hand. Maverick clamped his mouth around Ronnie's cuff and pulled, erasing the grin just beginning to form at the corners of his mouth.

"Maverick!" I said.

Before Ronnie toppled, Maverick released him.

Startled, Ronnie took a step back, then stopped. "Do you smell that?" he asked.

I sniffed daintily. I had no idea what to expect, but just when I thought I caught a whiff of something, it wafted away. I heard, however, the purr of an engine.

"It's exhaust," Ronnie said. He pulled on the garage door handle but it didn't move. He turned to his partner, and said in a rush, "Jake, get me a crowbar."

"Should we call it in, Ronnie?" Jake asked with too much eagerness.

"Yeah, but first, bring me the Halligan," Ronnie ordered.

He jammed the tool under the door and when Ronnie pried enough space, he tossed the crowbar and heaved the door up and out of the way. Waves of cloying fumes billowed out of the storage unit. Throwing his arm over his nose and mouth, he plunged through a haze so thick it distorted my vision. He peered into the driver's door of a bright red BMW. He banged on the door and wrenched the handle. He disappeared and returned, holding what looked like a rake, and swung at the driver's window. Nothing happened. He swung again and dropped to one knee. Maverick tore from my grasp and raced inside. I took one step forward and was spurned by the dense, hot air.

I grabbed a ragged breath. "Ronnie," I called. I coughed and staggered against the door rail. The wood panels dislodged and slammed down in front of me, settling into the water-resistant groove at the bottom. "Maverick," I screamed.

I pulled at the handle and rammed my shoulder against the door. It wouldn't budge. I banged on the wood. The suffocating smoke burned my nose. Jake dropped next to me and thrust the crowbar under the door creating a narrow opening at the bottom. I shoved my fingers underneath and yanked with all my might. The pry bar clanged to the pavement and Jake joined me in raising the door. When it retracted, it sent sparks flying. He raced inside.

Before I could take another step forward, an enormous whoosh blasted my face. It took seconds, but it felt like forever. Tongues of fire licked the air as the two men stumbled through the smoke and out of the blazing garage. Ronnie's left arm hung over Jake's shoulder; Maverick pulled at a pant leg.

I grabbed Ronnie's other arm and wrapped it around

my shoulder. Together we dragged him to the squad car and steered him into the passenger seat. I pulled at the collar of his shirt, unbuttoning the top two buttons as he gasped.

"Sophie Grainger's in there." He panted, helpless, unable to lift himself to return to the garage reeking with noxious vapor.

Maverick stood in front of the unit and barked, sharp and shrill yelps. He bounded back to me and circled, his sign to follow. Jake and I stepped toward the garage, and an explosion pounded the air around us and the ground shifted. We fell behind the car doors, shielded from flying wood, metal, and glass.

"The fuel," Ronnie said, panting.

CHAPTER TWO

Three firetrucks burst onto the property minutes after the explosion sent slate siding, shingles, splinters, and glass shards soaring. Firefighters hooked up to the hydrants, and silver rivulets ran into the street from the flood of water poured onto the flames. Squad cars circled the storage facility and blocked the growing number of unit renters drawn by indecipherable smoke signals, demanding to know if their stored belongings made it through the blaze. The air was thick with acrid smoke and deeply unhappy vibes.

Ronnie recovered enough to speak to the manager of the facility, a short, wiry man who tore at his sparse red hair, repeatedly clasping his hands behind his head. I stood too close not to overhear their conversation.

"Man, she was such a nice lady. What happened?"

Ronnie said, "That's what we're trying to find out. Can you tell me how long Mrs. Grainger rented this unit?"

"'bout four months, I think. I'd hafta check the records in the office but you guys have that all blocked off."

"We can look at the records now. I need contact information." Stepping toward a small rectangular building, they veered off track when a firefighter staggered onto the miniscule parcel of lawn in front of them, ripped off his facemask, and retched.

"Jeezuzz, Craig. Get outta here. You'll contaminate the whole scene," said Ronnie.

The man's shoulders convulsed as though he was going to heave again. Instead, he sucked in a stream of semi-clean air and stood, rolling his shoulders before heading behind the trucks.

I dusted gray ash from Maverick's coat, and my nose turned up at the smell of singed hair. I swiped at the grime but didn't find any injuries. We retreated to the wall. From my vantage point, I could see anyone who drove in or out, and we were still standing there when the county coroner van pulled up to the officer guarding the lockbox. The window rolled down and the driver displayed his credentials.

I hadn't seen Dr. Pete Erickson in two whole weeks. We'd enjoyed spending time together until he'd been awarded a primo position in a pilot fellowship program designed to elevate medical practice in outstate Minnesota. With the advent of tele-health, computer and communication technologies provided opportunities to increase knowledge, diagnostics, treatment delivery, and care of patients. That's what he said, anyway. In addition to his ER position at our hospital, for three weekends of the month he worked in Minneapolis. He hadn't gone alone, and it felt like he was avoiding me.

When the door of the black Ford opened, I took a step back as the lithe drink-of-water unfolded his long-limbed frame and stood, glancing my way with recognition and the hint of a rakish smile. I could also tell the moment he understood the significance of my presence. He shook his head in disbelief. It wasn't the first time I'd been found at the scene with a dead body.

Then the passenger door opened and out slithered Nurse Susie Kelton, his right-hand, his trusted helper, his indispensable, reliable assistant, and his partner in the fellowship. They'd dated in the past and though he might not have a clue, she still had the hots for him. I had to admit the medical synergy between them impressed me. I'd seen them work in tandem, saving a young girl's life, and I couldn't have been more awestruck by their teamwork. And yet…

Tall-dark-and-handsome stood in front of me. "Katie, tell me it isn't so."

"Hello to you too."

His hand cupped my shoulder. Maverick nudged Pete's other hand for a scratch. True to form, Pete gave it. Maverick melted into Pete's knee.

"I've missed—" he began.

"Doc. Glad you're here," said Ronnie, striding up the incline.

"What do we have, Ronnie?"

"An apparent suicide."

I inhaled sharply.

When Ronnie and Pete stepped out of earshot, I

dropped to my knees. Maverick licked my face. I guess there might have been tears there.

"Ms. Wilk? Katie?" Officer Jake sounded like he was twelve. "You're free to leave. The gate is locked open." He offered me a hand up. I swiped at my eyes and brushed imaginary dust from my knees. "Just so you know, the video corroborated your story." He reached out and scratched behind Maverick's ear. "He's quite a dog, this one."

"Yes, he is."

"Do you need a ride home?"

"No, thanks." *Now I really needed to clear my head.*

Traipsing past the deserted commercial buildings no longer appealed to me so Maverick and I hiked out the gate and turned toward Main Street, filled with its cars and trucks and stores and people—lots and lots of people—and headed home.

I rented the rear unit of a private residence. When we finally reached the beautiful Queen Anne style home on Maple Street, my landlady, Mrs. Ida Clemashevski, sat on the porch swing. She patted the cushion on the seat beside her. I sat and Maverick laid his head in her lap.

"Ronnie called me," she said.

The numbness with which I held my feelings in check fell away and more tears spilled down my cheeks. She pulled me close, and I buried my face in her shoulder.

Her diminutive height of less than five feet didn't measure up to the depth of caring in her heart. She murmured soft words of encouragement. "It'll be all right. You'll be fine."

I believed her. She'd already saved my life, once by taking me in and making me feel at home, and once by doing the two-step on a madman intent on killing us both.

When my shoulders relaxed and ceased their quaking, she said, "Go in and fix your face. Your father had a good day and we wouldn't want him to see you like this."

I sat up and snuffled. I certainly did not want my dad to see me like this. Recovering from a traumatic brain injury had left him much more sensitive than the man I grew up with. My tears would most likely bring on his tears and he would be embarrassed.

I splashed cold water on my face and forced a smile. My dad had been a large man, quick-witted but sardonic, handsome, strong-willed, supportive, and determined to raise me the best way he knew how. He was still all of that, but in different proportions as he labored through his recuperation. At the end of the summer, he had been released from the long-term facility into the arms of my stepmother. Long story short, she was sorting through what she was still willing to give up for him, and he was now in my care. He had missed me and I missed him.

I've owed him my life from the very beginning. My mom was gone before I was a month old and, until he married Elizabeth when I was ten, Dad had been everything: father, mother, sister, brother. Honestly, Elizabeth had tried, but she had two children of her own. Together they raised the three of us to be independent, self-actualizing adults, as prepared as any for the trials and tribulations, the accomplishments and joys of a life well-lived. And then, although we never proved it, I knew, deep in my heart, my dad had taken a bullet meant for me.

The front door clattered open. I took a deep breath and plastered a smile on my face. "Hi, Dad."

"How was your walk, darlin'?" he asked, looking up from the book in his lap.

Honesty is always best, but I decided to be judicious in my telling. "When Maverick and I were walking by the storage facility across from Olsen Tiling there was an explosion. The alarm sounded and the police and the fire department showed up. It was pretty hairy."

"I heard."

"What? W-where'd you hear it?" I stammered.

"It's all over the waves." He raised his phone. "Did you know there was a fatality in that fire?"

I busied myself rustling under Maverick's collar and nuzzling up close, noticing he still bore traces of ash and soot and smelled of smoke. I ran my hand down his back as if I could brush off the impending question.

"Well?" Dad said, but patience was no longer part of his personal arsenal. "I'm waiting."

I sighed. It was going to be a long weekend.

CHAPTER THREE

My workweek began again before I could forget the smell of smoke, and the story resurfaced throughout the school day, dragging me through endless uncomfortable conversations.

My students demanded to hear too many morbid details, so I sidestepped answering some of their questions by introducing a complicated one-time pad encryption. The students took to sending secret messages in earnest.

As I organized my work to cart home, my intercom crackled. Mrs. McEntee barely got the words out, "Stanley Mossa's on his way to see you," before a huge presence darkened my doorway.

"May I help you?"

The shadow of a sneer in his jowly face made me

take a step back, but the look was so fleeting, I might've imagined it.

He extended a huge paw, swallowing my right hand in a tight grip. "Stanley Mossa, Esquire."

"May I help you?" I repeated.

He sandwiched my hand between his, patting, not letting go. "I'm going to save your bacon."

"Excuse me?" I asked. I jerked my hand free and massaged my fingers.

"You're the advisor for the mock trial team?" he asked.

"Yes. And you are?"

"I represent the nonpareil of Columbia's legal community."

My eyebrow shot up involuntarily.

He went on, "I'm the attorney assigned to work with you for the upcoming mock trial season."

"Thank heavens." I breathed a sigh of relief, and eagerly shoved my hand back at him. "Katie Wilk. Boy am I ever glad to meet you. Have you done this before? We have our organizational meeting tomorrow. Where do we start? When do we get the case? Is it—"

"Relax. I've got this. Call me Stanley." He ran his fingers through his scant comb-over and then took my hand and encased it, again, in his meaty hands, dwarfing my own long fingers. "This must be your first time." My stomach grew queasy and I retracted my hand.

"And this is my stepson, Oscar." Stanley stepped aside, revealing a teen wearing a Columbia High School Cougar sweatshirt and baggy jeans. "Get over here, Oscar. Meet Ms. Wilk."

A round-faced youth peered at me from behind tinted lenses. Odd shades of gray swirled in his eyes, reminding me of glass marbles. His thin pouting lips nearly disappeared in the smooth face framed by short spikey blond hair cemented in place with a pasty gel. He looked down and punched at the phone in his hand, averting his eyes.

"Oscar," Stanley's voice boomed.

Oscar pulled his eyes away and recited in a disinterested tone, "Pleased to meet you." He gave me a curt handshake then reconnected with his phone.

"Oscar sat first chair when the team placed fourth at state last year." Stanley puffed out his chest.

"Impressive," I said. "I've read through the information manual, but there is so much to learn, so much I don't know." Not that I couldn't deal with the unknown. "I'd appreciate any help I can get."

"That's what I'm here for."

As Stanley removed his coat, Oscar mumbled, "I gotta go," and spun out the door.

Ignoring the departure, Stanley handed his coat to me. "Burberry," he said, and squeezed himself between a chair and the table.

I grabbed the coat by the collar and laid it over my desk, pressing it flat with the palm of my hand.

Stanley loosened his tie and unbuttoned his jacket, flashing the Hugo Boss logo. He leaned back, lacing his fingers together, and rested his hands on his ample stomach. I watched him make a show of crossing his ankles, circling the toes of his shoes. "Gucci," he said.

"Mock trial allows students to examine litigation as a possible career choice. Opposing teams simulate a trial," he recited. "From both sides."

"We're nurturing the future Perry Masons?" I smiled.

He snorted. My smile faded.

"A team of judges evaluate the performances." He stressed the word performances. "A team can lose the case on its merits and win the competition with the ability to look and act prepared. First meeting is tomorrow? I'll take the lead. It shouldn't take long and I have information sheets to distribute."

"I found some supporting materials that might be helpful, including a few elementary scripts we could use to give us a feel for the courtroom." I shuffled the files on my desk and yanked free a blue folder.

"I've got this." He huffed and squirmed loose, grabbed his Burberry, and left without so much as a backward glance.

"But I have more questions," I whispered. My shoulders slumped and I felt as though the air had been sucked out of the room. Relieved to have met our attorney coach, I'd hoped to be more at ease. Stanley's commanding personality sucker-punched me, and I felt like a minion. I thumbed through the files. He might still be in the market for the practice material.

* * *

The following day, when the clock hands read time for the initial mock trial meeting to begin, there was no sign of Stanley. I panicked but resisted the urge to run. I threw my shoulders back and walked into a packed classroom. The number of interested students was both marvelous and daunting.

My eyes swept over the filled seats, alighting on the familiar faces of my science club students clustered near the exit. Brock Isaacson shook his head and crossed his arms. Lorelei Calder blew her bangs from her forehead. The others formed a circle, simulating a nineteenth century protective wagon train.

Oscar sat on the far right. In a loud voice he smirked, "It's her first time." Exchanging chuckles with the other students, he continued, "Stanley said she doesn't know what she's doing." I felt heat rise from the base of my neck.

I straightened my navy-blue blazer, and marched to the front of the room, ignoring the hum of Madonna's *Like a Virgin*. I clicked the computer mouse and my classroom SMART board came to life, playing the theme song from Perry Mason, in spite of Stanley Mossa. The slide show lit up with scenes from a courtroom: the judge's bench, a uniformed bailiff, a gavel, an empty jury box, a witness with her right hand raised, the gallery, and the counsel desks. While the slides faded from one to another, I distributed the student extra-curricular application. The display held the students' gazes until the screen sparked and went dark.

"What's this?" Oscar asked with an overstated look of dismay, holding the end of a power cord.

I plastered a smile on my face. "Welcome. I assume you're here for mock trial. Oscar, would you be so kind as to plug the cord back into the wall? It must've come loose." There was a rumbling from the restless natives. Stanley had better hurry. "This form contains the Minnesota State High School League Rules for participation in an extra-curricular activity. When you finish reading the form, sign it, and pass it forward. Does anyone have any questions?"

A timid hand rose like a python to a snake charmer.

"My name is Zoe and I did mock trial last year." Her affect changed so quickly it was as if the python struck. "A team is made up of up to *twelve* participants. Why are you all here?"

A few students nodded and grumbled. Oscar stood, facing the group. "You might not realize what a commitment mock trial can be. We work hard and we've gone to state the last three years. My stepdad is the coach and he's tough. I know. His expectations are off the charts so if you don't think you can cut it, it's time to get out." His gaze penetrated the circle in the back of the room. Lorelei grabbed Brock's arm and whispered something.

"Man, has she got you hog-tied," Oscar said with a challenge in his voice. Brock's eyes were ablaze. Oscar's tone changed to sickly sweet. "If that's all you have for us, Mizzzz Wilk, I think we should be going." Chairs slid back and a herd of students stood.

A low voice bellowed from the back. "Sit down."

"Mr. Rollins," Oscar said in a syrupy sweet voice. He dropped back into the seat.

A thin man walked to the front of the room and shook my hand. "Gene Rollins." The words rolled out on smoke-tainted breath. "I'm here to make sure our legacy stands, and to catch up with your stepdad." Rollins nodded to Oscar and turned to me, a steely glint in his eyes. "You ever done this before?"

"No," I said with as much nonchalance as I could muster.

"Thought I'd volunteer my expertise. I teach business law." He cast a glance around the room and settled on my science club students. "First off, there are too many of you here. You'd better not be wasting our time."

"Mr. Rollins, please. This is an informational meeting, and everyone is welcome."

"By all means." His right hand tumbled forward. "Inform."

I took a deep breath and read from the manual. "Mock trial is an introduction to our American legal system. Opposing teams perform a trial and the students act as both attorneys and witnesses. Mock trial can help you gain knowledge about law, develop questioning techniques, hone critical thinking skills, and establish the foundation to build a solid argument." My face heated as Rollins squinted at me, scrutinizing every word I had to say. I swallowed and continued.

"Mock trial may cultivate an appreciation for the difficulties judges, lawyers, and juries face, as you attempt to present relevant facts and legal arguments to safeguard justice, resolving the criminal or civil issues involved."

A whirlwind rushed around the corner. "Sorry, I'm late." Kindra panted and heaved a backpack onto an empty desktop.

A girl in the front row broke the stunned silence. "How many teams can participate from each school?" she asked.

"There can be up to—"

"I'll only coach one," thundered a voice from the doorway. Stanley dressed down for this meeting; he wore a gray chambray shirt and blue jeans over burgundy snakeskin cowboy boots. "And that team will have its case honed to stiletto precision." He set a stack of papers on a desk by the door and rubbed his hands together. "We'll hold auditions Thursday. Take an information sheet on your way out."

Chairs screeched across the floor and slammed against desks as some of the students piled out of the room. Those looking confused moved more slowly. Rollins bent over a desk examining a sheaf of pages Stanley had brought, nodding intermittently as Stanley whispered to him.

"Stanley," I said. "I don't think all the students know what they need to do." Neither acknowledged hearing me. "Stanley," I spoke loudly. "Mr. Mossa."

He raised hard dark eyes. He clenched his jaw, then inched one corner of his mouth up into a smirk. "Yes, Ms. Wilk?"

"I don't think all the kids understand what's expected of them, especially if you're planning auditions for Thursday."

"I'm well acquainted with the capabilities of the returning team members. I have room for one, maybe two more."

"It really isn't fair if you've already made up your mind."

"Is life fair?" Rollins snickered.

"I have enough students to enter three teams and give more kids a chance to participate."

Stanley grunted. "I don't have the time for three teams. I provide funds for only one team. I will coach that one team, and it will win."

"You're auditioning almost twenty students for one or two positions?"

"One student graduated last year. I can do just as well with nine."

I sputtered. "Would it be satisfactory if I search for an attorney to coach another team? I'll work on financing as well."

"If you can rope some poor sucker into coaching a losing team, that's fine with me."

He packed up his papers, and he and Rollins strode out of my room.

My insides roiled. My head spun. My fists clenched and I tugged at my tightening collar. I picked up the leaflet with the rules and reread it. I needed to enlist at least one more attorney willing to volunteer time to coach the students, and I couldn't afford two extra fees. I couldn't even pay for one. I fretted, having spoken so rashly, but it seemed Stanley Mossa brought out the worst in me, and his decision was unfair.

I wrote out my argument and called Mrs. McEntee, Mr. Ganka's administrative assistant, for an appointment.

"Mr. Ganka is free now. Are you able to meet with him?"

"Yes." Oh, boy. It was now or never. "I'll be right there."

CHAPTER FOUR

Phil Ganka, our school principal, sat in on my initial job interview. He had the flat top of a Marine sergeant, square jaw, and a stiff upper lip, but his eyes glittered with kindness, and he listened to both sides of a dispute before rendering a fair judgement to students and teachers alike.

"What can I do for you, Katie?" he asked. The chair squeaked as he leaned back and tented his fingers in front of his face, raising one eyebrow.

"I have some questions about mock trial."

"That's what Stanley's for."

"About Mr. Mossa, sir."

"His track record speaks for itself."

"He and I are not seeing eye to eye on a few things."

"Such as?"

"There were twenty-eight students at the informational meeting today and we could easily field two or three teams."

His chair squawked when he leaned forward. "The number is way up from last year. That's wonderful."

"But…"

"But?"

"Mr. Mossa will only work with one team of maybe eleven students."

His face contorted as the wheels turned and I didn't know which way they would go.

"He's holding auditions Thursday. But he's already chosen his team, so the auditions are moot."

"We have three trophies in our case. He knows what he's doing."

"I'm certain he'll get another trophy. But shouldn't we encourage as many students as possible to take advantage of this opportunity?"

"Stanley usually pays the entry fee. How much do you need to enter a team?"

"Two hundred seventy-five dollars per team," I said softly.

It sounded like air being slowly released from a balloon. He sat forward without making a sound. "I have four hundred dollars at your disposal. If you can be creative and come up with the rest of the fees, we can field three teams. And you'll have to recruit the volunteer attorney."

"I can do that." I took a deep breath. "Mr. Rollins sat in our informational meeting. I have the impression that he and Mr. Mossa would like to work together."

Mr. Ganka ran his forefinger over his lips. "If you don't mind…"

"I don't mind. But why is he interested?"

"Rollins used to advise the team. Last year he gave us an ultimatum. More money or he'd quit. We didn't have the money. He quit." Mr. Ganka shrugged. "But if he'll assist Mossa gratis, and you enlist another attorney…"

"Great. Thank you, Mr. Ganka." I rushed my words because I knew I had a few resources to tap, and I wanted to complete my task as soon as possible.

Before I'd gone ten feet out of his office, I pulled out my phone and thumbed through my contacts, punching in JM.

"What's up, girlfriend?"

"May I borrow one hundred fifty dollars?"

"Why do you need one hundred fifty dollars?" My best friend, Jane Mackey, tried to sound skeptical. "What have you found to do in Columbia?"

I told her about the interest in mock trial and my lack of resources. "I'd like to borrow the remainder of the entry fee and I need to find another attorney." Jane chose a job as a history teacher in Columbia instead of working in her family business—shuttling celebrities and high rollers anywhere they'd like to go in sublime luxury. Although it was her father who owned Sapphire Skies, I hoped Jane might have the money to spare.

"Coinage I have. Attorneys I tend to avoid." I could almost hear the windmills of her mind whizzing. "Except, of course, Dorene."

"I thought about her too."

"It won't hurt to ask. If she can't help, maybe she'll be able to point you in another direction."

Dorene Dvorak was an opinionated, intelligent, hard-working, highly sought-after criminal defense attorney who had tallied victories in the most hopeless cases. She had successfully argued to have the court drop first-degree murder charges leveled against our friend, and Maverick's vet, Dr. CJ Bluestone. And she really loved kids. She'd be the best addition to our team.

Jane said, "You know I'm going to help. Right?

"You don't have to." But one could hope.

"It's for my piece of mind. I have to watch over my investment. And I need something to keep me occupied." When Jane's beau, Bureau of Criminal Affairs Agent Drew Kidd, worked undercover, his time was never his own, but Jane had resolved to stick with him until she decided to have him 'commit or git.' "You're always a huge distraction," she said and chuckled before the phone clicked off.

I punched in Dorene's number.

"Dvorak," she said in her clipped manner.

"Hi, Dorene. It's Katie," I said. "Do you know anything about high school mock trial?"

"Why?" she asked warily.

"We're in need of an attorney coach."

"Mossa loves that stuff," she said and heaved a sigh of relief. She thought she'd be off the hook.

"He's helping us, too, but we have enough students to enter more than one team and we need another attorney coach."

"Sorry, Katie. I just don't have time."

"I get it," I said, trying to make her feel a little guilty.

"No, I don't think you do. I really would love to help you. But I'm preparing for a big case and real law tops play law every time."

"Oh." I swept the disappointment out of my voice. She was right. Her clients should come first.

"Have you tried Harley Brown?"

"Who?"

"Harley hung his buffed new shingle in Columbia about a year ago. He might have the energy, the inclination, and the time to help you out." She rattled off his phone number. "Go ahead and use my name."

He answered after the first ring. "Hello, Mr. Brown. I'm Katie Wilk. I'm a teacher at Columbia High School, and I've the distinct pleasure of advising our mock trial. Dorene Dvorak thought you might be inclined to help us."

After a few seconds he said, "I could use some exposure, and publicity like this would be great. I've never been involved with mock trial, but I've heard Stanley Mossa is pretty good so maybe he'll give me a few pointers." I doubted that would happen, but I didn't want to scare him off. He sounded so enthusiastic. "I can meet you at the high school in ... ten minutes."

"Thanks. I'll be here." I checked two major items off my to-do list.

While waiting, I considered a number of possible fundraising schemes and rejected all of them. Time was at a premium. I'd accept the money from Jane and think of a way to repay her later.

The overhead speaker crackled and Mrs. McEntee interrupted my woolgathering. "Ms. Wilk you have a visitor. He's being escorted to your room by Brenna de Silva." She sounded distracted.

Wanting to appear prepared, I arranged the mock trial files on one of the tables in the math commons. The door crashed open. Brenna bumped into a table, then stumbled over the legs on a chair. She barely acknowledged what had to have been a painful jolt because her eyes were riveted on the man in the blue serge suit. I opened my mouth to admonish her, but the words jammed in my throat.

The visitor had neatly trimmed wavy blond hair threaded with copper highlights. The cut of his coat accentuated linebacker shoulders and a narrow midsection. I looked up and was swept into twinkling cerulean eyes. Eyes were my nemesis, my downfall. My knees felt like noodles. My beating heart thudded in my ears. If I could paint, this would be my model for Adonis.

I heard faint words drifting around the room. When they were repeated with a chortle, they became clearer. "Ms. Wilk, I presume? I'm Harley Brown." He extended his hand and I stared at it.

"Ms. Wilk," Brenna whispered.

I seized his hand, pumping it up and down. "Welcome. I can't wait for you to join our team. What can you do for me?" Oh, boy.

Brenna giggled.

His warm laugh burbled from deep within. "Let's look at what you have." He carefully peeled my fingers away from his hand and said, "May we sit?"

I reluctantly pulled my eyes away from his adorable face as Brenna plopped down on a chair, equally captivated by Mr. Brown. "I have a few questions about Mr. Mossa's audition," she said.

The math department door swung open. "Ms. Wilk, did you know that spiders hibernate in the winter. It's a ..." The boisterous pronouncement halted mid-sentence and three pairs of eyes gawked at Mr. Brown.

He had a warm laugh. "Hello. Are you also wondering about the mock trial audition?"

Lorelei had the presence of mind to answer. "Yes, sir. Thank you, sir."

"And you are?"

Having regained some of her composure, Brenna said, "That's Lorelei Calder." Lorelei nodded at Mr. Brown. "Ashley Johannes and Allie Vomacka." Ashley and Allie gaped.

"We'd best get started," said Mr. Brown.

Words failed me.

"I'm Harley Brown," Mr. Brown addressed the students. "What do you know about mock trial?"

Brenna finally caught her breath. "It's a live performance taking place in a courtroom. We've never done one before, but it seems like it might be interesting and we've had fun working with Ms. Wilk and she's the advisor so we thought we'd give it a try." Three heads bobbed in agreement.

My voice came back to me, and I stammered, "I-I'm trying to coax Mr. Brown into coaching a second team. I've never been involved with mock trial, either, but I'm committed. I have all the competition materials except the court case which each team will receive in two weeks. However, I found additional scripts of sample trials to give us an idea about the format." My heart rate slowed and so did my words. "We can read through an example to get an idea what to expect."

"How many roles are there to play in your samples?" Brenna asked.

I thumbed through the first few pages of one example until I found a list of participants. "This case has seven major characters: judge, Mom Abear, Pop Abear, Babe Abear, Gold Elocks, plaintiff's counsel, and defendant's counsel."

Ashley said, "I bet I know what the case is about. Gold Elocks messed with all the Abear's stuff and she's in trouble." She patted her own curly blond tresses. "I'll read Gold if that's okay, but we'd better go roundup a few more bodies." The girls disappeared.

"I'll be the judge," said Mr. Brown. "May I look at the sample case?"

"You'll do it?"

He nodded as I slid the folder into his hands, and he scanned the script. "This case is written for elementary-aged students, but I think it'll demonstrate procedure nicely. It appears the performances are scored according to how well the students know the parts rather than what the law dictates."

I sighed, listening to his honeyed delivery, like a soothing bass crooning on late night radio.

"Do you have more of these?" he asked.

"What?" I snapped back to reality. "Yes. I have sample cases for Humpty Dumpty, Rumpelstiltskin, and one called Big Bad Wolf versus Curly Pig," I said, sliding each file across the stack as I read the tab.

"You do have other materials." He nudged the second stack leaning in front of me, a knowing smile tugging one side of his face into a grin.

"I have articles about the legal system, notes about evidence, objections, and a collection of loony laws."

"Give me an example of a loony law."

Pleased I had color-coded the resources to find them more easily, I yanked free a lime-green file, flipped it open, and pulled out an index card. "This one's from Michigan: a woman is not allowed to cut her own hair without her husband's permission."

"Would that open a can of worms today!"

"Most of these laws are being ignored, but they still

exist on the books."

Choosing another card, Mr. Brown read, "'It's Texas law that when two trains meet each other at a railroad crossing, each shall come to a full stop and neither shall proceed until the other has gone.'" He leaned in to read more outlandish laws and I caught a whiff of earthy pine. I inhaled sharply.

"Are you okay?"

"Yup," I squeaked. I was very much okay.

Ashley and Lorelei burst through the door with five students in tow. Brock trudged in and dropped a load of books on the table. Zoe hadn't been very welcoming at the first meeting and her presence surprised me.

"Mr. Brown, Ms. Wilk, meet today's team," said Lorelei. A few hands waved, some heads bobbed, but the faces looked insecure. Stanley had sure done a number on them. He'd done a number on me too.

"Mr. Brown, Esquire, has volunteered to coach," I said. There was a collective female sigh.

"I'll bet you didn't know that in Tulsa, Oklahoma, it's against the law to open a soda bottle without the supervision of a licensed engineer," Harley offered, straight-faced. The students gawked and then snickered. "You'd be all right with me. I have a degree." He reread the Michigan and Texas laws as well, and the students gathered around us. "And in California, you technically need a hunting license to set a mousetrap."

"This is going to rock," said Brock. His face beamed and he scooted onto the tabletop.

"I want you to know that I *will* coach. There *will* be more than one team. These cases are short and we can switch the parts around," said Mr. Brown, "We'll run through a few of them so you might know what to expect for the audition."

Lorelei distributed the copies of the scripts and the students volunteered for the different roles.

"See you tomorrow," he said. The room emptied.

"Tell me about yourself," Mr. Brown said, handing me files to stack in my storage bins.

"There's not a lot to tell. I've been teaching for two months, and so far, so good." I sorted through what I had to share but I decided to gloss over a murder or two. "I agreed to advise mock trial." That could turn out to be a good thing yet.

"What about you, Mr. Brown?"

"Harley, please."

"Harley, what brought you to Columbia? Dorene said you're fairly new to the area."

"Objection. Hearsay." Startled by the abrupt comment, I gasped, and Harley chortled. "Gotcha. Practice makes perfect. I've been here a little over a year. I decided to try my hand in a community I could fit my arms around and really practice the law. If I'd stayed in the Twin Cities, I'd more than likely be pigeon-holed into a specific area of practice. Here I can spread my wings." He glanced at his watch.

"I do appreciate your decision to help us, but I must be keeping you from something."

"I think this is a great opportunity and I'm excited to help. I do have a meeting with a client at my office shortly, but would you like to join me for dinner tonight and we can continue our conversation?"

"Well…" I hedged.

"Dutch treat."

"Sure," I said as my phone buzzed. "Excuse me, please."

I answered with my eyes on Harley instead of the screen. "Hello," I sang.

"You're in a good mood."

"Pete?" If I had Adonis in front of me, I had Apollo on the other end of the call. Dr. Pete Erickson was as darkly handsome as Harley was fair, and my heart skipped a beat. "What's up?"

"I'm finished for the day, early for a change, and I'm not on call. I thought we might grab a bite." I didn't answer immediately. "I've missed you, Katie."

"I've missed you, too, but I'm sorry. I've already made plans for tonight."

"Oh." He sounded deflated.

"How about tomorrow night?"

"Great. We'll go to Santino's. I'll pick you up at six."

Santino's was the first restaurant we'd gone to together. "Six it is, but I have mock trial practice. How about if I meet you there? And Pete?"

"Yes?"

"Thanks."

My phone buzzed again and I punched 'end call' and 'answer', this time reading the screen. "Hi, Dad."

"I didn't have time to make anything. Order take-out tonight?"

"Oh, Dad. I made plans. Can we postpone until Friday?"

I popped his balloon, too. "Sure. When will you be home?"

"Not late. I'll see you soon." I punched off.

"You must need a reservation card to keep your dinner

dates straight," Harley said, chuckling. "They'll have to wait in line. I'll meet you in thirty minutes, Ms. Wilk."

"That'll give me just enough time to finish prepping for tomorrow. And please call me Katie." My eyes tracked his departing figure and I sighed.

* * *

Harley was charming dinner company. I laughed until tears poured down my cheeks, but panicked after glancing at my watch. "Whoa. I've got to get going," I said, tossing down enough for my dinner and a tip and racing out of the restaurant.

Dad stood guard at the door, chomping at the bit to grill me about where I'd been and with whom, but he yawned through every other word and I sent him to bed.

Maverick blinked twice and stretched. "Work," I said, but I felt guilty all the same.

CHAPTER FIVE

After the final bell of the day rang, I found Harley sitting on my desk entertaining my department compadres with expansive gestures and funny stories. He had them eating out of his hand.

We arranged my room, shoving the furniture into a configuration resembling a courtroom. Harley pulled a rosewood gavel and a round sound block from his briefcase and I laughed when he slipped on a black robe and half-moon spectacles and sat at the front desk.

"Our senior high production was *Witness for the Prosecution*," he said matter-of-factly.

"I suppose you played Sir Wilfred Robarts."

"I wish," he said wistfully, raising an eyebrow. "But the play did give me a taste for advocacy." He drew a powdered wig from the bell-shaped sleeve and nestled it on his head. He pulled his phone out of an interior pocket and sighed.

"What's the matter?" I asked.

"I was going to call my office, but my phone is out of juice," Harley said.

"Here," I said, powering mine on, opening it, and handing it over. "Use mine."

"Thanks. I'll just be a minute."

He slipped out the room, and I heard the rumble of a one-sided conversation. He returned my phone and barely had time to settle into the chair at the front of the room.

The students entered the room reverently, curious about Harley's attire and serious about the job at hand. Zoe had competed in mock trial before and Lorelei took advantage of her invaluable assistance, settling the participants around the room.

"All rise for Judge Harley Brown," Lorelei said in a monotone.

Harley recited, using a slight British accent, "I call case number one."

Harley answered questions as they came up in simple language without condescension. I appreciated his interest and support of each of the students.

At the conclusion of the presentation, Harley said, in an authoritarian voice, "Does that conclude your evidence?"

Both attorney-players stood, exchanged glances, and said politely, "Yes, Your Honor."

"We have a jury, albeit a small one. In light of the evidence, have you reached a verdict?"

The heads hung together and the self-proclaimed forewoman stood. "Yes, we have, Your Honor. We find for the defendant."

"Oh, man," Brock moaned.

"However, I believe the plaintiff team came better prepared and would therefore win the competition." Harley read from his performance rubric, explaining how to garner more points. "There are no scripts for the real mock trial. We are attempting to build context."

Zoe snickered.

"What's the matter?" Galen asked. "You don't think we did a good job for our first court case?"

Zoe shrugged. "I've done mock trial for three years and I can tell you there won't be any fairy tales." Ripples of discontent filled the room. "I suppose you weren't horrible," she said in a conciliatory way. "You might check out the script of B. B. Wolf next. The hostility between the wolf and the pig provides lots opportunities for objections." She'd done her homework.

At the conclusion of the second reading, Harley listed possible objections, cited exaggerated examples, introduced the students to the rules of evidence, and explained how to behave in the courtroom, when to sit and when to stand, and how to address the opposing counsel and the judge. The students were riveted by stories of bizarre courtroom antics and strange but appalling trial outcomes.

Kindra's phone blasted. She read the screen, and said, "I'm sorry. I really have to go."

I blinked, not believing the clock face. I texted, **Sorry, still at mock trial practice**. I didn't receive a response.

The students packed their belongings and rushed out of the math department.

"Why such a long face? I think they sounded great. They won't be embarrassed at the auditions tomorrow."

I heaved a sigh. "I'm late for dinner."

"Six forty-five," he said after checking the clock.

I looked for an answer from Pete and sighed. "I'll go with you for moral support."

* * *

Despite the fat rain globules splattering his windshield, Harley successfully maneuvered his dented Bronco into a narrow space in the crowded parking lot. I'd been laughing at more of his law school war stories and my cheeks hurt. I laughed harder as we splashed through the puddles to get to the front door of Santino's. Upon entering, I mussed my hair to shake some of the water free, and peeled the soaked fabric from my skin.

Romano Santino pranced in his tuxedo. "Welcome, Miss Katie."

"Good evening, Mr. Santino." I squinted through the warm ambient light, and the first person I made eye contact with was Pete.

He downed the last of his beverage, then grabbed his coat and made his way across the restaurant, stopping in front of us. "Katie."

"Hi, Pete." It came out as a whisper. "This is Harley Brown. He's the attorney working with one of our mock trial teams." Pete took the hand offered, but his chocolate-brown eyes never left mine. "Time got away from us—"

"Sorry I can't stay. I have an early morning. Have a good night." He stepped through the doors and was swallowed by the rain.

I recovered from the awkwardness, inhaled and exhaled. I'm not sure extracurricular advising paid enough. In less than a week I'd missed two possible dinners with an amazing man, skipped three longstanding evening walks with Maverick, and reneged on attending waltz class with Ida. I hadn't checked in with Jane since I'd begged for a loan, and I missed my evening repartee with my dad. When Mossa completed his team, my job had to become easier.

"I should get home."

"Let me get you to your car," Harley said.

CHAPTER SIX

The thought of Mossa's audition hung over me like Poe's pendulum, swinging back and forth, dropping nearer and nearer, throwing me off balance and out of sync. Throughout the day, my bored students yawned and eyed the clock even more than usual.

It didn't help to find Mossa sitting behind my desk in the office at the end of the day, cracking the knuckles on his bear-sized hands.

"The kids will be here soon," I said. "I was able to enlist the aid of Harley Brown for an additional team. Do you still think we need the audition?"

"Nine students would be sufficient, but I wouldn't be averse to including another worthwhile candidate. I think it makes sense to keep the seasoned participants together, having a cohesiveness that has gelled over time."

I had an argument regarding what novices learn from his more experienced students, but he didn't really want my opinion.

"With the right score, we could be invited to nationals in Atlanta this year."

It appeared Mossa had already scared off some candidates. Fewer students converged on the math commons for the audition, and we wouldn't field a third team after all.

"I want last year's performance team to meet in Ms. Wilk's classroom," Mossa announced. He handed me a sheaf of papers. "Here's the test and answer key."

My mouth dropped open. "What test?"

"The instrument I will use to narrow the field of likely candidates for my team."

"You said there would be an audition."

"What better way to conduct an audition? This test will bring the cream to the top, and then I'll have the best duke it out." He turned to the students. "When Ms. Wilk finishes correcting this exam, she'll send in the top scorers."

Ten students made a beeline to the room but Mossa put his hand out to stop Zoe. "You were only an alternate, my dear." Her eyes grew large, and her lip trembled. "But I'm sure you'll make it this year," he said with saccharin sweetness. Rollins had managed to sneak by and followed Mossa into my classroom.

I distributed the tests. You could've heard a pin drop in the commons area, but the loud, rude noises coming from Mossa and the nine students had to be disheartening. When Harley arrived, he cocked his head, questioning the sounds of jostling desks, chaotic shouts, and playful voices while the remaining students conscientiously penciled in their answers. He helped me correct the exams and at the conclusion, there were three perfect scores; the rest were not even close.

Zoe walked as if she were being led to her execution escorted by Lorelei and Kindra.

Harley reintroduced himself to the remaining students and read more loony laws. He opened a file and produced a video of an effective cross examination by Raymond Burr as Perry Mason and a classic closing statement by Andy Griffith as Matlock. Then he distributed another sample script. "Let's read through this case."

Harley interjected tips during the reading, making additional comments about the law, procedure, and etiquette. Before he dismissed the students, he delivered his *piece de resistance*—last year's mock trial case—and assigned a part to each student. "We should be able to perform the entire case from both sides. Scribble all the notes you want.

"Tomorrow. Same time. Same place," he said, and they vanished.

Zoe stumbled into the commons. "I didn't make it," she said before tears coursed down her cheeks and she ran from the room.

Lorelei stomped out next. "What a crock!" She looked at me and grumbled. "I'm with you," she declared. She grabbed two packets and sprinted after Zoe.

Mossa's team streamed through the commons unconcerned or unaware of the disruptive effect of their behavior.

"Katie," Mossa ordered from my room. My eyebrow rose involuntarily to the summons, and Harley and I followed the grating voice.

"This venue is not conducive to productive thinking. Until further notice my team will be meeting at the courthouse." He eyed Harley. "You must be the barrister?"

"Harley Brown," said my partner. "I would love to pick your brain." Stanley scorned the hand Harley held out.

"No time. I must get a move on if my team is going to be victorious." He turned his dark eyes to me. "Excuse us, Mr. Brown. I need to have a word with Katie."

Rollins walked out with Harley, speaking as if he owned the entire building.

"There are too many students for you to take care of yourself, and if we have a split venue, it will be impossible," Mossa said.

"Jane Mackey offered to help."

"And I don't want you to be overburdened." He sounded like he didn't want me to mess up his team. "Gene and I talked it over and we decided—"

"You decided?" Unbelievable. "Mr. Rollins is not the advisor." I felt the tips of my ears flame. My heart raced.

"Gene volunteered to be the teacher liaison for *my* team again this year and I think that would be for the best. I'll take care of his remuneration. You have Mr. Brown, and you can involve as many students as are interested in the activity."

I sputtered. "But…"

"And I'll pay the fee for a second team."

Just when I thought he was pulling the rug out from under me, he offered me a hand up. I let out a breath. "Deal." I hated borrowing money from friends anyway.

"I need twelve copies," he said and held out a hefty folder.

I pasted a smile on my face, then turned my back as I replied sweetly, "Have your teacher liaison do it."

I arrived home a mere thirty minutes tardy. An envelope waited in my dad's hand. He watched as I slid the opener beneath the flap, pulled out the correspondence, and scanned the contents.

Dad examined the return address. "You could get out of it," he said.

I'd never received a summons before. The correspondence asked me to complete the online questionnaire and wait for instructions for possible jury selection. "I need to talk to Mr. Ganka. I don't think you can just get out of it, Dad."

"Probably best if you make the call. Have you eaten?" I shook my head. "I'll make grilled cheese sandwiches," he said, and rubbed his hands together with enough friction to start a fire.

When I was growing up, Dad had been the major meal maker in our home. Since his injury, however, his paltry food fare resembled mine, but the grilled cheese sandwiches were black on one side only.

"Earth to Katie," Dad said. I came back to a serious exchange. "I heard Sophie Grainger may not have committed suicide."

My sandwich stopped on its way to my lips. "Where did you hear that?"

"Ida said the ignition key was found under the remains of her car on the floor of the garage, and they haven't been able to lift any fingerprints. What does Pete say?"

"I haven't talked to Pete in a while." Who would want to kill Sophie Grainger?

"That's too bad. I should have invited him for dinner." Words dried up from there.

I left a message for Mr. Ganka before Maverick and I made our way through the deepening shadows, melting into memories of the day. He sniffed every blade of grass and who was I to tell him he should get a move on. He'd almost been a hero, and if we'd arrived sooner, maybe Sophie Grainger would still be alive. When he stopped, I stopped. When he moved, I moved. When he growled, I turned and faced a pack of hooded teenagers mounted on bicycles.

They closed the shrinking circle and my gut churned. Maverick pulled and barked, but he was not up to their level of menace. They blurred around us, making forward progress impossible. I slipped my hand into my pocket, thumbing any number among my favorites. When I heard the muffled greeting, I pulled the phone out and shouted, "Help!"

After one last revolution too near us, the bikers took off in every direction, jumping curbs and sluicing stones when altering directions.

"Katie?" snarled the voice on my phone.

I took a breath and said, "They're gone."

"Who is gone?" Dr. CJ Bluestone asked.

"Some kids were pestering Maverick and me. I just wanted to scare them off. I'm sorry for bothering you. I called your number from my redial list. Thanks for answering."

"No problem. Do you need a ride?"

"We're close to home. We should be fine." After finding Sophie Grainger, I'd wanted to talk to CJ. He understood the heart of a search-and-rescue dog and the mind of his partner. I needed his advice. "But I've been meaning to call."

He had an exceptional skill for waiting.

"We were practicing our communication skills when we found Sophie Grainger. I praised him. I treated him. I thanked him. But I'm sure he could feel my insincerity. I'd like for him to find lost children, wives too busy to pick up the phone, or husbands who say they need to let off steam. But he keeps finding dead bodies. What does that say about him? About us? About me?"

"He's good at his job." After a long pause he added, "And you are good at yours."

I snorted. "Maverick pulls me in the right direction. I hang on for the ride."

"Teaching," he said. "Carlee says only good things about you."

My face felt warm. "How are you doing?" I asked.

"Carlee stays with Miss Grace only part of the time now. But we still have much to learn, and my bachelor accommodations don't grant her much privacy." CJ had served as a Navy SEAL. Years after Carlee's mother died in childbirth without telling him she'd been pregnant during his deployment, he met his seventeen-year-old daughter. They'd saved each other, but building a family took plenty of concentration.

"Perhaps Maverick is in need of a training session Saturday?"

"That would be great."

"We will head to Sibley State Park at nine thirty. Bring an open heart."

How CJ saw a search-and-rescue dog in Maverick, I'll never know, but I will be forever grateful. Maverick possessed the natural ability to sense when someone needed him, including me.

CHAPTER SEVEN

I guess mock trial isn't for everybody," Jane whispered. The ten remaining students fidgeted in the desks as we waited for Harley.

"Mossa will pay two fees. Harley can coach the second team and you and I—you will still help me?"

"Of course. You'd get into so much trouble without me," she said and changed the subject. "Did you hear about the woman who died in the storage unit fire? They're looking at her husband."

My heart jumped. Jane caught something in my eye and said, "Not again, Katie."

Before we could say more, Harley barreled around the corner, herding Zoe in front of him. "Look who I found," he said, staring down any grumblers. "Are we ready?"

Heads nodded, and Zoe slumped into a desk.

Jane caught her first glimpse of Mr. Brown and her eyebrows arched in appreciation as Harley explained the courtroom basics. "They seem to enjoy this."

We observed and took notes for the next ninety minutes.

Even grumpy Zoe performed well and provided helpful hints to her teammates. Lorelei gave her a thumbs up.

As we packed up, Zoe said, "Where's the competition case?"

I scanned instruction manual. "It'll be released a week from today."

She furrowed her brow and pouted. "I'm sure we had it way earlier than that last year." She shrugged and shook her head before heading toward the exit.

Harley waved as the rest of the students raced off to their respective weekend activities. Piling stacks of files in his briefcase, he asked, "And who is this lovely creature?"

"Jane Mackey." He kissed the hand she offered, and she blushed. He picked up his battered brown briefcase and sauntered out of the room.

"Boy, can you pick 'em." Jane smiled and sighed, flipping the light switch.

"I hope the kids are learning as much as I am." I fanned pages of notes, and we walked toward the office.

Jane chuckled. "This is almost as much fun as hanging out with Drew, but he's not working tonight so I'm out of here. See you."

"Have a great night," I said.

I packed up my weekend work but before I turned off the light, a noise caught my attention. Stanley Mossa crept into the commons area from an adjoining classroom. His eyes flashed with a look I couldn't identify. He stood with his Burberry coat draped over his right arm, his beefy left hand gripping a tan leather briefcase. He said, "I caught the last few minutes."

"What can I do for you, Mr. Mossa?"

"Stanley, please," he said, dripping with honey.

My respiration rate increased. I waited.

He smirked. "I thought I should check on the girls who did not make the A team."

How pompous! What made him think he had the A team? Okay. His team had demonstrated their success for three years running, but still…

"The blonde with the glasses has quite a remarkable mind. She stalked out before I could provide any feedback and I was hoping she might reconsider."

"Reconsider?" I sputtered.

"I'd still like her to be a part of our team. She did a spectacular job."

"You didn't cut her?"

"Oh, no. But she created quite a stir and stomped out."

That's our Lorelei.

"She'd be perfect for the role of a…" He searched for words. "Defense attorney."

"I think she's happy where she is."

The grimace on his face sent a jolt down my spine. I had to leave the room if I wanted to keep any dignity at all. "I'll give her your message. You'll have to excuse me." I stepped through the office entry to the front of my desk, pulling out my phone, pretending to be busy. I kept Mossa in the corner of my eye as he swaggered toward the exit, a smug expression pasted on his oily face.

I plopped into my wheeled chair which flew out from under me, and I landed on my rear end. Mossa turned and sniggered. He provoked people for a living. I had to grow a thicker skin if I wanted to stand up to him.

I crawled from the floor and sat again.

On my short drive home, I counted my lucky stars to have Harley on my team, Jane in my corner, dinner with dad, and a treat for Maverick in my pocket.

Maverick bounced at the door, tail wagging, drooling around a bright blue ball. "In a minute," I said, scratching under his collar.

"Dad?" I called. I followed the echo of my voice to the empty kitchen. The counters, oven front, and stovetop gleamed. The refrigerator held nothing but cold air. "Dad?" I glanced at the clock. "Dad?" I plodded up the creaky stairs, Maverick on my heels, a little afraid of what I might find.

As I reached the top step, Dad and Ida burst through the kitchen door, laughing, swinging matching takeout bags. They glanced up and stopped in their tracks. "Hi, Dad. Hi, Ida."

"You nearly gave me a heart attack," Dad said. "I thought you were going out for dinner again?"

I stammered at his newly acquired forgetfulness. "What do you have there?"

"Leftovers from that Mexican place."

"Las Tapas," Ida added. "Felipe took very good care of us."

"I'm starving. Any leftovers for me?" I sat down. "I thought we were eating dinner together tonight, Dad?"

"Yes, but Ida popped in when my stomach started growling, and I couldn't wait. She and I decided to eat when we were hungry. You've been late all week."

I could feel the tips of my ears redden. "Sorry."

CHAPTER EIGHT

CJ's weak attempt to look stern when Maverick and I arrived four minutes late failed. His Labrador puppy, Renegade, plowed into the back seat. She tried to rile Maverick for fifteen seconds, pawing, nipping, and barking, and when that didn't work, she circled him twice and curled up next to him. I followed CJ's directions down gravel roads into the state park where he'd prepared a training ground for Maverick and me.

"He is ready. Are you?" he asked. Chantan John Bluestone's six-and-a-half-foot frame leaned on a sturdy black cane topped with an intricate carving of his former dog, a Belgian Malinois. His black eyes danced, and his straight black hair glinted blue in the sunlight.

I strapped on the National Association for Search and

Rescue required backpack and nodded. I poured water from one of my bottles into a collapsible bowl which Maverick lapped dry, and clipped on his scarlet NASAR vest.

"You remember my friend Westin?" I nodded. "He has already secreted himself in the park. Remember your training," he said, shaking the plastic bag containing the article of clothing with Westin's scent.

Grateful our newest find still walked among the living, I signed "sit" and pulled the cap from the bag. Maverick sat. I examined the trees and shrubs surrounding us, getting my bearings. Being extremely efficient, Maverick would likely take the shortest route, plunging through the undergrowth, avoiding paths of any kind.

I offered the scent. "Maverick," I said. "Find."

Maverick bolted. "Really?" I let out a huff and took off after him, skirting trees, sliding through damp patches, and traipsing through thick grasses. Forty minutes later, Westin, CJ, and I were seated at a picnic table in the park, downing ice-cold water.

"He's good," Westin said, pulling off his cap and wiping his head with a camouflaged sleeve. "But it's hard work. You need practice running over more demanding terrain, Katie, but you'll get used to it. Let's try again next Saturday. Maverick's a natural. Aren't you, big fella?" Westin rustled Maverick's ears and Maverick leaned in for more.

My sweat-soaked shirt stuck to my back, and my shoes weighed five extra pounds from all the gunk clinging to the bottoms. My socks slid down and bunched under my heels, the backs of which had been scraped raw and could use band aids. The tear along the inseam of my jeans stretched to the crotch. I'd wiped the blood from the scratches on the backs of my hands on my white T-shirt. And Westin expected me to work harder.

"I know," I admitted and took a long drink of water. "Have you lived in Columbia your entire life?" I asked.

"Not yet," he said and chuckled.

"Do you know Stanley Mossa?"

He snorted and my eyebrow jerked toward my hairline. "You do too, I see."

"What can you tell me about him?"

"He's primarily a divorce attorney specializing in taking his opponent to the cleaners. You might say I know him from personal experience." Westin grimaced. He slapped his hands on his knees and hoisted himself from the bench, saluted CJ, and trudged down the bike path to the beat-up Chevy in the lot, his shoulders sagging.

"What did I say?"

CJ stood as he emptied two enamel drinking mugs, hooking them on his index finger. "His former wife married Mossa after their divorce."

"Is Oscar Westin's son?"

CJ stopped, considering his answer. "Oscar was his stepson but Westin loved him as his own. He took the role of proud father for fourteen years. You know Oscar?" I nodded. "His mother was granted full custody. I do not know the terms of the dissolution, but I know that Westin was hurt. Having Carlee in my life has given me a different perspective and I understand."

A silent "oh" formed on my lips and I wilted, understanding how bringing up Mossa might have offended Westin.

Maverick nudged my hand which in turn nudged my heart. When CJ tossed a ball and Renegade retrieved, Maverick panted with eagerness. I encouraged him to join in the exercise, hoping to wear him down even more. The dogs waited patiently for CJ's instructions, and I watched in fascination.

When CJ plopped down on the bench next to me, we wobbled, corrected the imbalance, and laughed.

CJ said, wistfully, "Stephanie wanted what she thought would be best for her son. Stanley can give her financial security and status."

I couldn't like him any more for it, nor any less.

One biker whizzed by on the path and a second slowed to a crawl, stopping as close to us as the path would allow, and removed his helmet. Gloved hands raked through shiny dark locks, and white teeth broadcasted a pleasant grin.

Maverick and Renegade made a bid for attention. Maverick circled the figure, closing in. Renegade jumped, and CJ whistled her away.

A gloved hand removed dark wraparound glasses, revealing Pete Erickson's luscious face. He reached down and vigorously scratched Maverick's favorite spot. Maverick leaned in and Pete secured his one-handed grip on the bike before it tumbled.

CJ lurched from the bench and walked the few steps to shake hands. If you didn't know he'd been injured in combat, his limp would be undetectable.

I joined them. "Hi, Pete." I thought of a million things I wanted to say.

"Hi, Katie. What a gorgeous day. We don't have to report until three o'clock for the night shift so we thought we'd take advantage of every second."

A man of few words, CJ simply nodded and scooped Renegade into his arms, nuzzling her.

The first biker had backtracked and joined Pete on the

path. Unclipping one bicycle shoe, Susie Kelton planted her foot on solid ground and said, "Why are we stopping? Aren't we almost to the snack shop?" She turned to us and, with a slow and sly voice, said, "Hey, you two."

I sighed. "Hi, Susie. I thought you didn't like to bike."

"I hate to bike for exercise, but Pete is a great inspiration. We have put on…" she glanced at the gauge between her handlebars. "…two miles already." Her breathless voice whined. "He promised me a smoothie before we head back so it won't be so bad." Then she said with the snarky lilt, "What are you up to?"

"CJ is helping Maverick and me practice—"

She interrupted, her eyebrows raising above the rim of her sunglasses. "I'll just bet."

Renegade wriggled free and dashed toward Maverick and Pete. Susie gave a frightened squeal, pulled both hands up in front of her face, and still attached by one shoe, floundered. Pete reached over and grabbed the handlebars. CJ anchored Susie by her elbow, whistling to Renegade whose rear-end promptly kissed the ground.

She pulled her hands from her face, locating both dogs. "Thank you," she cooed, putting one hand on Pete and one hand on CJ. Sheesh.

"Let's go, Pete," she said as she slipped her foot back into the pedal. "Race you."

When Pete took too much time preparing to leave, she hollered over her shoulder from thirty feet away, "Told you."

He shrugged and deftly shoved off, completing his shoe clipping mid-rotation as he coasted by her.

CJ tethered Renegade with a long leash, and said, "She needs a walk. We will return shortly."

I sat on the ground with Maverick's heavy head in my lap and closed my eyes, letting the warm sunbeams fall on my face. I heard birdsongs, far-off children's voices laughing and screeching, and leaves rustling in the gentle breeze. I also heard tiny pebbles crunching and felt a low rumble begin in Maverick's chest. I dragged my eyes open.

The army-green helmets on the five bicyclists surrounding me hid their faces behind heavily tinted plexiglass visors. I pitched forward as my heart jumped to my throat.

CHAPTER NINE

I threaded my fingers through Maverick's collar and heaved myself off the ground. "What do you want?" My voice shook from anger more than fear, although the cyclists weren't much less ominous in the light of day.

Maverick bared his teeth. One of the bicyclists raised his hand as if drawing a weapon and pretended to fire. The bikers moved in unison, circling and laughing, until Renegade raced into the mix, chasing with unimpeded bliss. One of the cyclists went down and Renegade darted to the fallen rider, eager to lap at a face.

"Get the hell away from me, bitch." Renegade cocked her head at the ill-tempered response.

After wrenching the bike off the ground, the rider led the retreat with Renegade in pursuit and Maverick chomping at the bit to join her. "Renegade!" I ordered with authority I didn't think I had. She turned and sprinted to Maverick's side, prancing around him.

I heard the whistle. She sat. CJ hurried toward her, and then she playfully darted in and out of his reach. "Who were they?"

"I think they were the same group that followed me the other night."

"Do you have any idea what they wanted?"

I shook my head.

We bounced down the driveway of the veterinary clinic and CJ said, "Carlee is making dinner for Miss Grace, Ida, and the Farleys. Would you care to join us? She is becoming quite accomplished in the kitchen."

"She's quite accomplished in a number of endeavors. I have an afternoon of mock trial legalese to pour over; after which, I'll be more than ready to devour anything I don't prepare myself. Do you want to wait and ask if she'll have enough?"

"She has learned from Ida."

"She'll have plenty then and I'd be pleased to join you. Thank you. Can I bring Dad?" He nodded. "What else can I bring?"

His dubious glance would have sliced thinner skin. I couldn't wait to see what delicacies Carlee would create. Even I had mastered a few edibles with Ida's culinary assistance, and I needed another lesson soon.

Maverick and I spent the early part of the afternoon on the padded swing hanging in the back yard, highlighting a glossary of terms from acquittal to writ. I wrote an opening and a closing statement and practiced aloud to make certain each fell within the allotted time parameters. The rest of the work required more attention than I was willing to give so I took advantage of the pleasant day, which would soon be a memory if Mother Nature Minnesota had her way. I closed my eyes under the guise of concentrating and scratched Maverick's belly.

Next thing I knew, Maverick lapped at my face. Crisp air had replaced the direct sunbeams. I roused to the busy hands of my next door neighbor weaving ribbons in my hair.

"Rise and shine, Katie," said the precocious three-year-old.

"To what do I owe the pleasure, Emma?"

"It's date night and you need to put your best self forward."

"What if I don't have a date?"

"You have to fix yourself up even more," she said, giggling. With expertise beyond her years, she turned the bottom of a gold tube of blood-red lipstick and aimed for my lips. When she finished mashing the slick paint on my face, she sat back to assess the damage.

"How do I look?" I batted my eyelashes and put on a dreamy grin.

She huffed, "You'll do. Let's go."

"Go where?"

"Date night, silly. CJ is waiting at Miss Grace's."

CJ? Date? In a slight panic, I noted the hour. Patting the multiple knots in my new hairdo, I squirmed. "I have to get ready."

Emma put her chubby hands on her hips and pouted, "No time to dilly-dally. I only get one night out a week, and I don't intend to waste a minute." She sounded exactly like her mother. "Let's go."

I breathed a sigh of relief. "*Your* date night. Let me get my dad—"

"He went with Mrs. C," Emma said.

I opened my back door and Maverick marched inside. "Wish me luck, buddy."

Emma grabbed my hand and led me to the crosswalk. She bent at the waist, looked both ways, and hauled me safely across the street. She planted us on the stoop and rang the bell. The door opened and CJ stood tall, resolute, handsome, dressed in a pressed Carhart under a leather vest, faded blue jeans, and thick-soled boots. And I tried not to laugh.

His black eyes glittered, daring me to continue my chuckle.

The baby-blue shadow that ringed his eyes clashed with the artificial orange smeared on his lips. Most of his hair had been caught up in two pink scrunchies and cascaded like fountains over his ears onto his broad shoulders.

"CJ," Emma cooed, sounding even more like her mother.

He swooped down and scooped her up, holding the door for me.

"Looks like we have the same cosmetologist," I murmured.

He grunted.

With our outrageous makeovers, I wasn't prepared for the richly appointed dining room set with a white linen tablecloth, gold-rimmed china, and gleaming silverware. I recognized Ida's cherished Waterford crystal; yellow candlelight flickered off the glassware.

Ida and Miss Grace sat in matching blue wing-back chairs, locked in an animated conversation. With barely a glance, they waved a greeting and didn't break stride. Adam and Pamela Farley stood as bookends around Emma and CJ, making sure their daughter's date behaved well. Dad's head fell forward onto his chest, snoozing. Galen, Carlee's boyfriend, slouched against the far wall, his arms crossed over his chest, observing. He shoved away from the wall and approached me with uncertainty.

"Nice 'do," he said.

"Thanks. I'm sure I could get you in." His eyes grew large. "I could probably even get you the family discount."

"No, thanks!" He shuffled his feet, and I could barely hear him. "Do you know Annalise Rigelman?"

"Sure. She's one of my students."

"She said for you to be careful."

"Scary," I said slowly with a touch of fake fear thrown in, unsure of where this was going. Annalise struggled with numbers, coming in before or after school to iron out difficult concepts. She always seemed grateful. I sniggered. "Why would Annalise tell you that?"

"I dunno," he mumbled.

I'd have to take Galen at his word. He was still reeling from the repercussions of a huge personal mistake and tried hard to do what he thought was right.

"Just be careful." His demeanor lightened. "You know, it's hard to have a serious talk with you. You might want to take a look at … this." His opened hand made an oval encompassing my face.

"Thanks." I flushed. I'd already forgotten my new 'do'.

I excused myself and headed to the powder room to adjust the absurd reflection in the mirror. The red paint traveled somewhere in the vicinity of my lips, making them appear three times their normal size. A black pencil had shaped my eyebrows which joined together in a vee and sparkly pink powder circled my eyes. I squirted soap onto my hands and gently rubbed, smearing the rainbow of waterproof makeup, but I had toned down the hues. I removed half of the ribbons and ran my fingers through my loose shoulder-length hair. I clicked off the light and closed the door.

I followed new voices to the dining room and stood face to face with Susie whose features morphed from apprehension through affirmation to triumph in a matter of seconds. "Hi, Susie," I said with the same gloomy pessimism as Winnie-the-Pooh's friend Eeyore.

"Katie," she sang. "The look suits you both." She waved her hand. "Pete, look who's here."

Pete Erickson knelt between Miss Grace and Ida, listening and laughing. His eyes danced, and his dreamy baritone reached out and pulled smiles from each of them. As he followed Susie's finger pointing to me, his face changed from amusement to resignation.

Galen and CJ slid chairs closer together and Pamela arranged additional place settings as Pete said, "Please don't bother. We can't stay."

Carlee peeled around the corner, hauling a heavy roaster muttering, "You most certainly can stay. I have enough food to feed the neighborhood. You can't find food like this anywhere in Columbia." Ida cleared her throat. Amending her statement, Carlee said, "Except at Mrs. Clemashevski's." She and Galen returned to the kitchen twice for more savory dishes. "Sit," she ordered.

Maverick and Renegade sat, waited for acknowledgment, and ignored the weird tension in the room.

"Please," she said. "This is my dry run for Thanksgiving."

We all sat at the table and Carlee said, "Please join hands. Let us pray." We bowed our heads. "For what we're about to receive let us be truly grateful. I'm bursting with thanks that I found my dad." Her sparkling eyes looked at CJ. "And I have a charming boyfriend too." She waggled her eyebrows.

"I am thankful my daughter can cook," said CJ.

My dad muttered, "Wish mine did." I squeezed his fingers with a little more oomph than he expected. "Ouch. What was that for?"

Miss Grace continued. "I am thankful for old friends."

I liked to be prepared, so I ran through a litany of blessings trying to narrow it down to one profound thought when a ringing doorbell saved me. I jumped up and said, "I'll get it."

"May I help you," I said as the door swung open. "Oh!"

Harley Brown stood on the top step, looking every bit the solicitor he was, dressed to the nines in a charcoal gray three-piece suit with light-gray pinstripes running through it, a crisp dove gray shirt, and a red and steel-gray paisley tie. "Here you are," he said, stifling a laugh. "I've been trying to get hold of you all afternoon. I left a few messages. I thought maybe something had happened."

"I must have set my phone to silent. How did you find me?"

"Everyone in Columbia knows where Ida Clemashevski lives. When neither of you answered there," he pointed to our house across the street, "I detected a gathering in the neighborhood." The floor creaked behind me.

"You must be Miss Grace. I'm so pleased to meet you. I've heard so much about you. I'm Katie's friend, Harley," Harley said. He stepped in and kissed the fingers of her hand.

"Enchanted. Please, join us. We're practicing for Thanksgiving."

"I couldn't bother you."

"It'll be no bother. In fact, you'll round out our numbers." I could count and I gave her a what's up glance which she ignored. In a low raspy voice, she said conspiratorially, "We have enough food to feed the entire town of Columbia."

Miss Grace locked arms with Harley and she led him through the house. I gaped at my face as I walked by the mirror in the entry. No wonder he laughed.

Harley flirted shamelessly with Miss Grace and Ida. He fascinated Carlee with a magic trick. He spoke fashion with Susie and coins with my dad.

"Say, Doc," said Harley. "I hear you bike every month of the year. I'd love to join you some time. I could use some new routes." Pete gave a strong handshake to a cycling enthusiast with whom he could trade war stories.

Harley charmed Emma and Pamela and, when she blushed, he tamed the simmering bear in Adam by telling him what a lucky man he was. That man was smooth.

"You're crazy, Mr. Brown," said Pamela, blushing.

"Harley, please," Harley said.

Galen thrust his hands into his pockets. "Yeah, crazy like a fox," he said so quietly I second guessed what I heard. I nodded my head when he mouthed, "Sorry." He shuffled his feet. "How's he know so much about everything?"

I could feel the smile grow a smidge from my lips. *How, indeed?*

CHAPTER TEN

Mr. Ganka squeezed time in his day's frenetic beginning to talk about my summons. "They need you when they need you and since we are public servants, I can't have you saying no. We have substitutes to cover for just that reason." He held off my protest by raising his hand. "Be prepared for every contingency. Have your lesson plans ready. It's usually a four-week stint, although it's extremely rare for any case in our county to make it to trial. You're not the first teacher to be called to jury duty.

"Did you get your difficulties ironed out with Stanley?"

I forced a smile. "Harley Brown is working with one team and Mr. Mossa is working with the other and he promised to pay for both."

"He's already made good on that promise. That leaves

more petty cash for other extra-curriculars."

"Jane Mackey insists on helping."

"I like that idea. It won't be much but let's get her on the payroll. Talk to McEntee. My admin knows everything," he said, waving me out before reaching for his ringing phone.

* * *

At the end of my first period class, I took Lorelei aside.

"Mr. Mossa said you left before he could tell you how well you did, and he would very much like you on his team."

Her eyes darkened, and I stepped back. I'd tangled with her ferocity before.

"That pretentious blowhard is so full of himself. I wouldn't be a member of his team if he paid me. He was so mean to Zoe." She shook herself and relaxed. "But our team rocks and we're going to give them such a run for their money."

Atta girl!

"You've been duly informed and have made what I think is the correct decision."

You know you've had a good day when your students engaged in conversations, asked relevant questions, told you to have a good week, and you looked forward to an afterschool activity, even on a Monday.

Harley hauled in a dozen different newspapers and periodicals, doling them out, and asked the students to peruse the print media, pretending to be an attorney, looking for possible scenarios which could lead to mediation, an arrest, a lawsuit, or another legal procedure. "When we find a suitable legal question, we'll construct our own mini-mock trial built on the fiction we create," he said. "Practice makes perfect."

"Ambulance chasers?" Galen asked.

Harley said, "Something like that."

Pages crinkled. Brock said, "Here's a case for a possible lawsuit. City employees claim their income is insufficient compared to neighboring communities of a similar size." The room came alive.

Another junior barrister raised an issue with an obituary. "The death of a ninety-two-year-old might be considered suspicious. We could pretend his heirs expected a huge payoff when he died. If he exercised daily and was of sound mind, his death might have been unexpected. My grandpa is ninety and a force."

Harley nodded.

Stories swirled around the room as Harley quizzed the would-be attorneys. Everyone jumped in with their own personal take on the possible crimes. They strayed from the printed word and invented fanciful plots with little old lady murderers.

"Sounds like a plot for a movie," Harley said and smiled. "Do we have a consensus?"

But Lorelei had continued to seek more realistic challenges. "Listen to this," she said, her nose buried in the rattling newspaper. "Natasha Sandburg drowned in her hot tub. Questions arose regarding the electronic self-closing cover. Police Chief Erickson, however, found no evidence of foul play. Though the victim had an blood alcohol level of .07%, the coroner ruled the death an accident." She looked up, her mind spinning. "The family could sue the electronics company or the hot tub company for a faulty product and damages resulting from her death."

"We have a few different possibilities to examine. Let's take a vote," Harley said. Though the results could have been close, no one wanted to tackle the steely set of Lorelei's jaw.

"Is the lawsuit civil or criminal?" Harley asked.

"Civil," said Zoe. "The family is seeking damages from a company with a bad product."

"Could it be criminal?"

Brock said, "Maybe. If the company knew the product could cause someone to die?"

"Defendant?" Harley asked.

"The electronics company," Ashley said. "Without the ability to operate remotely, the cover would not have closed on its own and there would not be a victim."

"Plaintiff?"

"The victim's family," Brock said.

"I don't want to minimize the tragedy of her death, however. Let's change the basics and make the victim Mr. Tom Jones and the company Miller Electronics. Mr. Jones left a wife and two little kids. What else could we use?"

Energy hummed as the students put together a case file. I continued turning the pages of the *Columbia Sentinel*, halting to read about the cessation of divorce proceedings against Ransam Grainger, at the behest of his attorney, due to the suspicious death of his spouse. The overpowering smell of the gasoline returned, and when I could breathe again, three faces swayed behind the noxious fumes in my mind—Sophie Grainger, Ransam Grainger, and his attorney, Stanley Mossa.

* * *

By the end of the week, I felt the students better understood the legal gymnastics. I certainly did. The students had crafted scripts for the realistic lawsuit from the story found in the *Columbia Sentinel*. They rehearsed both plaintiff and defendant sides with ease. Although Dorene was still swamped, she consented to act as judge for our first practice performance.

At our pre-performance conference, we talked about what professionalism looked like.

"Attire," said Lorelei. "Witnesses dress in good clothes, clean and pressed."

"Our attorneys should have suits," said Brock. "Does anyone need their shoes polished?"

"Which brings up another point. Never ask a question to which you don't know the answer," Harley said. The students nodded their heads.

"No phones," said Zoe with an intensity.

"Sit up straight. Speak loudly and clearly."

"Exude confidence. Control the courtroom," said Harley. "Practiced. Poised. Prepared. Professional."

"Memorize your opening statement," said Brenna.

"Be polite and courteous. Ask permission and walk deliberately if you intend to move," said Carlee.

Jane added, "Respect the judge and the system. Even if you could disagree, agree. Before you begin to speak, make eye contact."

"Think quickly and react," said Galen.

Jane said, "Address the judge as Your Honor. Shake hands before and after the case, no matter what the outcome. Ask permission to admit your exhibits."

"We're ready," said Harley. He stretched his right hand out in front of us. "Teamwork," he said. One-by-one the students added their fists to the center of the circle. Jane and I joined them, and Harley said, "Ms. Dvorak will be here at four. Are we ready?"

Lorelei pulled her hand out of the circle, a sly smile reaching her eyes. "Never ask a question to which you do not know the answer."

Harley nodded and asked again, louder, "Are we ready?"

"Ready," came the resounding answer. Harley's forehead scrunched and his eyes held disapproval.

Lorelei said, in a singsong voice, "Yes, Your Honor." He smiled.

"One. Two. Three. Teamwork." We punched our fists down and raised opened hands in a cheer.

As we shuffled papers and files into backpacks, Kindra waltzed in, frowning. "Oh, I loved him so," she mourned. "I don't know how I'm to live without him." A stridency entered her voice. "It's all your fault," she said as her finger slid around the room from one alarmed face to another. The façade fell away, replaced by a schoolgirl's tittering, and she swept out of the math area.

"What was that about?" Carlee asked.

"Who knows," said Galen, "and who cares?"

* * *

Arriving in much less formal attire than my students who were scrubbed, pressed, and polished, Dorene Dvorak tugged at her jeans, straightened her pullover sweater, and self-consciously ran her fingers through her short black hair. She commenced with a pre-case discussion.

"Opening and closing statements should take no more than two minutes. The presentation of each side of the case is allowed another ten minutes, plus cross examinations. At the conclusion, I will try to render a verdict. Good luck."

In a clear, stentorian voice, Brock shouted with Harley whispering in his ear, "O yea, O yea. Please rise. The Court of Common Opinion is now in session, the Honorable Fake-Judge Dorene Dvorak presiding."

Dorene wriggled around the table we'd moved to the front of the room, sat, and said, "You may be seated."

"Attorney for the Plaintiff," Dorene began.

Galen, garnering a few surreptitious second looks dressed in a crisp light-blue button-down shirt, a red paisley print tie, pressed khakis, and shoes polished to glossy black, playing the part of the plaintiff's attorney, took a deep breath. "May it please the court. Your Honor, Galen Tonnenson for the plaintiff," he said. And the show began.

When they finished presenting the trial, Dorene passed judgement, and Lorelei gave a celebratory handshake to her acting John Miller when it was determined the defendant won, and there would be no damages.

Dorene called them together to provide feedback and they quieted immediately.

"Be sure of yourself; you have good reason to be. I think you could challenge some practicing attorneys I know."

At that moment, Mrs. McEntee knocked on the edge of the doorway. With her eyes agleam she said, "This just arrived special delivery."

I tore open the envelope and read the title of the pages within, "The *Titanic* Bandsmen Played On—Mock Trial." The pulse in the room sped up and my heart hammered in my chest. "This is it." My voice quavered.

Harley asked Mrs. McEntee, "Is the copy machine still available?"

"Absolutely," she said, and began her stately exit. Like

a row of baby ducks, we followed her into the office where she made a copy of the entire case for each of us, and a few extras just in case.

"This looks like fun," said Brenna, flipping the pages in her hand.

Lorelei gnawed on her lower lip, concentrating on the words. Brock took her elbow and directed her out the door followed by the rest of the kids.

"Can we get together tomorrow at noon and work out our strategy, assign roles to the students, and study the rules for the mock trial procedure?" Harley's confidence in us seemed to have waned. "We have to be ready for our first scrimmage scheduled in eight days."

Jane said, "I'll be there."

"Me too."

"Noon," he repeated. "On the dot."

CHAPTER ELEVEN

I pranced through the doorway, breathing deeply, my heart racing, and said, "I think we were given a really cool case."

Before I dropped my briefcase, Dad handed me an official looking envelope, his left eyebrow raising in question as it had when I was seven and carried home a note from Sister Monica Marie. "Well?"

I peeled back the flap, dragging out the process as long as I could before sliding the paper out. I opened the trifold page and scanned the contents. "My juror number came up and I need to call Sunday evening and listen to a recorded message which will indicate whether or not I need to report for a case on Monday morning. They apologize, but the online jury pool information has been compromised and they're pulling the data together by hand. They hope it will not be too much of an inconvenience."

"Did you speak to your principal?"

I nodded. "If I get called up, Mr. Ganka said they have substitutes ready, willing, and able to take over. I just can't help thinking about the math sub we had in September who said the students were unruly and rude and that she'd never sub in math again. Honestly, she never understood the lesson or the assignment, nor did she try to do anything other than babysit. I don't know what I'll do if the sub can't help my kids with numbers. I guess it'll be a study hall."

"Well, darlin'. *Que sera, sera!* Let's have some dinner."

He'd prepared chicken fajitas, one of his new specialties, and the authentic taste had me refilling my plate. The spicy Margarita marinade tenderized the chicken and seasoned the julienned vegetables with just the right amount of heat. When I couldn't eat another bite, I put down my fork. I gave Dad the abbreviated version of the mock trial rehearsal, recalling a few of Dorene's comments. Then I outlined the competition case.

"Musicians aboard the *Titanic* were contracted independently and not considered crew or passengers and couldn't claim compensation. The fiancée of a fictional violinist is suing the White Star Line.

"I have to read through the case so I look prepared for tomorrow. Thanks for dinner, Dad."

"My pleasure." He looked sheepish. "Carlee helped."

My eyebrows rose. *Of course, she did.*

He said, "I'll take care of the dishes. And remember, Ida has a special place in her heart for all things *Titanic*."

* * *

I woke before sunrise, surrounded by pages scattered across my comforter. The ink of the last note I'd taken trailed down the page and I searched, unsuccessfully, for the errant pen. As I gathered my notes and put them in order, I solidified my opinion. The case would be challenging and exciting.

To prepare for CJ's SAR training session with Maverick, I wore my lightweight Gore-Tex pants and jacket.

"Good morning." My words echoed in the kitchen. "Anyone here?" I said as I slathered jelly between the halves of a warm croissant.

Maverick scarfed down his kibble and we were out the door with plenty of time on the clock.

The training session to find our subject took a little over an hour and it took CJ a little under four minutes to drive out to meet us.

He poured water into a bowl for Maverick and handed our subject, Jane, an icy cold bottle, dripping with condensation, while I sipped my own lukewarm beverage.

The three of us sat at a picnic table.

CJ tapped my map with his pen. "There are a few tricks to make the job of annotating your trail easier. Jotting a letter to indicate some of the landmarks requires less time. Use a personal shorthand."

"Such as?" I asked, dubious.

"T for tree, OT—"

"For oak tree. S for shrub. MT for maple—I get it," I said. "Very helpful, and it would be faster than drawing figures. Is there other standardized notation to use?"

CJ handed me a pamphlet. "These seem to make sense in general. It's a good place to begin."

"Thanks." I glanced at the time. "Oh gosh, Jane and I

have a meeting in twenty minutes."

We raced to school and met Harley. He relaxed after our short discussion, and I looked forward to our next practice.

CHAPTER TWELVE

Father Steve does such a fine job storytelling," Ida said as we headed to her car after Mass.

"And exactly what was the point of spilling the contents of those five grocery bags all over the altar?" said Miss Grace.

"Waste. According to the EPA, the average American adult will produce almost six pounds of trash daily, recycling only one and a half pounds, and he showed us what six pounds looks like using popped corn. We need to become better stewards of our wonderful world. The altar boys were already sweeping it up after Mass to use at the next service. He just never ceases to amaze me," said Ida.

Pete, looking fine in his khakis and navy-blue sport coat, strolled up to our group. "Hello, lovely ladies. Wasn't

Father's homily brilliant!" We mumbled our affirmatives. "What do you have planned for today?"

"Baking," said Ida.

"Watching Ida bake," said Miss Grace. "No class this weekend?"

"Nope. Our team needed a break. They said we've been working them too hard," said Pete. "Katie, what are you up to?" Pretty bold considering whatever he had going with Susie.

"I'll be watching Miss Grace." I wasn't prepared for Ida's disapproving glance.

"This may be the last good weather we have for a while. Would you like to head up the bike trail?"

Four eyes lit with excitement. I wanted to shout, "Would I! Would I." My confused heart thumped hard against the inside of my chest but, struggling to hold back, I said calmly, "Sure. What time works for you?"

"I suppose you'll need to return home and get all gussied up."

I'd gussied up for church. I would be dressing down a bit to ride, wearing black padded thermal pants, a multi-pocketed jersey, black jacket, pink riding gloves, gray shoes, and an ugly metallic green helmet. "I'll have to change but I can meet you at the trail in fifteen minutes?"

He saluted and spun on his heels.

Ida shook her head. "What was that all about?" she asked in her fake Irish brogue, planting her fists on her ample hips in frustration. "You couldn't have been frostier."

"He's seeing Susie now. And I wasn't frosty."

"He's what?" said Ida, shaking her red head. "They just work together."

"I've seen them out together a few times. We're just friends anyway." Weren't we friends? I could bike with a friend, couldn't I?

"Let's get you home so you *can* get all gussied up," said Ida as she led me to her chariot and our ride home.

It took fourteen minutes for me to pass inspection, with Ida making multiple suggestions I chose to ignore. "You could try a little harder to win him back," Ida mumbled. I pretended not to hear her.

* * *

With one foot secured on the pavement, Pete rocked his bike, itching to get onto the trail. The temperature hovered above fifty degrees, and the gentle breeze tugged at the few remaining leaves. We were close enough that floating particles from harvested corn and the aroma emitted by the freshly fertilized fields in combination with the brilliant sunshine made my eyes water.

"Ready?" he asked.

I slipped my flyaway hair behind my ears and checked the snap on my helmet. I adjusted the Velcro on my gloves and stepped down on the pedal.

We rode side by side for about a mile before I let tentative words escape. "How's your fellowship going?"

"We're supposed to have eight weeks remaining but we've already learned so much we can use out here on the prairie. How's everything here?"

"Our mock trial team is coming along." I thought I saw him stiffen. "Stanley Mossa's team is made up of ten students, nine of whom competed before. He and Gene Rollins took their teams to state for the last three years. They know what they're doing.

"Harley is coaching the second team. What we lack in

finesse and experience we make up for in determination, but I'm certainly learning about the law. We received the competition mock trial case on Friday and it's a negligence case revolving around a death on the—"

Wild Thing erupted from Pete's back pocket. I hated that ring tone. We skidded to a stop, and he retrieved his phone. "Dr. Erickson." His responses were all yeses, and I could tell by the look on his face it wasn't good. While he slid his phone into his pocket, he said, "I'm so sorry, Katie. I've got to go." Without waiting for a response, Pete whirled his bike around and screamed toward the trail parking lot. I watched until he was out of sight and wondered what might have been as I continued up the trail.

There was no reason I couldn't make the best of a bright and beautiful day. Jane had helped me conquer my fear of riding caused by the attack made on Dad, Charles, and me. More and more often, pleasant reminisces of Charles eclipsed the memory of his death.

My mouth watered during the remaining two miles to the coffee shop, and I couldn't wait to sink my teeth into the almond puff pastry I'd have to purchase to accompany the delightful white chocolate raspberry steamer I needed to assuage the petulant feeling of being left to my own devices.

Café Lot was hopping. Walkers and riders had taken the most recent prognostication seriously and intended to make the most of one of the few remaining fine days before cold weather settled in for the winter. I carried my mug and pastry to the last empty high-top two-seater table in the corner near the back window, overlooking a glassy lake surrounded by trees stripped of their mop of leaves, scratching at the periwinkle sky. Before I could take a bite, two clip-on bike shoes clopped next to my table, and the clear voice above them asked, "Is this seat taken?"

"No, I…" I looked up into the laughing eyes of Harley Brown, and a smile leaped onto my face. "What are you doing here?"

"Same thing you're doing, I guess." He carried a mug and a paper plate wobbling from the weight of the tasty treat on top. "Mind if I join you?"

"Be my guest. What a great day to be outside!"

"Are you by yourself?"

For a fraction of a second, I almost unloaded but said, "Not anymore." Harley sat.

"Are you a long-distance rider?" Harley asked.

I hesitated. *Not anymore.* "I like the eight miles to this wonderful coffee shop and the eight miles returning to the trail's head but I don't ride much farther."

I laughed as Harley started comparing the competition case to the fictional negligence case we had concocted from the information in the newspaper. He had literally cornered an audience of one.

Another set of shoes crept next to the table, and I looked into the red-rimmed eyes of Jane. "You didn't answer your phone, Katie. You didn't answer."

I stood and engulfed my friend in an embrace. "What is it, Jane? What's wrong?"

"Drew is missing."

CHAPTER THIRTEEN

We made a date for last night and he never showed." Her shoulders shook as she sucked in each breath. "They won't tell me anything except that he's on assignment. Even on assignment, he would've let me know. We've already gone through so much. He wouldn't have let me hang like that. I'm scared."

"Jane, sit." Harley held the chair and slid it under the table as she sat. He brought her a cup of tea. "What happened?"

"Drew was on a local assignment but promised to be back late Saturday afternoon and I haven't heard from him."

Harley glanced at the timepiece on his wrist. "It's only been sixteen hours and, honey, you look like hell. What kind of assignment?"

She cast her eyes down and whispered, her concession to confidentiality. "Drew is undercover again, some drug thing. His team isn't concerned. But I need to find him, Katie. I need you and Maverick to find him."

"Did he give you any indication where he might be going, who he might be seeing?"

She shook her head and her sobs erupted anew. I held her clammy hand.

"He said the duke might be as high as he'll go, or something like that." She shuddered.

Harley shifted his weight back. "I might have an idea on the location," he said. He patted his pockets. "Shoot. I left my phone in my car." I opened my phone and handed it to him. He pulled up a map and his fingers danced across the screen. "There's a geographical marker in Sibley, explaining the history of Duke Hill." He spread his fingers on the phone screen, zooming in on the location. "Should we call it in?"

Before he'd finished his question, I'd taken my phone back and pulled Jane out of the chair. "We'll find him." I grabbed my bike on my way to her Ford Edge and as I hefted it into the back, Harley's bike rattled behind me. We sandwiched the two bikes between the wheel wells and headed for Ida's, dropping Harley at the parking lot.

I knew Dad would worry so I jotted a note to him. I clutched the straps of the ready pack Drew had helped me assemble. It weighed a ton now. I knelt and hugged Maverick. "We have a friend missing, big guy. Jane needs him and we're going to find him." He lapped the water from his dish so I refilled it and, as he drank, I snapped on his vest and grabbed a jacket, slinging the pack over my shoulder. CJ didn't pick up so I left a message, giving him the possible location and the bare bones of our search plan. Jane and I were just overreacting and I knew he couldn't call out the other members of the crew until Drew was declared a missing person, but Drew was his friend as well as mine.

* * *

Jane and I followed Harley through the park into a wildlife protection area. My wheels sank into deep ruts in the path and the steering wheel yanked my arms with every bump we encountered. The Douglas firs and stately Norway pines joined branches across the trail and needles clawed at my doors and windows with a squeal like chalk on a blackboard. Jane rocked forward and back, urging speed, but we plowed on at a steady pace, careful just to keep moving. Clouds drifted overhead, and shadows edged closer to the van.

The path took us up and over a hill and I slammed on my brakes to avoid running into the rear of Harley's stationary Bronco. The driver's door hung open and he stood on the edge of a bluff overlooking a stream flowing twenty-five feet below. He gestured for us to join him.

"Are you sure you want to do this?" he asked, solicitous, his hands on my shoulders.

I stepped away. "Absolutely." I tossed him a walkie-talkie. He balked. "We need someone here to maintain a command post, to roust the right folks if we need help."

Jane handed me an extra-long skinny purple and yellow paisley tie. "He'll be okay. I'll keep you posted," I said, laying my hand on her arm.

If looks could kill, I'd be a goner.

Maverick paced and barked in the back seat until I released him. He continued barking and circling until I knelt next to him, scratching behind his ears, and whispered, "This one's for real. We're not playing." I let him sniff the tie. "Maverick, find Drew. Find him."

Maverick bolted, zigzagging down the bluff. I slipped and slid, chasing the flashing black tail, Jane glued to my side, slaloming around moguls of rock and dried brush. At the base, I sought purchase on the slippery stones, sloshing through the churning water. I grabbed a flimsy overhead branch to check my balance and followed Maverick to the other side. He splattered the cool water from his back, allowing us a moment to catch up.

Waves of terror radiated off Jane. In the time I'd known her, even when her own life was on the line, she'd never lost her cool. We had to find Drew.

Maverick plowed through the trees, tearing up the reeds, loosening stones, and racing over the terrain, then he looped back to make sure we were still in pursuit. Jane looked spent but pulled determination from her gut, dogging my steps.

The walkie-talkie crackled. "Katie, I lost sight of you."

I had no answer.

We slogged through the five-foot high prairie grasses, tailing Maverick by listening to the crunching of the stalks. Every once in a while, we'd see the tips of the vegetation disappear as he trampled them.

We lost Maverick at the edge of the field abutting a sheer wall of granite. There was no clear way to climb, no paths, no handholds. Thundering water drowned out my calls. We followed the stream which had cut a tube-like passageway through the house-sized boulders. Bracing against the smooth walls of the tunnel, we navigated the cold, roiling water until it tapered and calmed in a chasm at the base of a waterfall.

A shrill bark ricocheted off the stone walls. Jane scampered up the stone cliff, grabbing anything she could find, hauling herself from one slim perch to the next like a mountain goat. I did the same, aiming for her tried-and-true handholds.

I struggled to maintain Jane's pace, breathing heavily. My toes withered in my wet shoes. Water soaked my pants. My shoulders ached. Sharp limbs jabbed at my face. I could no longer feel my hands and had difficulty holding on. Jane kept climbing. She dragged herself onto a rocky outcropping and hung over the edge, dangling her arms to drag me up. She wrapped both hands around the one I offered and hoisted me on top of her. After a moment of chuckling, she sputtered, "No time. Let's go, Wilk."

She crept nearer the hammering cascade that spilled into the mirrored pool. We still heard barking and Jane continued to wend her way toward the falls. She fixed her gaze on the curtain of water, hunting for Maverick when one leg dropped into a hole. She screamed, her forward momentum carrying her over her leg.

I reached for her and helped her crawl from the hole, writhing, moaning, exhaling a stream of blue words. She gritted her teeth. "Go," she said. "I won't be moving from this spot." She bit her bottom lip, trying to hold back tears. "Just don't forget me."

She shoved me forward. I took a last look then elbowed my way through jagged limbs, plunging down a steep incline, avoiding the edge until the path stopped.

The barking continued. I blindly dove through the pouring water and found Maverick standing guard over Drew.

"Good boy, Maverick," I said, petting him. "Good boy," I repeated, scratching the scruff of his neck. I slid the pack off my shoulders, eyeing Drew's still form.

"I'd like a drink of water, if I may," came the distinctive voice of our dear friend. "I expected you hours earlier," he said with a soft reprimand. "And could you get this off?" He said, opening his eyes as he pulled at his lavender tie. I jerked the square knot and tugged the fabric loose. I twisted the cap on a bottle of water and, lifting his head, allowed him small sips. Still, he choked.

"Drew?"

"I'm pretty sure my right arm and leg are broken. And I may have a concussion." He spoke matter-of-factly. Then with a touch of panic, he asked, "Are you alone?"

I shook my head, sat back on my haunches, and put my arm around Maverick. "Let's get you out of here." I radioed Harley and gave him contact information for CJ Bluestone. CJ would know what to do.

The walkie-talkie blipped and, surprisingly, CJ came on. "We'll be right there. How is Drew?"

"He's talking. He may have broken an arm and a leg and sustained a concussion, but he's still a know-it-all. I think Jane may have hyperextended her knee." I started to rattle off the topographic terrain I mapped in my head to our location until CJ cut off my recitation.

"I have your latitude and longitude and we're on our way."

"How?"

"From the GPS device on your pack," he said. "Out."

Drew moaned. "Help Jane. I'm not going anywhere. I'll be fine."

"What happened, Drew?"

"I didn't have a good plan," he said as he drifted off.

"Oh, no you don't. Talk to me."

Drew continued to mumble about his plan, or lack thereof, and I sent Maverick to sit with Jane. I wondered what plan? What GPS device?

CJ knew the area, hosting NASAR training runs in the park. He brought his truck to the base of the granite pile. I sat with Jane as he and Harley hauled Drew out, secured to a stretcher.

The over-the-counter pain killer CJ gave Jane had begun to take effect by the time he picked her up, and she nestled in his arms like a child, her arms wrapped around his neck, her head on his shoulder.

"Thanks, CJ," she murmured. He traversed the rocks with a stutter-step, unable to use his cane. I followed in his wake and helped lift her into the truck.

Drew lay unmoving in the back of Harley's Bronco covered with a metallic blanket. Harley hung his head, penitent. "I never had occasion to utilize the tracker before. I should have asked you but you'd made up your mind so quickly and told me to stay back, you didn't give me time to tell you about it. I just wanted to help." I swallowed my disbelief as I put my hand on Drew and said a short prayer before closing the tailgate.

"I'll meet you at the hospital," I said. Harley swung into the driver's seat and retraced his tracks to the road. I directed Maverick to the rear of CJ's cab and I crawled in after him, cradling Jane in my arms as we bounced and bumped back the way he'd come. I closed my eyes and sighed.

Pete met us at the ER entrance, his ferocious face full of emotion as he whisked Drew into the capable hands of the on-call orthopedic surgeon and Jane behind blackout drapes.

CJ and I sat on the plastic waiting room chairs, and Harley paced. As Maverick curled around my feet and rested against my backpack, CJ pulled out a NASAR debriefing checklist, noting our areas of deficiency. I hung my head and scratched behind my partner's ear.

"You did well, grasshopper," he said finally, his hand heavy on my head in blessing.

"If I did so well, why all the checkmarks?" I whined, looking up to find Susie snickering behind the reception desk.

"In a perfect world, you would have a perfect rescue, a perfect outcome, and would have been able to follow the guidelines more easily. But life is not perfect." He removed his hand. "We will continue to practice."

Pete returned. "I put Jane in an immobilizing brace and I'm keeping her overnight and I'd like the orthopedic surgeon to have a look at her too. What happened?" He slumped into the chair across from me and took my hands. "How do you do it, Katie? I thought I left you safe on the bike trail."

I started to speak when Harley plopped into the seat next to me. "You should've seen them ski down that hill. A fiery girl with the speed of light, a cloud of dust, and a hearty Hi-Ho Maverick.

"With her faithful companion Jane, the daring and resourceful trio raced across the open prairie into the unknown to save the day." His right arm painted a picture of the terrain. Pete released my hands in the middle of the narration and sank back in his chair. With unsurpassed storytelling skill, Harley kept us spellbound by a tale that seemed almost new to me.

When Harley concluded his exaggeration, CJ commented on the refinement of the skills I used rescuing Drew. Pete brought up the explosion at the storage unit, and all three discussed my inability to stay clear of calamities. Here I was, surrounded by three of the hottest looking men in all of Columbia, my heart pitter-pattering, wishing I was anyplace else.

When Harley declared me a hero, Pete said, "Drew was fortunate Harley had the presence of mind to give you that tracker, Katie. It made the rescue so much more efficient."

I had to agree, but I wish Harley had told me before he'd just stuck it on. "Where is it, Harley?"

He leaned over the backpack and flipped the strap.

I snatched the offending techno-gizmo and shoved it into his hand. Then I exhaled and shook my head. "Tell me next time, please."

He bit the inside of his cheek and cocked his head. "Next time, take a breath before you speed away."

CJ snorted. "Carlee and I will retrieve your van. Harley will take you and Maverick home." Maverick's ears perked up.

Realizing Drew and Jane would remain at the hospital overnight, sudden weariness pelted me like a spring rainstorm, heavy and thick. On our ride home, my heavy eyelids drooped only to flicker open what seemed like a moment later when Maverick licked my ear.

"We're here," Harley said, leaning away from Maverick's slobbering lips.

"Thanks. See you tomorrow?"

"Absolutely. You're not angry?"

"No." He brightened. What could I say? "All's well."

My dad held the door as I dragged myself up the stairs. "Supper is ready," he announced and led me to a table, serving a fragrant and finely finished French onion soup. I didn't want to ruin a good thing so I sat to eat but our entire dinner conversation consisted of the words "Don't forget to call in," and "No, I won't. Thanks."

I connected the number slowly, half hoping to get the nod to appear for jury duty and half hoping I would not be among the special numbers needed for the case.

I received a bye week.

CHAPTER FOURTEEN

D on't let the truth spoil a good story," said Carlee in defense of the tall tales she'd told and that grew more unbelievable by the hour. "You should hear Ms. Mackey tell it."

Every class hammered me for information on the imaginary man I carted miles out of the swamp on my shoulders or the made-up gunslinger I disarmed single-handedly, or the fictional baby Maverick saved from floating down the river in a wicker basket.

"I can't help it if everyone adds a little spice to your story. The bottom line is you and Maverick saved two people. If you don't like the celebrity, keep your life boring."

When the initial shock of seeing Jane in a brace wore off, and with her assurance that she was fine, my mock trial students bubbled with excitement. Based in fact, the *Titanic* case provided incentive for an in-depth study of the characters in addition to studying our local historical resources.

"On its maiden voyage, the ill-fated vessel struck an iceberg on Sunday, April 14, 1912, and sank at 2:20 a.m. on Monday morning," Harley read. "Over fifteen hundred souls perished in the disaster. At the time, the survivors and the families of those who died sued for more than ten million dollars, but settled for a paltry six hundred sixty-four thousand to be shared among all the litigants. The plaintiff is the fiancée of a fictional orchestra member derived from a composite of the original bandsmen, all of whom died that night. The musicians were not considered passengers or crew and had no legal recourse. They didn't receive a penny."

Lorelei read from the brief she'd prepared. "The estate of twenty-three-year-old Connor Robert Mitchell is claiming negligence by the White Star Line in its operation of the R.M.S. *Titanic* and are seeking damages for breach of duty of care and causation of fatal injuries, having suffered loss of life, loss of wages, pain, and mental anguish."

Harley nodded. "What else do we know?"

Zoe came equally prepared. "The White Star Line and its representative, Executive Officer Lightoller, claim Mr. Mitchell's conduct and that of other passengers caused his death. He continued to entertain the passengers, even while the ship listed, therefore assuming the risk of dying and contributing to his own negligence. Negligence, at the time of this lawsuit, was an all or nothing proposition. If Mr. Mitchell did anything, and I mean anything to contribute to his own death, the plaintiff may recover nothing. It's totally different now."

"Supporting the plaintiff's case are statements from Maggie Murphy—the fiancée and executor of the Connor Mitchell estate, Captain Rostron of the *Carpathia*, and another famed survivor, Margaret Brown. Second Officer Charles Lightholler, lookout Reginald Lee, and a Swedish military attaché who survived the sinking, were deposed for the defense," said Carlee.

"I can play that guy," said Galen, and in a guttural Swedish accent he added, "I can be very believable."

Harley assigned the students to plaintiff or defendant teams. Each witness was paired with an attorney. They formulated a list of questions, hammered out details, drilling facts and assuming identities to lend credibility to their performances.

"Great job. Take the day off tomorrow," Harley said, grabbed his coat and case and followed the kids out the door.

"I'm going to see Drew. C'mon." Jane still wore a neoprene brace, but she led the way with scarcely a limp.

* * *

Pink hearts covered the red plaster cast that encased Drew's right hand and leg. "I'd offer you coffee or tea or water or something, but as you can see…" He wiggled his toes.

"I've got it covered." Jane made a beeline to the kitchen.

"I want you to know I'd have been fine but you saved me a whole lot of blood, sweat, and tears," Drew said. "Thanks."

"Jane made me."

"I know." He looked longingly at the kitchen. "I'm a lucky guy."

"And she's a lucky girl. Have you remembered anything yet?"

He shook his head then leaned so far forward I thought he'd fall out of the chair. "What have you got for me to do? What's been happening? I'm going stir crazy stuck here doing nothing."

I pulled up a chair. "What do you know about Sophie Grainger's death?"

"I'd be looking at the husband as a suspect. Rumor has it, the money in the family was all hers and Ransam had been finagling for a profitable divorce settlement. But he was locked in a solid prenup, and he'd already found a new honey named in the countersuit," Drew said.

"I've met Mr. Grainger's attorney." My lips puckered at the sour taste Stanley left in my mouth. "Stanley Mossa would've been a formidable adversary." I grinned. "Sophie's team would have had their work cut out for them."

"Mossa's reputation precedes him," Drew said. "But he's a thorn in the side of law and order. His criminal client is usually shady, devious, guilty as sin, and *über* rich. Maybe he doesn't take on a case he can't win, but his victory percentages are extraordinary. And his civil cases work the same way. He almost always finds a loophole or a seedy witness. It seems like he'd do just about anything to win. I could go on, but I shouldn't. Don't mind me. I don't much like him."

Carting a tray of cheese and crackers and iced tea, Jane found us deep in conversation. She wrapped a cold pack around Drew's upper arm and said, "According to her business partner's daughter, Lynn…Yeah, I know, gossip, but we're speculating here, right?" Drew nodded, reeling his good hand as if to speed up her delivery.

"According to her, Sophie called in a team of accountants to comb through the books and initiate a dissolution of her business too. She started the company when she completed her degree and, although she had a lot of talent in design, she couldn't get the business off the ground. She got together with Lynn's mom who's an ace in implementation. They've worked together and have been very successful for almost ten years, but after she tied up all the loose ends, Sophie planned to resettle somewhere in the lower latitudes. Lynn's mom was not happy."

As I mulled over Sophie's demise, the doorbell rang.

"I'll get it." Jane trotted to the entry.

"It doesn't seem like Sophie had a reason to commit suicide, does it?"

"Can't see it," Drew said, and, looking up, added, "And look what the cat dragged in. *Rowr.*" Jane blushed.

"I came to see how the patient is doing." Pete looked down at his shuffling feet. I couldn't figure him out and I wished I could melt into the woodwork.

"We were discussing who could have murdered Sophie Grainger."

Pete stilled and looked up. "Suspicious death," he intoned with a poker face.

"I knew it. It was murder, wasn't it?" Drew's eyes lit up. "You can't get one by me."

"The police don't have much to go on. It really is considered a suspicious death."

Drew accepted the stonewall and launched into a complaint about his inadequate Tylenol prescription. Pete slid onto a nearby chair, listening and nodding. When Jane pulled at my sleeve, I followed her to the kitchen, my eyes on her heels.

"What's up?"

I looked up through the unexpected tears blurring my vision and her right eyebrow raised. "He's dating Susie," I sniffed and swiped at my cheek.

Both of Jane's eyebrows shot up.

"It's true. Ever since they began their fellowship program, they've been spending all their time together. They've been out to dinner and they bike together." Jane's eyes grew round. I sniffed and pulled my shoulders back. "But I'm all right. He's still my friend. And I'm not even sure I'm ready for more, yet."

A tear spilled down my cheek, and Jane laid her hand on my arm. "Oh, darlin'," she said, dripping with her Southern drawl.

CHAPTER FIFTEEN

There wouldn't be many more fair weather days and I had to take advantage before the roads iced over and the arctic winds tore through Minnesota. Unplanned free time left just enough daylight remaining for a solid ride. I jotted a note of my intentions as a just-in-case for Dad and headed toward the trail.

I pedaled the familiar bike path where I could let my mind wander, and my entire face wrinkled when I thought about Sophie Grainger. I had images of her death at the hands of another rather than suicide, and I ran through a list of possible perpetrators.

Husbands are always cast as suspects, and money often played a significant role in motivating a murderer. I hadn't met Ransam Grainger, but having met his attorney,

I probably thought less of him than I should have. And what would Mossa do to win his case?

Rounding a corner, I came upon an oak tree splayed across two-thirds of the path which jolted me back to the task at hand. I jumped off my bike and picked my way around the limbs. When my heart stopped pounding in my chest, I slipped back onto my bike and, maintaining a mundane pulse, let my mind wander again.

If Jane heard correctly, Sophie had a falling out with her partner and had intended to move on. Maybe her partner didn't have the capital to keep the business afloat, nor the skill Sophie maintained in design and networking. Their business acquired much of their clientele by word of mouth but they wouldn't be following Sophie. I'd have to talk to Jane.

I wondered if Sophie planned to move on alone. She also could have had a significant other. The photo in the *Columbia Sentinel* showed a vivacious woman with an attitude. Highlights gleamed like a halo in her long, wavy locks. Dark lip coloring set off her fair, flawless skin. The photographer caught a woman with an engaging smile and a magnetic personality, one comfortable as the center of attention.

My thoughts returned to Ransam Grainger. If he had someone on the side, and Sophie hadn't altered her beneficiary yet, then his attraction improved dramatically.

The coffee shop materialized in front of me, but I hadn't kept track of how quickly the sky changed. The sun had dipped behind heavy clouds. The temperature had dropped. So, I turned around and, with a wind at my back, I raced along the empty trail. Riding hard, I'd make it home before dark.

When the trail intersected a county road at the mile marker, I slid through the loose stones, my hands squeezing the life out of the handlebars, struggling to maintain control. The naked branches of the trees formed hag-like fingers extending over the trail, as though admonishing my late presence. The colors faded to gray and as my tires chewed up the asphalt, I heard a rumble behind me. I turned to investigate, and headlights popped on, momentarily blinding me.

The path accommodated the Department of Natural Resource vehicles; I'd met them at various times, removing branches and debris, scything weeds next to the path, repairing the blacktop, or cleaning the portable toilet at the halfway mark. I appreciated the illumination until I sensed the lights nearing. I knew they could see me. The driver revved the engine. I pedaled faster.

I heard hoots from the vehicle. The ground reverberated. I rushed forward. Just as my shadow shortened and became more defined, I shimmied past the fallen tree on the path. The brakes squealed behind me. Car doors slammed and I raced down the path. I slowed at the next crossroad and decided I'd be better off on the trail I knew than on the wide-open road I did not. They'd have to choose from three options. I hoped I made the right one.

CHAPTER SIXTEEN

The DNR chained a picnic table, two benches, and a garbage can to a cement slab at the rest stop on the path. I swung onto the slab and steered my bike off the trail. The wheels carried it into the brush, and I searched for a place to hide, eyeing the porta potty.

It's not that I didn't realize they could open the door and find me, but I needed a wall between us to feel protected. I opened the door. The stink made me gag and my eyes water, but I covered my mouth and nose with my sleeve, took shallow breaths, and barreled in. The full pot reeked. As the door clicked behind me, the gleam of headlights shined through the gap around the door.

The vehicle stopped and its headlights illuminated the rest area. Doors banged.

"She ain't here."

"We didn't see her down the county road, either. She couldn't've gone far."

"Kaaaayteeee," sang a female voice with artificial sweetness.

"I ain't going in there."

"I'll do it. He said we have to give her the message."

"Yeah, heh heh."

Footsteps approached. The heavy plastic door flew open.

"Arggh. Gross. Hurry up." Someone retched.

A flashlight beam fanned the walls and the floor. I squeezed my eyes closed.

"It's empty. Let's get out of here."

The car doors slammed again and, as the headlights rolled past, I lifted my foot from the top edge of the plastic wall and rolled off the narrow ledge, spilling toilet paper rolls and cleaning supplies to the floor as I lowered myself to the bench, careful not to step into the open hole of the seat. My arms shuddered. "Thank you, dear Jane. I'll never again complain when you request a three-minute plank."

My shaky fingers made the call difficult to connect as I rolled my bike down the path, scanning for car lights. When Jane answered, tears mixed with the big, wet snowflakes drifting onto my face. Explaining my predicament took more finesse.

Jane and Drew and her Ford Edge made it to the crossroad in record time.

"What are you doing out here?" she asked.

"I thought I'd make one last bike run…"

"What are you doing out here?" she demanded.

"I lost track of time."

"Do you know who they were?" Drew asked wearing a

scowl the size of Texas.

"No, but they were kids. At least one girl. And I have no idea what message they needed to send me."

"You didn't check the weather, did you? They predicted snow. And you know daylight in November is at a premium." He shook his head, but leaned forward. In cop-mode, he asked, "Can you identify the perps? Clothes? Hair color? Old? Young? Tall? Short? Any voice peculiarities to identify?"

"No. I squeezed my eyes shut the whole time. If I couldn't see them, they couldn't see me, right?" My attempt at levity did nothing to diffuse the interrogation. "I need to call Dad," I said.

"Already done," said Jane.

"What have you gotten yourself into, Katie?" asked Drew. "Unhappy students? Did you see something at school? Disrupt Ida's book club meeting? Did you eat her donation to an ecumenical dinner? What?"

I'd say I wasn't the target but they had used my name.

"I don't know, Drew. It started out as a great day for a bike ride. Nobody but Dad knew about my ride and I didn't notice anyone following me, not that I'd been looking. They must've seen me along the way and just decided to scare the bejeezus out of me. I'm fine."

"You aren't fine," said Jane, splashing the slush accumulating on the road.

"And what's with you and Pete?" Drew said.

I took a long pause. "Pete's seeing Susie."

"Where did you get that idea?" said Drew. "She's his companion, his partner, his nurse, and she's always around and you're not anymore. What gives?" They waited.

"Cat got your tongue?" asked Jane.

"I thought Pete and Susie were together," I stammered.

"And Susie told him you and CJ were an item." Drew sketched air quotes around item. "Girls." When he caught the squinty look on Jane's face, he said, "Women."

I coughed. "CJ's a good friend. He's coming to terms being the dad to a seventeen-year-old and is reconnecting with Carlee and I promised to do anything I could to help them." I had thought, for about a second, CJ and I could have become more than friends, but I really, really liked Pete. I just couldn't figure it all out. "Why would Susie say that?"

Drew hummed.

Jane pulled in front of Ida's home, lit like Times Square. "Looks like you have a welcome committee."

Familiar silhouettes filled the parlor windows. "Would you like to come in?" I said hopefully, clutching my handlebars for protection.

"You couldn't pay me enough. Good night and good luck," said Jane.

After I put the bike away, I entered softly. Cocoa powder dusted the marshmallow cream melting in the mug of frothy hot chocolate Ida handed me and patted the seat beside her. "Harley called and he would like to take the team on a field trip."

"A field trip? I haven't requested any funds. Why did he call *you*?"

"I have connections. He's contacted the students and you're coming to *Bruckner's New Titanic Exhibit* after school tomorrow."

The blocks fell into place. As a newly appointed member of the board of directors, Ida occupied an influential perch from which she could direct educational opportunities and, though I applauded her ability to make that happen, still felt blindsided by Harley. "Does he have a specific agenda?"

Her left eyebrow rose and she narrowed her eyes. "*Titanic*, correct?" I nodded. She rose and went to the door. "I believe he wants to provide depth and breadth to your skeletal story line. See you tomorrow."

I watched her leave.

"It's snowing outside and Jane had to pick you up from biking? What were you thinking, Katie?" said Dad.

I deserved the reproach and I blinked back tears when I heard the hurt in Dad's voice. "It seemed like the thing to do on one of the last nice fall days." Maverick trailed me, took one look at Dad, turned tail, and withdrew.

"Uh-huh," he said.

His sighs punctuated the crackling in the fireplace. "Dad?"

I strained to hear his response. "I don't know what I'd do without you."

That hit hard. I understood those feelings, and I was glad he didn't have to find out.

Maverick wandered back in, jumped up, and laid his head in my lap. I rubbed his silky ears.

"I'm fine, and with all this snow, it'll be spring before I ride again. I'm sorry I worried you." It's a good thing I didn't tell him what really happened. He'd have grounded me.

CHAPTER SEVENTEEN

Backed up traffic and fender benders clogged Columbia's roads and our local radio station encouraged everyone to stay home. The powers that be delayed school two hours.

However, even with the two-hour late start and shortened morning classes, it seemed the storm clouds followed us inside as waves of discontent lapped at the edges of our scholastic assembly. One student interpreted an accidental bump as a purposeful shove. Curt apologies answered whines of wrongdoing. Grievances popped up over the slightest infraction: a lost pen, standing too close, a misunderstood glance, a wrong answer. Tempers simmered just beneath the surface. Our usually cheery department head fumed out of the office rather than repeat an assignment to a pair of "inattentive knuckleheads."

Everyone was riled up and it was my day to monitor the lunchroom but I didn't even get that far.

At the end of the hall outside of the math department, I could just make out one figure backing another against the lockers. I scurried to break up the confrontation and I recognized the voices.

"Calm down. Maintain. Get a grip," Galen said.

"Wuss!" Annalise kept prodding, poking her finger into Galen's sternum. Galen dodged out of reach.

I stepped between them as Annalise said, "She's a tramp."

Galen's head jerked up. Fire lit his eyes. I stretched my arms out between them and kept them from connecting. Brock appeared and found his way behind Galen, pulled on his arms, and talked him down.

"Annalise," I said firmly.

Blood-red nails slashed the air as she dropped her hands to her sides. "Are you taking me in?" She sounded almost hopeful.

Sounds of crashing and shouts broke from the end of the hall.

"Today's not that day," I said. "Are we okay here?" Galen and Annalise nodded and I hustled into the fray.

"He's mine," one girl shouted, yanking the other's ponytail.

Roars bellowed from clusters of students. "Fight! Fight! Fight!"

"Stop. You—" My words were drowned out by a screeching fire alarm.

I pulled two girls apart, scratching and clawing at each other, careful to miss me, almost choreographed. I clamped one hand on each girl's arm and dragged them through the rush of bodies filling the exit. The students shivered outside, corralled by pacing teachers.

After the fire chief gave his all-clear to an unplanned fire drill, there wasn't much time left, and the closer I came to the end of the day, the harder my heart thumped in my chest.

I trudged up the bus steps with my team, and horrible thoughts of the evening after my first visit to the history center played on the screen in my mind—memories of when Maverick and I discovered the body of Ida's friend, the founder of *Bruckner's New Titanic Exhibit*.

The ride seemed to take forever but my troubled thoughts vanished when Ida met us as we exited the bus. She sizzled with excitement. "Welcome," she said, distributing tickets in the guise of boarding passes of actual passengers who had sailed that fateful night.

When stepping onto the gangplank into the exhibit, the mood changed and all eyes were awestruck as they scoured the space, so like the ill-fated ship seen in every other rendering. The re-creation of sections of the leviathan allowed a step back in time, displaying splendid replicas among authentic artifacts salvaged from the ship: clothing, shoes, papers, valises, dishes, cutlery, and pieces of the structure. A trip to the *Titanic* exhibit provided context for our students to plunge deeper into character.

Jane met us at the exhibit in exchange for my promise to visit Drew again and grant her a welcome respite. We benefitted from her fascinating historical data and skill in storytelling.

Drifting in groups of twos and threes, the students scribbled in notebooks, whispering respectfully. Of particular interest were the succinct profiles posted on various walls throughout the exhibit detailing what happened to each of the passengers and crew, survivors and casualties alike, and each student compared biographies to their ticket in hand.

Anticipating disappointment when the students sought the nonexistent biography of Connor Robert Mitchell, Jane came prepared. "Bobby, as he was known to his friends, is a fictional compilation of the eight musicians who performed aboard the *Titanic* so all of their biographies are essential. Our Bobby lived to twenty-three years of age before he went down with the ship. He was the son of Brian and Dorothy Mitchell, and was recruited by the Liverpool firm of C. W. and F. N. Black to provide music for White Star ocean-liners, learning more than three hundred fifty songs to perform at the different venues aboard ship.

"After striking the iceberg, the bandsmen continued to play on deck in bitter cold temperatures wrapped in bulky cork lifejackets. The music calmed the passengers until the ship could no longer stay afloat. Survivors rowed away in lifeboats, and by the time the band played the final note of what might have been *Nearer My God to Thee*, Captain Smith ordered the remaining passengers and crew to abandon ship.

"Bobby and Maggie planned to marry as soon as he completed one final job aboard the super liner. For our purposes, his body was found and buried in Fairview Lawn Cemetery in Halifax, Nova Scotia.

"Maggie Murphy, named executor for his estate, is suing the White Star Line for negligence. The mock trial author completed a detailed biography and we know Maggie was expecting their child when Bobby perished.

"In today's legal world, Maggie would have been

provided ample opportunity to enlist the aid of a solicitor." We followed Jane through the ship, across the ice-cold deck, pressing our hands into depressions in the man-made iceberg, and passed state rooms, dining halls, and workspaces, capturing a moment in time from April 1912.

Harley scouted the exhibit and directed the students to more comprehensive biographies and photos. "According to the rules, we're able to use information about the disaster beyond the material included with our trial information. Here is Lightoller's account." The students crowded around the placard on the wall. A few phones snapped photos and pens scrawled across notebooks. "Originally appointed as first officer, he had been demoted." Harley's finger underlined the next sentence. "Lightoller replaced David Blair who was subsequently reassigned to another ship. It appears Blair may have inadvertently retained the key to the storage locker holding the binoculars intended for use in the crow's nest." He eyed the students. "And when you finish here, step into the parlor—"

"Said the spider to the fly," Galen finished, quietly. Harley's eyebrows rose. "Sorry. It sorta slipped out," Galen whispered.

"—and read about our friend Mauritz," Harley continued, shaking his head.

The students scanned news articles posted in climate-controlled plexiglass cases mounted on one wall of the parlor, taking particular notice of the January 16, 1913 copy of the *New York Times* citing a claim against the Oceanic Steam Navigation Company. Björnström-Steffanson, the military attaché deposed for our trial, also sued the company, citing a one-hundred-thousand-dollar value for a painting lost in the sinking.

On our bus ride home, the animated kids talked, laughed, and even sang. My own mood improved and the return trip took no time at all.

"See you all tomorrow," said Harley, smiling at the kids as they stepped off the bus.

Jane concentrated on her phone screen, her brow furrowed.

"What's so important?"

She smiled when she looked up. "I don't know about you, but I'm not used to twenty-two degrees. With this app, I can start my car and it'll be warm when I get in. That saves my sensitive behind from freezing in this tundra."

Galen and Carlee shuffled back and forth in front of the bus doors. "Why such long faces?"

Galen hedged a bit and Carlee said, "Tell her."

"Did you hear what Annalise said today?"

"Yes, I did," I said sadly. "Why?"

Galen thrust a folded paper at me. "I'm pretty sure she wanted you to have this."

"Why didn't she just give it to me?"

Carlee said, "Gang members watch from every corner and talking to teachers is way off limits."

"I could barely hear her but she kept whispering 'C'mon, fight me'. I didn't want to, but when she grabbed me…" Galen began.

"And Annalise badmouthed me," Carlee continued, grinning.

"She shoved this into my shirt pocket and whispered your name."

"Thanks."

Carlee and Galen headed to a clunker in the parking lot.

I slowly peeled back the folds of an origami envelope, and found an arithmetic problem I had presented to Annalise's Applied Math Class penciled inside. I didn't need to work out the numbers; I'd done it countless times before and could find the solution in my sleep. I needed to add the requisite zeroes, subtract the number provided, and substitute letters for the digits in the answer to unlock a hidden message. I was caught in the mathematical moment and by the time I looked up, the parking lot was empty, and goosebumps ran up my spine.

CHAPTER EIGHTEEN

The weather settled, but not my last period Applied Math Class. The kids consistently challenged me to make math fun or surprising or magical or useful to them and I introduced as many different ways to do that as I could. I thought we'd had some interesting examples. They admired my nerdy ability to determine that the odds of holding a royal flush are better than selecting winning lottery numbers. They virtually promised to give up wagering—for a day.

I scrounged up copies of last year's 1040 EZ and, with fictional data and W2s, we completed tax forms for John and Jane Doe. I borrowed baseball scoresheets and we played a game of whiffle ball in the gym. Scorekeeping required using numbers not only for runs, but bases attained, strikes (of which there were many), balls, at bats, hits (few), home runs (fewer), and the path the ball took between positions in securing an out. We created our own trading cards using stick figures, and made-up ages, heights, weights, at bats, runs, balls, strikes, and averages. We even used measurements, weights, and fractions to bake a tasty apple pie in an idle Life Science lab.

In our elementary spreadsheet of careers, we checked off the type of math used in each. Applied Math made more sense when applied. I challenged the students to find a career that didn't use math.

"My dad hates math and never uses it," said a tall, gangly blond.

I played along. "What does your dad do?"

"We milk two hundred two cows, morning and night," he said, sneering.

I pretended to be stumped, cupping my chin in my palm, hooking my forefinger over my jaw, fishing for insight. "Anyone have an idea here?"

Kindra sat in the rear of the classroom, coughed lightly, and said in a small voice, "You counted the animals." The tittering from the other students empowered her. "You have to weigh the milk and chart pounds per cow and compare the output in relation to different mixtures of food. You have to change the mix of food depending on the daily circumstances. Most farms keep track of expenses, updates, and gestation times." She talked over her sniggering neighbors. "When you have to add on to a building to accommodate a growing herd, construction is full of numbers. You have to use perimeter, area, and volume formulas, angles and circles, measurements of length and width, cost, and time."

You could have heard a pin drop. Emboldened, she

added, "So there."

"You seem to know a lot about the dairy business," I said.

"Yeah." When I met her glaring eyes, her defiance dissolved. She looked down at her hands and let a curtain of straight blond hair fall over her face.

Addressing the entire class, I said, "Can anyone else think of a job that doesn't use math?"

Eyes darted around the room.

Pacing back and forth in front of the class, I said, "There's always a need to determine if your pay is equitable for the work you do. Unless you do nothing or you volunteer your time and talents, just the remuneration requires math. Filing tax returns, shopping purchases, sale prices, sales tax, tips, driving, and even cooking require the use of numbers."

With eight minutes remaining in the hour, I wrote their assignment on the white board. "Any questions?"

I tried not to stare at Annalise, but I so wanted to drag an explanation from her. She avoided looking at me. Her pencil flew across the page, diligently completing her assignment. Every other student had me in their sights. I circled my desk, aiming to sit my weary bones down after a long day. The chair screeched as I pulled it back. The students were uncannily quiet. Before I sat, the words in Annalise's message took on new meaning: WATCH YOUR ASS.

I sniffed and, instead of sitting, returned to the front of the class, then sauntered through the rows, looking over the students' shoulders, their heads now bent to the task. I scanned the room, determined to catch the miscreant who had poured some kind of stinky liquid on my seat. No one jumped out. I knew Annalise had given me a heads up. I hoped it hadn't cost her.

The bell rang. The students slapped together their belongings and hurried out. I almost called to Annalise but the look on her face silenced me.

Jane bounded into my room all smiles, whistling until she took a deep sniff and wrinkled her nose. "What is that?"

"I'm not a hundred percent certain, but I have an idea." I poked at the trash and removed a small bottle. I took a whiff. "Hunters sometimes use fox urine to disguise their own scent, and I think someone poured some onto my chair."

"By someone, you do mean a student?"

"Looks that way."

She glanced at my rear end and raised her left eyebrow as I tore paper towels from a roll in the cupboard and wiped the chair.

"I caught on early enough but it seemed like the entire class knew and had been waiting for my mortification. Their exemplary conduct should have given it away." I opened the top drawer of my desk and fished out Annalise's message. "If I hadn't already known how this worked, I wouldn't have taken the time to figure it out and, sure as shootin', my rear end would've been the laughingstock. Meanwhile, I have to get this cleaned up before—"

"Ew!" Carlee shrieked. "What is that?" She held her nose.

Brock and Galen followed her in. Brock understood. "Someone wanted to do a number on you, Ms. Wilk. Did it work?" He chortled as he looked behind me. "It's a rite of passage."

"To where am I passing?"

"Not you, but whoever put this on the seat and whatever group they want to belong to." Brock tossed protein bars around the room, pulled off his wrapper, and took a big bite. "Need the energy," he mumbled around the crumbs. "What was with Annalise today?"

"It was all show," Galen said. "Annalise baited me and when I wouldn't bite, she shoved me against the lockers and said some stuff to get me to react. I'm already on suspension, and I don't want to wait out wrestling any longer than I have to. But right before Ms. Wilk got between us—"

I cleared my throat and gave him a look that I hoped would stop a train. I didn't want Annalise to get in trouble for passing along the message.

"I have a puzzle." To save Galen, I penciled in a missive as they circled my desk and I demonstrated the math that would help them understand. "Take any three-digit number where the first and third digit differ by more than one. Reverse the digits and subtract the smaller from the larger. Reverse the digits again and add. The answer is always one thousand eighty-nine. Multiply that by ten raised to the power that will tack on enough zeroes to encompass your coded message and subtract the number whose answer produces the necessary translation using the numbers corresponding to the letters in your legend."

Groups of two and three huddled together to generate their own encrypted messages.

"'Watch your ass' could mean anything," whispered Jane. "But it certainly fits the crime here."

"Annalise wouldn't even look at me."

"Do you think it was Annalise's rite of passage thing?" Jane asked.

"I never thought about it, but sure. And after all she did to save me from embarrassment, I owe her big time."

Harley breezed in, his eyes aglow. "I've finagled our first trial for Saturday." He put up his hand to squelch the chatter. "You'll do great. I have absolutely no doubt."

The students looked at each other for reassurance. The practice flew by as my students worked the case until the silver-tongued interchange passed back and forth with ease. Harley, Jane, and I did our best to spotlight their worst, but they made moves as if dancing, and their hard-fought preparation infused a confidence we couldn't teach.

CHAPTER NINETEEN

Our first foray into law failed.

"It can happen to anyone," Carlee said to Lorelei. "Everyone gets to forget which side they represent once."

Ashley turned crimson. "I was so embarrassed. I gave my own name instead of Molly Brown's when they swore me in."

Jane took me aside and whispered, "Galen threw a pen across the room when they tried to fluster Carlee by interrupting her with frivolous objections that the judges wouldn't sustain. But Allie was sensational. She pulled off the role of a righteous man who couldn't possibly be held solely accountable for the sinking of an unsinkable ship. She almost had me believing she'd sat freezing in the crow's nest, peering into the distance without benefit of binoculars before announcing, 'Iceberg, right ahead,' with just a hint of an English accent."

The judges provided constructive criticism. Though it would've been a huge upset if we'd won, disappointment hung like a guillotine. Anxiety gave way to crabbiness while they waited for the announcement of the morning results.

I encouraged the students to visit the concession stand. "If you liked this opportunity, let them know by putting your money where your mouth is. They're serving fast food, snacks, soft drinks, and water, and the money will be used to support their school's mock trial program. Maybe we'll receive another invitation."

One by one, our students threaded their way through the cafeteria, selecting goodies to tide them over until the results were released. They sat quietly, tense, dreading what they perceived as the only possible outcome.

Harley and Jane drifted in, grim and somber. If I hadn't known Jane as well as I did, I wouldn't have caught the glint in her eye and the surreptitious wink.

When the judges released the results of each head-to-head meeting, determining the pairing for the second round of the competition, our score reflected our overall performance. The total put us in the winners' bracket by a fraction of a point. Our afternoon opponent earned a state berth last year and although most of their team members graduated, they would be a tough adversary.

Harley switched up the teams so everyone would have a chance to play a different part.

After the second session, Brock barreled into our assigned classroom. "I suck," he said and flopped onto the floor, slapping his shoes against the tile. "The judge said that part of his job was to investigate the facts of the case and he knew very well the idiosyncrasies of mock trial.

This wasn't his first carousel ride." Brock hung his head.

"Rodeo. This wasn't his first rodeo," Galen corrected.

Brock's head flew up, sparks flying, and Galen put up both hands in surrender. "Hey man," Galen said and they bumped knuckles.

"Anyway, he said it was his job to determine the validity of the objections. Mine was to play my part as well as I could and trust that the judges researched the lawsuit, and to stay in character."

"Which you didn't do for all of about three seconds. Next time you'll be great."

Brock shook his head, unsure.

Jane brought out a stash of miniature chocolates and passed them around before saying, "The results should be tallied soon. Let's get a good spot."

"I think I'll change my title to the Pied Chocolatier of Columbia." With her bag of goodies, Jane could have led them anywhere, but she steered them to the auditorium.

"Just in case," I said. "Do you think you could manage our practices with Harley if my juror number comes up."

Her eyes widened and she nodded ever so slowly.

While they waited for the judges to share the final results, Brock paced at the rear of the auditorium and Allie chewed on a thumbnail. Lorelei sat by herself, waves of anxiety carrying anyone who tried to sit nearby to the end of the row so that ten feet of empty space encircled her.

When the host coach approached the podium waving the results, the circle closed and our team pulled together.

"Fourth place goes to..." The coach peered over cheaters at the contents of the results page. "Writ Ten from Little Falls. Third place goes to Habeas Score from Marshall." He juggled the envelopes and continued.

"Second place goes to Columbia."

Before he could say anymore, the host team screamed and yelled, slapping hands and rushing to the stage to collect their trophy. With heads down and shoulders slumped, we bundled our personal belongings, and turned to the exit.

Harley had other plans and marched onto the stage. When he reached out his hand, Galen joined him, following his example. The receiving hands were wary at first, but they emulated their coach, smiling and returning the congratulations, promising a repeat performance somewhere, sometime. Then every one of our students trekked to the front of the auditorium, and before we left, all exchanged accolades and set the stage for another encounter.

As Jane and I cleaned up our area, movement in the balcony caught my eye. I glanced up as Kindra's solemn face retreated from the railing.

CHAPTER TWENTY

A spy?" Carlee whispered, settling herself on the bus
seat. "Why would they need to watch us?"

"We're already better now than we were at the
beginning," Galen said.

"Do we call them out on it?" Brock asked.

Harley shook his head. "I say let them be. You've
improved significantly and you'll continue to do so.
When we face off, we'll win." His volume increased. "We
need a team name so we're not confused with the other
competitors from Columbia. Any ideas?"

"PLAWsible?" said Ashley.

Brock squinted. "How about Torts Illustrated?"

Ashley leveled a gaze at him. "That's rather sexist, don't
you think?"

Brock's eyebrows shot up and his eyes widened. "I'm sorry. I would never..." he sputtered.

"EsqChoir? E-s-q-C-h-o-i-r." Lorelei spelled the name and grinned.

Off the hook, Brock breathed a sigh of relief and nodded. "That works."

Harley said, "All in favor of calling our team EsqChoir, please signify by raising your right hand."

Every hand shot up.

"We want to keep our presentation fresh. Let's meet Tuesday after school to continue our battle preparation. We'll come up with a plan to win the next competition."

"Where is the competition?" asked Allie.

"The Marshall coach invited us to a meet next Saturday. It'll be another four-team event but we almost won this one."

The students hooted and hollered and strategized the entire ride back to Columbia.

We'd just stepped off the bus and Jane's phone pinged. "Drew made a big pot of pumpkin soup and Ida's dropped off some of her pumpernickel raisin bread. Would you care to join us?"

Before I could give her my lame excuse about three's company, it seemed Harley had read my mind. He draped his arm over my shoulder and said, "We're going to head over to the local eatery and dine on the just desserts of our work." I nearly crossed my eyes trying to determine his meaning until he waved a handful of manila envelopes. "The judges' comments? Good night, Jane."

His head jerked toward his wheels. "C'mon. I'll drive."

We sat at a table for six, sliding extra place settings to one side and arranging the score sheets among our plates and glasses. We noted negative comments and weak arguments we could turn into a strength, color coding the data by character. Our kids had some exposure now and proved they could think on their feet.

Pete and Susie found us, heads together, scouring the pages between bites of burger.

Susie gushed. "Katie! How are you?" Not waiting for an answer, she continued. "We only have two more weeks until break and I cannot wait to have two weekends off in a row. You don't know what it's like having your weekends all tied up." Susie plopped down into the chair next to Harley, tossing her head of wavy chestnut hair. "What are you doing?"

"We're studying the judges' remarks from our mock trial competition today," Harley said with pride, a sentiment I assumed Susie could appreciate.

"And how's that going?" she asked, examining her nails.

Pete said, "I think they've been working weekends too."

Her gaze drifted back to Harley. "Sorry. Sometimes I get wrapped up in my own thing."

Pete snuck a glance my way and raised his eyebrows—just enough. One corner of my mouth inched its way into a smile.

"Join us. We're just about to put this away and indulge in a glass of wine," said Harley. He waved and the server delivered a bottle Harley must have preordered. Chemical formulas covered the orange and black label of an ambrosial cabernet sauvignon. I hadn't expected to finish our meal with wine, but I nodded approvingly.

"Tell us about your trial," Susie said.

Harley gave her the low down like a delighted dad and when he completed his rendering, Pete turned to me and started to say, "How are—"

Susie cut him off. "That's so cool. You've got to be a great lawyer. Where's your office?" she said with so much feeling I needed to excuse myself before my eye roll became too obvious.

I stepped into the hallway near the restrooms so I wouldn't hear Susie continue to wend her wiles with Harley while I tried not to gag, and called to check on my jury status. The automated message affirmed my potential first appearance, but with the possibility of a settlement, I needed to call Sunday evening for an update. When I rounded the corner on my return trip, I came eye to eye with a white button. I looked up, and my heart leapt to my throat. Those dark eyes have given me plenty of trouble.

He handed me a glass. I examined the wine as if it held a glimpse into my future.

"How are you?" Pete asked. "Really."

A smile tickled my lips while I tried to figure out what to say, and my eyebrows raised as I lifted my face to answer. "Busy, I guess. Are you getting what you need?" My face flushed, but Pete went on as if I hadn't said something to regret.

"I can't wait for a slow-down. I'm learning enough to fill an encyclopedia but I miss—"

"We miss all the fun in Columbia," Susie said as she linked arms with Pete. He didn't seem to notice. "We haven't made one Cougar football game since we started at HC. And Mr. Quarterback here has to listen to Viking broadcasts all the way home on Sunday. And I'm tired of discussing the Grainger case. Ronnie thinks that in addition to the fire blowing up Sophie's car, it also took out a storage unit full of drugs."

"Susie," Pete said in a warning tone.

"Sorry. I think I'm beat. Can you take me home now?"

They turned and walked out as I blinked back tears. I did miss Pete.

Harley had cleared the table and disappeared by the time I returned. Momentarily panicked, I made a grab for my phone and, as it tumbled away from me, Harley caught it in mid-air. He held two small take-out boxes.

"Just desserts." He nodded toward the door. "It's been a long day."

CHAPTER TWENTY-ONE

I listened twice to verify the message. Sure enough, my randomly generated identification number filled one of the spots and requested my presence for selection of a jury to sit on the case beginning Monday.

I called Mr. Ganka. "My number's up."

"We'll have a sub for you on Monday." I could almost see him smile. "You have nothing to worry about."

That's what he thought.

In addition to a restless night, fretting about the day, it snowed another four inches. It took an hour to shovel a path to get my van out. When I finally backed down the driveway, I navigated the streets with caution. The near-freezing temperatures made the snow slushy and slippery. Cars and trucks attempted unpredictable evasive maneuvers and slid through the intersections. My substantial vehicle stopped when I stomped on the brakes and only a blind person wouldn't see it for its size. However, getting used to driving in snow brought out the worst in many of us and some of my fellow drivers, hah, voiced their opinions by laying on their horns and flipping me off. Universal message received. Unfortunately, I sent a similar message to a shiny black sports car that cut me out of a premiere parking space in front of the courthouse, a communication witnessed by two watchful police officers who trailed me with a whoop and flashing lights as I turned into the nearest parking lot.

"License and registration, please," the officer said as I cranked down my ice-caked window.

He read my license, comparing the photo with the real thing. "Ms. Wilk, it's nasty out here made only nastier with your impatience. Where are you going in such a hurry this fine *fall* morning?" he said with a glib smile, flipping the ticket book open to the next page and pulling out a pen.

"Jury duty, sir," I said, resigned to the fact that I would not be with my students and would have to pay a fine to be here as well.

Signing with a flourish, he handed me a page. "Thank you for doing your civic duty. Just a warning this time, but, Ms. Wilk, please be thoughtful."

"Thank you, officer," I said, closing my eyes and exhaling. "Thank you," I whispered again.

The alarm tooted when I forgot to remove my keys from my pocket and, after finally passing through the metal detector, I followed the signs to the jury assembly area where I hung my dripping coat, poured a cup of hot water, and flipped through cellophane wrapped chamomile and mint flavored teabags, searching for a plain black tea loaded with caffeine. I settled on hot chocolate and stood in line, watching a rapidly diminishing mound of glazed donuts. My stomach rumbled so I snagged a pastry labeled prune kolache from a neatly stacked pyramid at the end of the table.

I took a bite of the carefully bundled roll with trepidation. The fragrant prune filling spurted out of a light buttery sweet dough. I closed my eyes, savoring the moment, when a quiet, low voice said, "Wipe that smile off your face or we'll have to share." I opened my eyes, swallowing the mouthful, and wiped the goo from my chin with the back of my hand. Dancing hazel eyes belied the frown on his face. "Wonderful, aren't they? I grew up eating my grandmother's kolaches and now they are a specialty item very few take time to make."

I tried to mirror his fake dissatisfaction. "These are soooo bad," I said before a giggle erupted. He threw back his head of short-cropped, sandy-colored hair and chortled.

When we'd regained our composure, he said, "I've seen you with Ida." He held out his hand.

I confirmed clean fingers and offered mine as well. "Katie Wilk."

"Steve Anderson." I knew that, but without his clerical collar I might have been mistaken.

"You'd better call me Steve." He looked at me over the tops of his glasses. "When I'm in a secular setting, it's easier if I'm not identified by what I wear."

"Sure. Hi, Steve," I said again, slurping the filling from my fingers.

"Kolaches come in lots of flavors, and there is quite

an art to making them," he said. "I grew up, feasting on all manner of ethnic foods like *knedlíky*, *žemlovka,* and *jitrnice.* And you should try our Christmas *oplatki.* The wafer is so thin you could shave a kiwi."

"If the other foods are anything like this, I want to taste them all."

Before he could say any more, the door opened and a uniformed officer stepped in. Everyone stopped talking.

"Your jury numbers indicate the order we will use for the preliminary examination of our panel," he said, holding a clipboard. "The first twenty prospective jurors should accompany me to the courtroom for *voir dire.* It means questioning potential jurors and discovering those who may have experiences or biases which might undermine a fair outcome." He tried making his memorized speech sound exciting. "If we haven't completed impaneling a jury, I'll return for the next twenty prospective jurors. While you wait, please answer a short questionnaire to expedite the selection. Should you be dismissed, we request you remain in the gallery for the duration of the session. Restrooms are located out this door to the left. Lunch will be provided at eleven thirty. Please do not leave the premises until directed. We have no way to predict if or when you might be needed. Officer Martha will assist you if you have any other questions."

A stalwart, dour, fiftyish matron in a khaki uniform clasped her hands behind her back and rocked on her heels. "Thank you for your service," she said. Her gel-doused, short-cropped, gray hair stood straight out from her head, and her intense blue eyes inspected every inch of the room, searching for a reason to pull the shiny handcuffs from her belt.

The first twenty potential jurors followed the bailiff, and Steve and I dutifully penciled in answers about education, marital status, number of children, residence, employment, involvement with civil, social, and professional organizations, hobbies, activities, and prior jury service. We continued our conversation, with tidbits about music, literature, Ida, school, and our obnoxious weather, until the door banged open. Officer Martha's head rotated slowly, validating lunch delivery as the source of the commotion. Time had flown.

One delivery person lined up stainless-steel trays of sandwich fixings on the long tables. A second person dragged in a cooler containing cans of water, soda, and iced tea and opened a box, containing a variety of single-serving chips and cookies.

The first wave of potential jurors returned with grim faces and more than half of them grabbed coats and made their way out the door, but not before making their lunch.

When the bailiff reappeared, we quieted again. "We will need the second half of the jury pool at eleven fifty-five. Again, thank you for your service."

While I chomped on a cookie, I hoped the shortened day would be easier on my substitute. Next time I wanted to meet the person, tailor my lesson plans, and make sure my students wouldn't waste a whole hour of instruction or cause an hour of pain for the sub.

Steve and I filed into the jury box as directed. After the judge described the case, the questions began in earnest, beginning with whether we had a medical, personal, or professional hardship that would make it difficult to serve.

The judge had looked over our questionnaires and asked. "Does anyone have difficulty reading, hearing, or understanding the English language?"

"Does anyone know the plaintiff, the defendant, or their lawyers?"

A hand raised, and the judge asked, "What is the nature of your relationship?"

"Stinky's my cousin," the woman answered, pointing to the prosecuting attorney. The gavel shut down the laughter burbling from every corner of the room and he dismissed the potential juror.

Some of the questions made us all sit back and consider the implications.

"Have any of you served as a juror before?" A few hands went up and the judge asked more specific questions, dismissing another potential juror.

"Have you read in the newspapers or on the internet, seen on television, or heard anyone talk on the radio about this case—Cross versus Simonet?" Many hands went up, but when asked if they thought it would affect decision making, only two hands remained.

"Do you feel comfortable using technology? Phones? Tablets? Apps you use at home or at work?" Some Luddites complained, but everyone owned at least one smart device.

"Did any of you know one another before today?" My hand crept up warily. "Identify the person and the nature of your relationship, please."

"Steve Anderson," I said, pointing out the priest, blushing crimson. "He's the pastor at my church."

Two others identified Steve the same way. Steve said, "They're all members of my congregation."

"Would anything they said impact your ability to render a fair verdict?" The judge addressed each of us in turn.

The other three replied in the negative.

I was expected to make my own intelligent, well-informed decision. "I believe I could render a fair verdict," I said. All kinds of justifications were swimming in my head. Even if I didn't know someone, my contact with them could color my opinion. I might not like what was said, or disagree with the way they thought, or the mismatched clothing they wore, or an outrageous hairstyle, and I would listen, however negatively, and still try to render a fair verdict. As soon as all four of us finished answering the question, the judge dismissed us to the gallery. We would not make up part of the jury.

In my heart, I knew I would've done my best to do the right thing, believing I would've been impartial. However, amid the bustle of our reseating, I whispered to Steve, "I think I just lied through my teeth. Of course, everything you said would have held more weight than anyone else. I would have tried to be fair but…"

His eyes crinkled. "Good to know. But they still kicked us all off." He moved his hands and it looked like sign language. I planned to check its meaning with Kindra. "I wish I had the influence on my congregation the judge is giving me credit for."

"We have impaneled our jury. Counsel, are you ready to begin?" the judge announced.

The fresh-faced attorney stammered and worked herself into a standing position, gathering papers. A handful fell to the floor. "Sorry, Your Honor." She bustled around the table and bent down to pick them up when the rear door of the courtroom flew open.

CHAPTER TWENTY-TWO

"May it please the court. Harley Brown for the plaintiff, Your Honor," Harley said as he strode to the table, sliding the loose pages to one side to make room for his new shiny, black briefcase. The three-piece dark-blue suit, crisp white shirt, and flashy red tie didn't moderate his appeal and appreciation thrummed among the female onlookers. He dismissed the exaggerated gesture the judge made looking at his watch. "Weather, Your Honor. May I approach?" His briefcase opened with a snap and he removed some files.

The judge cocked his head. Harley's soles slapped against the tile floor as he, the woman from the plaintiff's table, and the opposing counsel advanced toward the bench. Harley distributed a folder to each. The judge's jaw tightened as he read the first page and he squashed the file in his meaty hands. He removed his glasses, and his discontented whisper was heard by all. "New counsel at this stage? I suppose you'd like an extension?"

"No sir, Your Honor. The plaintiff is ready." His colleague nodded rapidly.

The glasses sagged from the judge's hand as he squinted toward the table. "Are the plaintiffs on board with this change?"

All eyes turned toward the sound of chairs scraping across the floor. The plaintiffs stood and nodded. "Yes, Your Honor, sir," they said in unison.

"This is quite out of the ordinary." The judge let out a sigh. "But let's get this show on the road."

I relaxed, looking forward to seeing Harley in the flesh, observing his performance in real time. I settled into my seat to watch the events unfold. After introducing the case, the judge delineated the particular components of law to the jury. I leaned forward. A smile stretched across my face, as Harley, looking more than confident, stood to give his opening statement and lay out the plaintiff's case.

"May it please the court," Harley said. I sat bolt upright, riveted. As prospective jurors, we hadn't been given the particulars of the case. After the third or fourth sentence, however, I slouched back, careful to keep my face hidden behind the heads in front of me. I'd heard the opening statement before. Lorelei had provided this argument acting as the plaintiff's attorney in the case she'd unearthed in the *Columbia Sentinel*. Harley had changed the decedent's name from Natasha Sandburg to Tom Jones for our case. And it was Amelia Cross, Sandburg's daughter who'd brought the suit.

My insides flipped; surprise and disappointment

tumbled as one. I tried to give him the benefit of the doubt, but I couldn't help feeling someone cheated. Harley encouraged Lorelei to think beyond, to question, prepare, and practice. As he repeated her opening statement, I shelved my initial incredulity. Maybe Lorelei and Harley had collaborated and she'd taken her cue from him. Maybe he'd provided more one-on-one instruction than I'd realized, challenging her, championing her potential.

I could never have been a juror for this case. It seems I'd heard it all before.

Harley completed the powerful opening and the defense retained its right to present its opening statement at the onset of their case.

"Call your first witness, counselor."

"We call Mr. Frederick Sandburg."

Natasha Sandburg's son stammered, twisted his hands, and shifted in his seat, but had his eyes glued to Harley, whose encouragement guided his short direct examination to a positive conclusion.

The cross-examining lawyer pounced on what Mr. Sandburg did not know and when the plaintiff broke down, the defense attorney almost smirked. My irritation gene climbed and I gritted my teeth.

"Objection. Badgering the witness, Your Honor. It's clear Mr. Sandburg is still grieving."

"Objection sustained."

I released the breath I'd held, mentally thanking Harley for his consideration.

"You may step down," the judge said.

"We call Amelia Cross." Harley held a legal note pad in his hand. He stood behind the table as she was sworn in.

"Please tell us your name and how you are related to

Natasha Sandburg."

She leaned forward with the easy answers, her lips nearly touching the microphone. "My name is Amelia Cross and I am Natasha Sandburg's daughter."

"What is your occupation?"

"I am a nurse in cardiac rehab." She proceeded to tell of her loss, and the meticulous care her mother took in keeping a perfect household. She delivered her testimony with more passion than her brother, and Harley took her down a slightly different path, describing her mother's healthy heart and engaging personality.

"What did your mother do?"

"She was an influencer."

"Please explain what an influencer is."

"My mom ran a successful blog, reviewing products. She started out—Do you want me to tell about that?"

"Please."

"My mom loved to examine new things. She checked out three or four different brands of similar items and compared them on her blog. She reviewed soaps, scents, clothes, and gadgets. She wrote at length about her favorites, and her followers seemed to appreciate her recommendations. She examined tech products with particular relish."

"Do you know why?"

"She had a PhD in electrical engineering but put it on the back burner when she adopted my brother and me and became an at-home mom. But we always had new-fangled electronic devices in our home."

"Wasn't her specialty signal processing and wireless communication?"

"Objection." The voice from the opposing counsel

sounded unsure. "Leading the witness."

"I withdraw the question, Your Honor. What was her specialty?"

Amelia blinked a few times and said, "Yes. Of course. Her specialty was signal processing and wireless communication. She even taught classes at the university."

"Then she would have been extremely competent to process her reviews as well as understand the mechanism used in her cover. Thank you, Ms. Cross. Nothing further."

When the defense attorney began his questions, Amelia answered through gritted teeth, giving short, terse responses. She did not break down. Her anger and pain spilled onto the jurors who looked at the defendant coolly. At the conclusion of the cross examination, she said, "I think the spa closer apparatus killed her."

"Objection."

"Sustained. The jury will disregard Ms. Cross's last statement. You are excused, Ms. Cross." The judge asked, "Mr. Brown, will your examination of your next witness be lengthy?"

"I believe so, Your Honor," Harley answered. "He's our expert."

"Then we'll recess until ten a.m. tomorrow morning." The gavel struck the block. Thank goodness I would be back in school.

The gallery exited sluggishly and I ended up straggling behind Amelia Cross and Frederick Sandburg.

She whispered to her brother, "I'm glad Harley remembered what mom taught. I'd almost forgotten. Do you think we did all right?" He shrugged.

I scurried out of the courtroom and raced to my van.

* * *

Dad shook his head as I removed my soggy shoes at the back door after slogging through the slush left in the wake of the capricious Minnesota weather.

"They're predicting a temperature of forty degrees. The snow'll be gone tomorrow." He cocked his head. "What's wrong kiddo? You gotta go back to court tomorrow?"

"No. They're finished with me. I wasn't acceptable as a juror. During *voir dire,* the judge decided my judgement might be clouded by Father Steve. They released him too. I enjoyed being part of the process and once I was there, I hoped they could've used me. Either way, it was a great opportunity to step outside my comfort zone. And to top it off, I got a better feeling for the judicial system and how it relates to mock trial." I must have frowned a bit.

"There is a but in there," Dad said.

"Harley turned out to be the plaintiff's attorney. He did a fabulous job during the short time I watched him today." But hearing the similarities with our invented mock trial suit also made me uncomfortable, and I wanted to check out Natasha Sandburg's case.

Dad's next comment came out of thin air. "I sat in on your classes today. I see what you mean."

My mind went blank.

"The sub did an adequate job, but his specialty is history. I volunteered to help answer students' questions and he took me up on my offer."

"Really, Dad? You were there? Thank you. Did they behave?"

"Pretty much. You've got some lively ones in that last hour. And I had to put a kibosh on a conversation among some of the hooligans not doing their work. When I told them I'd talk to you, they moaned something awful."

CHAPTER TWENTY-THREE

An hour before school started, I hunkered down in my quiet classroom, but my search for a techno-gadget influencer proved a tricky task; so many wannabees posted photos and videos of their next greatest find for an exciting Christmas gift that I would've missed Natasha Sandburg's blog page if not for her substantial number of followers.

Navigating her streamlined webpage provided answers to questions about new merchandise she had on trial. She posted photographs wearing casual and fashionable clothes. She compared similar multi-faceted tools. Videos caught her observing the flame-life and odor of scented candles or testing the quality of construction and uniqueness of a collection of novelty items. She opened and read aloud letters she received from satisfied, verified purchasers. A number of companies whose items she panned with her bright cheery voice repeatedly sent her their next new product for commentary. Even bad press was good press.

I was so caught up in studying the items Natasha sponsored on her wall of fame that my pen flew from my fingers when Brenna cleared her throat and I looked up at her standing next to my desk.

"I didn't mean to startle you."

I reached for my pen and let out a chuckle. "That's okay. I needed to jumpstart my heart anyway." She wore an expression I couldn't read.

"What's up?"

She mumbled something into her collar.

"What's wrong, Brenna?"

She looked up and swallowed. "Do you remember my friend, Annalise Rigelman?"

"Sure." I still owed her myself, but I couldn't tell Brenna.

"She's not answering my calls or my texts. I'm worried."

"If she's not in school, maybe she's home sick?"

"She's here today, but she's avoiding me. Any advice?"

I thought about it. "Maybe she's working with a teacher. It's probably nothing."

"Yeah, it's probably nothing."

If Annalise attended my last hour class, I could talk to her and reassure Brenna, but Annalise didn't show.

* * *

At the end of the day, jarring laughter drifted from my classroom. I peeked around the corner. Lorelei and Harley exchanged congratulatory high fives which lightened my mood considerably.

"Ms. Wilk, you should've been there," Lorelei said enthusiastically. "Mr. Brown tore the defense apart. I'll bet the Sandburgs are going to receive millions. Their expert witness stumbled over his credentials and it was game on."

"What?" She swept me into her excitement and all the questions I planned to ask Harley retreated to the back of my mind.

"My parents let me skip some classes today and I sat in on Mr. Brown's court case. I witnessed firsthand how the presentation of an argument can bring out the facts and leave the defense lacking. And I understand how the staging works, especially having prior knowledge of the basics of the case. He wasn't the original attorney-of-record, but the plaintiff's counselor contacted him and they hired him at the last minute. Mr. Brown said he used parts of our opening." Her flushed face radiated. "I'm going to be an attorney," she said decisively. Harley beamed.

Before I could reply, the rest of our team crowded the doorway. Galen and Carlee brought healthy protein bars—the ones that didn't taste like cardboard—and they got a ribbing from Harley for all their trouble. When the rehearsal began, I kept my eye on Brenna. At first, she held back, but by the end of practice, she'd focused her energy on the run-through. As she left, she gave me a half smile and a thumbs up.

That evening I spent the first twenty minutes of my walk with Maverick raving about the polished production they put forth at rehearsal, expounding on the positive performances they could give in competition. Everything was going well. I started to sing.

I should have waited to celebrate until after the other shoe dropped.

CHAPTER TWENTY-FOUR

The next morning before school, Kindra barreled around the corner of my classroom carrying a multi-drink tote with two steaming beverages. "Ms. Wilk, it's done. My mom requested the best and now you'll have my little sister in your math class."

I forced myself to focus on what Kindra was saying and caught the tail end of her comment. "She's nervous, but I told her all about you."

"Your mother?"

"No." She laughed with more to say than just no, but she held back her smart riposte. She placed a drink in front of me. "Patricia."

"Patricia?"

"My sister." She snorted, exasperated. "You weren't

listening." I worked up a smile. "I showed her the signs I taught you and, being the bratty little sister that she is, she told me I had them all wrong, but my mom said I'm right, so you should be okay."

"I only know a few signs, Kindra. Will she have an interpreter with her?"

"She reads lips really well, so when you need her to know something, don't look at the white board or cover your mouth. Make sure she's looking at you. She'll get it. She's way smarter than me."

"Which class will she be in?"

"Our Applied Math Class." My stomach lurched. She would join my most challenging group of students. My computer dinged. "I'll bet that's about her transferring in now. Just don't have her sit by me, okay?"

I read the message introducing Patricia.

* * *

Because we didn't have physical doors, I ate lunch in my room, standing guard. I timed my absences to coincide with the presence of a fellow teacher, so that my room stood unprotected for only seven minutes the entire day. I repeatedly checked the seat of my chair and examined the drawers in my desk and the cupboards for anything I hadn't put there myself. I thought I was safe.

My last period students entered calmly enough, taking their seats, opening books, and retrieving homework. I started explaining the relationship between the percentage off a sale item and the purchase price when Patricia waltzed in, five minutes late, slurping from a water bottle. She dropped into a chair at the back of the room and her backpack thudded to the floor. I motioned her to the front.

She made a lot of noise, extricating her lanky body from the desk and hauling her pack. She dragged her feet to tower next to me and handed me a late admit.

"Class, this is Patricia Halloran. She joined the Columbia student body today."

From somewhere in back, a voice said, "She can join my body anytime."

Patricia couldn't hear the words, but she could see the snickering reaction. The edge of her jaw turned white. She raised her hand and flipped off the group. I touched her arm to get her attention and she jerked away from me.

"Hey, what's wrong with her?" a female voice called out.

I grabbed a note pad and pen from my desk and scribbled, "May I tell them you're deaf?" I showed it to Patricia.

"Most of them already know," she said in a strong voice. "They're just dumb asses."

I nearly choked on my tongue. She could have fooled me into believing she heard everything I had to say, but Kindra told me to take nothing about her for granted. She'd lost her hearing at age thirteen and she worked extremely hard to maintain her communication skills.

I glanced at Kindra, hoping for encouragement, but her attention was fixed on the boy in front of her. I mouthed, "Sit here." I signed, "Please," and pointed out a desk in the front row. Kindra told me the fewer distractions, the better.

Patricia rolled her eyes and spilled into the seat. Needing to be fair and to set boundaries, I provided a short course, reiterating class rules about expectations, language, tardies, absences, homework, and grading. A pencil rolled to the front of the room and settled against the wall. I turned to pick it up and everyone threw a fake coughing fit which stopped the moment I turned back and no one claimed the pencil.

I tried to keep my face turned toward Patricia while I talked, but when I caught myself facing the board, I turned and signed, "Sorry."

She rolled her eyes and shuffled in her chair. Then, before I could react, Patricia stood, paraded to the back of the room, and poured the entire contents of her water bottle into the trash. She stirred the contents. Apparently satisfied, she made her way back, slipped into her seat, and repeated, "Dumb asses."

The bell rang and all my students vanished except Patricia. I stood in front of her, waiting for her to look at me so I could express my displeasure at her choice of words and also let her know the bell had rung and the others had gone. When she looked up, she said with defiant eyes, "I smelled the smoke."

"What?"

"Someone threw a spark bomb in the trash can. I'm sure those eggheads just wanted to test their hypothesis," she said sarcastically. "I'm outta here."

I raced in front of her, blocking her way.

"What do you want?" she said.

"Can you teach me sign language?"

She let out an exasperated breath. "Guess what this means," she said disdainfully, saluting with her third finger while hefting her backpack onto her shoulders.

I signed "Bye," and whispered, "I'm going to learn." Then I moved aside the top layer in the trash can. A pile of soggy singed pages cradled a metallic ball. There must be something to the theory that if you lose one of your senses the others take up the slack. I hadn't smelled anything.

* * *

When I finally caught Maverick so we could get in a few steps after dinner, the sneakers I removed from his jaw oozed drool. I hoped pulling my jacket close would fend off the falling temperature and blackening sky. We stepped into the street, but before we reached the third block, Maverick barked and pulled.

"Quiet, Maverick," I shushed. "We want to stay on our neighbors' good sides." I dropped down on one knee to nuzzle, and he bruised my ego by backing away. "Okay then. Let's go home."

Maverick jumped and yanked. I held onto the leash, but before I could stand, a half dozen black clad bikers appeared and streaked around us.

"What do you want?" I yelled. "Leave us alone."

The bikers pelted me with balls of paper. I covered my face and tried to drag Maverick under my arm. As they tightened the circle, a car turned a corner down the street and its headlights bounced toward us. The bikers fled.

Maverick sat and I buried my head in his neck, taking one slow breath at a time.

My head buried deeper as the tires screeched and the vehicle parked next to me. The door opened and Maverick resumed his barking. I squeezed my eyes and shuddered at the sound of rapid footsteps. I gasped and fell back when a firm hand grabbed my shoulder.

"Katie? It's me." Harley pulled me up and crushed me in a huge hug.

CHAPTER TWENTY-FIVE

Maverick nuzzled between us.

"Who were they? What did they want?" Harley asked. He picked up a paper wad and peeled back the crumpled page. He picked up two more, opened them and smoothed the creases against his chest, revealing letters cut from newsprint.

"Keep quiet," one message read. "We're watching." He looked at me questioningly, and read another message. "Remember. You didn't see anything." He pulled out his phone and punched in three digits. He waited a brief time before saying, "My friend has just been attacked. We're on..." He squinted to read the street signs caught in the shadows beyond the lights. "Sixth and Raven." He listened and added, "We'll be here."

I petted Maverick and my drumming heartbeat slowed to the tempo of his. My breathing steadied. *How dare they? What did they think they were doing? Who did they think they were? What did they want?*

Harley settled me in the passenger seat of his Bronco. Maverick jumped in next to me and I leaned on him. Harley slid into the driver's seat and clamped both hands on the steering wheel. "Do you have any idea who they are?"

"None. They started tailing me out of the blue one day and I never know where they will turn up next."

"This has happened before?"

I nodded. "But I don't know what I shouldn't say. I don't know what I could've seen." Their attempt at intimidation angered me. Given another set of circumstances, however, I might have been terrified.

"When did it start?"

I thought back. "It might have started close to the time we began mock trial, about the time you and I met." *It couldn't be.*

"Don't look at me!" said Harley, raising his hands to deflect the bad vibes. "I'm here for you, babe."

Babe? A tingle radiated from my stomach to the tips of my ears.

"Sorry." He didn't look it. "That just slipped out. What else was going on?"

I closed my eyes and leaned into the headrest. I considered my short life in Columbia which included school, experiments with the science club, mock trial and Stanley Mossa, church, dancing lessons, working with Maverick to improve his SAR status, Dad moving in, biking, and finding Sophie Grainger.

"I'm pretty sure they're kids. But I didn't recognize

anyone. I can't imagine what I know that they don't want me to share. But this can't continue for long. They won't be biking so easily in the snow." I tried to laugh. "What brings you out this way?"

"I come bearing gifts. I've been preoccupied this week and you've taken up the slack. For that I am deeply grateful."

"The practices have gone so well; I can't wait for Saturday."

"I've got some other lawyering to do, but I'll be there."

"I did have some questions about your court case. Is it—"

A squad car trolled the street and stopped in front of us. Officer twelve-year-old-looking Jake stood between the cars in the glare of the headlights. "I was on my way home and heard the call. What can I do for you, Katie?"

"A pack of hoodlums chased Ms. Wilk," said Harley. "I think I scared them off, but I felt she needed to report it in case this behavior continues." Harley told a compelling story, repeating much of what I'd told him and Jake jotted notes.

"Anything to add, Ms. Wilk?"

"I wish they'd cease and desist. Do you have any advice?"

"Carry your phone and don't go out alone." He snapped his notebook closed and tipped his hat before sliding into his cruiser.

Harley gave Maverick and me a ride home. Before I got out, he handed me a small box. "Open it," he said eagerly.

I tore off the shiny giftwrapping and opened the cover of the faux velvet box. A brass-colored gavel charm hung on the short chain. "It's lovely. Thank you." I thought about giving him a bigger thank you, but Maverick licked his face instead.

"Good night, Katie," he said, swiping at the drool.

"Goodnight, Harley."

We bounded up the steps and inside. I closed the door and slumped against the door. My heart jumped to my throat when Dad said, from just a few feet away, "You've taken enough time, Katherine Jean. Charles would want you to be happy." I started to protest, but he held up his hand. "Just think about it." He smiled. "G'night, darlin'."

It took a long while to unwind. While I lay awake, I fretted about Drew's recovery, what I should bring to Carlee's Thanksgiving feast, Saturday's competition, and who might have wanted Sophie Grainger dead. Then I gave thanks for Dad's recuperation, Ida's kitchen skill, Pete's eyes, Harley's hair, and all my new friends, but I pulled my pillow over my head and moaned when Susie entered my thoughts.

CHAPTER TWENTY-SIX

We gave thanks and barely noticed the absence of Pete, Susie, and Harley. Carlee outdid herself when she brought out four picture-perfect pies: chocolate cream, pumpkin, pecan, and sour cream raisin and I missed them even less.

I shook my head to fend off the food overdose when my phone pinged with a message.

Happy Thanksgiving!

Thanks, Pete. U2.

Sorry I couldn't make it.

There are plenty of leftovers.

Pete's messages stopped so I pocketed my phone and joined a rousing hour-long game of Pictionary that revived my dad. It ended when Carlee, Galen, and CJ handed out homemade doggie-bags decorated with googly eyes, a nose, ears, and a tail, and they took off for a bit of family time.

My dad escorted Ida and me across the street, fully cognizant that we were as ready to support him as he was to support us. His strength returned in spits and spurts, and I trusted his judgement on his abilities most of the time.

Ida squeezed my arm and gave my dad a kiss on the cheek. "I'm done for. Have a pleasant evening."

With Thanksgiving tryptophan coursing through his veins, Dad took a nap. The clock read five-twenty. I had just pulled out a book when my phone pinged again.

Did you have a good day?

Yes.

Sorry I missed the meal. What RU doing?

Lesson plans.

Ever heard of geocaching?

Talking would be a lot easier so I hit 'call'. "Hi, Harley."

"What do you know about geocaching?"

"Where'd that come from?"

"I came across it while researching the marriage between technology and gaming. Have you ever geocached? Is that the right term?"

Boy, had I ever, but I played it cool. "I may have heard of it. I've watched the kids in the science club find a few." Then I stopped talking, remembering the body I found on one of my first geocaching excursions with Maverick. My enthusiasm took a detour.

"If I'm reading the attribute list correctly, there is a newly-placed medium-sized night-time cache that is winter accessible. I need to get out of the house and this game aroused my curiosity. Are you up for it? Or are you already down for the count?"

A smile spread across my face. "I'd love to."

"I can pick you up in twenty minutes," he said, and hung up.

I placed my phone on the charger and fished through the closet for a warmer jacket with deep pockets, a pair of gloves, a hat, and hiking boots. I replaced the batteries and pocketed a small flashlight then sat and waited.

I didn't have long to wait. I jumped up to answer the soft knock, grabbed my phone, and nabbed my house key from the hook, whisking open the door, and stopped short.

"Ah, hi?" I said.

Her eyes traveled down to her own shuffling feet. She mumbled something unintelligible.

"Brenna, what's the matter?" I asked.

She looked up at me and said quite clearly, "It's been a long day, Ms. Wilk." Long brown tresses whirled around her face and she shivered.

I looked both directions down the street. "How'd you get here?"

"Walked."

"Come in. Where've you been? What have you been doing?"

"My family went to my aunt's for Thanksgiving and I told my mom I was hanging out with Annalise today, but she must've forgotten and I haven't been able to get hold of her," she said as she removed her coat, gloves, and hat. Then she added sarcastically, "I had a great lunch at Bob's Burgers, though."

"Oh, Brenna," I sighed.

"It's okay. It's my own fault. I should have checked with her. She's been acting awfully weird lately. Can I hang out here for a while, just until my folks get home? Do you have anything I can do?"

"You can help me finish a fabulous piece of pie and—"

"But you can't cook!"

"So I've heard." I smiled and the look on her face gave an apology. "I have a secret weapon. Follow me."

I pulled together a small, tasty Thanksgiving plate from the doggie bags Carlee sent home, and Brenna's eyes grew to the size of saucers. "Carlee made it all," I begrudgingly admitted.

"Thanks, but I'm not hungry," were the last words she spoke before cleaning her plate and licking the tiniest bit of whipped cream from her lips. She groaned.

"You can stay here until—"

The doorbell rang. I'd forgotten about Harley. "It's probably Mr. Brown. Would you like to try a night-geocache?"

"Mr. Brown, huh. That sounds great, Ms. Wilk." She checked her watch and smiled for the first time. "But maybe you want to be alone." Her eyebrows danced.

I swung the door open and Harley said, "Katieeeee … Ms. DeSilva?" I couldn't quite read the look on his face, but he recovered well. "With such great company, we will, no doubt, have very little trouble finding this … this … thing."

CHAPTER TWENTY-SEVEN

Night cache?" prompted Brenna as she stuffed her long tresses up into her cap. She wrapped her coat around her and yanked up the zipper. "Where are we going, Mr. Brown?" He showed her his screen. She pressed keys on her phone and brought up the identical listing. "Do you have something to write with, Ms. Wilk?" she said as she pulled on her mittens.

I added a pen to my bulging pockets, and stepped onto the landing. When I saw the creamy-white Range Rover in front of me, I stopped in my tracks. "Nice wheels, Mr. Brown. New?" It was a rhetorical question. The paper tag in the rear window and the buffed exterior gave it away.

"We settled the case," Harley said, wiggling his eyebrows. Brenna giggled, another good sign.

"Maybe you don't want Maverick to take a ride."

"He's welcome. Have him sit in the back seat."

"I get to sit by Maverick," Brenna said.

We climbed in and I inhaled that new leather smell I'd probably never have in a vehicle of my own.

Harley's phone communicated with the Range Rover's GPS and it periodically announced the direction and remaining distance. Brenna chatted breezily from the backseat, drawing our attention to newly erected displays of decorations pulsing their holiday greetings. I wondered if Ida put up Christmas lights.

When the last of the city lights receded from view, we drove into the pitch-black night of a new moon. Harley's face glowed green in the dash lights. Maverick's head rested on the seat and Brenna leaned into him. Harley turned on the radio and tuned in to a holiday station.

The Range Rover carried us to the state park entrance. Harley grabbed an envelope from the center console and jumped out. He slid it into the slot and claimed a permit at the kiosk. As the gravel crunched beneath the tires, I shuddered, shaking away the morbid memory of the body Maverick found on our first visit to this park.

When we reached the parking lot, Harley shut off the engine. The dash lights dimmed, but his face still glowed with excitement.

Brenna read the listing, "This cache is best found at night. You can find it during the day, but it may be more difficult and not nearly as rewarding. You will need a bright flashlight. Follow the glow-in-the-dark FireTacks."

Brenna opened the door and she and Maverick bolted, scouring the trees with her flashlight, and darting from one set of reflectors to the next. Harley grabbed a stiff new backpack and we followed.

We hadn't been searching long when Brenna and Maverick stopped next to a short wall. "X marks the spot," she said, shining her light on the nine FireTacks.

We poked and prodded and pulled and pressed, but nothing seemed to unearth the cache. Brenna reached as high as she could and then crawled on her knees. I covered the area in between. Light beams crisscrossed the nearby trees. Maverick gave a close approximation of searching and pawed at the base of a tree stump before raising his hind leg and faked marking it.

Brenna's voice rose. "Look at that."

She shined her phone light on the top of the stump. Her hand brushed a brass hinge embedded in the bark that dripped reflective paint spatters. Her smile could have lit the night. "Way to go Maverick!"

"Open it," said Harley like an anxious parent watching his firstborn opening a birthday present.

She shoved the top of the stump, up and away from the hinge, revealing a crevice. She pushed with both hands. Then she used her shoulder as if blocking a tackle on the football field. We examined the door and the hinge. It had to open. Brenna flashed the lamp on the surface and tugged at the end of what turned out to be a long dowel. As it cleared the hole, the door sprang open. She turned to us, waved the dowel like a conductor's baton, and grinned. Maverick circled, wagging his tail.

"Since this is your first cache, I think you should sign the log, Mr. Brown," I said.

Harley wore a Cheshire Cat grin and Brenna let out a belly laugh.

"What am I missing?"

"Mr. Brown planted this cache." Harley nodded.

"And how do you know this?"

"It's in the description." Her face lit up in the phone screen as her fingers danced across the display. "'Search for Justice was placed in honor of the great work done by the Columbia High School mock trial team—EsqChoir—by its attorney coach.'" She looked up and added, "Not bad, Mr. Brown. I can't wait to show the rest of our team."

"I have two additional night caches in the planning." He looked pleased with himself. "I'm enjoying the game."

"You've been acting like it's a new thing to you. When did you take up geocaching? Where'd you get the idea?"

"During our first meeting, one of your students brought up the subject of geocaching and as I set out to learn all I could about what the students could and couldn't do, what they liked and disliked, or why they disagreed, I thought I'd look into something new. The creative process is awesome."

"Well, if this is a cache, where is the log we're supposed to sign?"

"Keep looking," he said, a grin stretching from one ear to the other.

I reached into the hole and extracted a small container holding an even smaller log. I retrieved the pen from my pocket and asked, "What'll we call ourselves?"

Harley answered, "How about the three musketeers."

Brenna shook her head. "I'm sure that's been taken. How about the night fliers?"

I signed the narrow strip of paper, and we put everything back the way we found it. "I can't wait to try your other caches," I said.

CHAPTER TWENTY-EIGHT

After the meet on Saturday, although it looked like herding kittens, Harley reined in the exuberant whoops and fist bumps and gathered the students, escorting them to the stage in the auditorium where members of Team EsqChoir claimed their first-place medals and shook hands with their opponents. Jane and I stood, bouncing on the balls of our feet, cheering so boisterously I almost missed the gentle tap on my shoulder.

Kindra stood next to me, grinning and clapping.

"Way to go, Ms. Wilk!" she said.

"What are you doing here, Kindra?"

"We're visiting my grandparents who live on a farm outside of town, and we came to watch you so we wouldn't have to help in the kitchen. It gets pretty crowded and my grandma's way too picky. We caught your second face-off."

"We?" asked Jane.

Kindra turned and nodded over her shoulder. Patricia came into view, rolled her eyes, and flopped into a seat. Kindra shrugged. "You're pretty good," she said with a hint of admiration.

Patricia watched me so I pronounced my words slowly. "Kindra, how did your team do yesterday?"

"We took second. It was a sixteen-team tournament." She sounded a little defensive.

"Her snobby coach made them practice this morning because they didn't win yesterday and we were almost late for lunch," said Patricia. "Of course, that wouldn't have been a bad thing."

Kindra snickered and said, turning to face her sister. "We'll win next time."

The celebration on stage broke up and the kids raced over to show off their hardware.

"I'll wait in the lobby, Patricia," said Kindra. She knocked into her sister's knees. "Just ask," she ordered. "Congrats, everyone!" she said as she waved and slid out of the row, stepping into the darkened alcove of the nearest exit.

Patricia gave me the oddest look. "Do you think I could do this?" she asked.

Surprise stole across my face.

"Never mind," she said, and rose to her feet.

Carlee and Allie looked at me expectantly. As gently as I could, I touched Patricia's arm to get her attention. "Of course. Can you be in my room after school on Monday?"

Her smile could have lit a room. She nodded. Carlee and Allie sighed.

"Great," said Galen. "She was a little worried, but we told her a room could be arranged so she could read the lips of all the speakers. She's really funny." Carlee nudged him. "And she's really smart. She's already studied the case and memorized Maggie Murphy's part."

Jane and I sat in the bus seat behind Harley to converse more easily. At first, his astonishment at our suggestion to include Patricia caught me off guard. "It's a bit late in the game, don't you think?"

Jane said, "It behooves us to be all-encompassing. Galen said she already knows Maggie's part and she might feel comfortable enough to try one competition. In any case, we'd have another veteran with young blood for next year."

"Behooves?" Harley snorted. "You're right. I don't know what I was thinking."

I said, "There seems to be less ad-libbing as a witness, don't you think, Harley?" He nodded. "The opposition is generally standing behind their table unless they're presenting an exhibit so her ability to lip-read shouldn't be hindered. I agree with Jane. I'd like to include as many students as possible, and we've had the luxury of winning. We really are good."

"What about the other kids? Shouldn't we ask them? They might feel slighted. They have been working hard for a while now," Harley said.

Jane looked at me and back at Harley and then turned around, kneeling on the seat to get some height. She raised her hand and everyone quieted. "Patricia Halloran would like to join our mock trial team. Anyone have a problem with that?"

Lorelei jumped in. "Even if her sister's on the other

team, we're all part of Columbia's mock trial. I know we'll win and if we can teach Mr. Mossa's team a thing or two, so much for the better."

"I can't see what difference it would make," said Brenna.

Carlee said, "Show of hands. Who votes yes to Patricia?" Brock's hand crept up last, but every one of the students affirmed the decision and they all began talking at once, assigning jobs to help Patricia in her new role.

Brock jostled his way to the front of the bus. "Ah," he began. "We were talking. Could we get together tomorrow afternoon and do a rehearsal for Patricia? Then she'll know if she'll like it."

"Great idea, Brock!" said Harley. "Katie, can you be there? You're the one with the keys."

Jane cleared her throat.

"Or Jane?" he added sheepishly.

"Hey, everybody. If you want, bring a beverage. We'll bring snacks," Jane said, pointing her index finger back and forth between us. *Oh, boy!*

* * *

I couldn't wait to kick off my shoes and put up my feet. Instead, I pulled up information about Natasha Sandburg's death in the hot tub, smothered by the electronic spa cover. After reading her obituary, I read about the huge settlement against the electronics company. Then I read about Sophie Grainger. Ronnie Christianson asked for witnesses to come forward and said they were talking to persons of interest. I imagined that included Ransam Grainger, his girlfriend, and Sophie's business partner. I wondered if

Sophie had a boyfriend as well. Two bright women, who were much more tech-savvy than I, died violent deaths—one seemingly by accident and one possibly at the hand of another. So sad.

The next article detailed the extent of the damage done by the explosion and subsequent fire at the storage facility. It also mentioned finding traces of fentanyl in one of the units with a common wall to Sophie's.

I shifted my concern to something more concrete and considered what snack I might bring to our practice and whipped up what I thought might be a close approximation of Ida's award-winning seafood dip. When Dad tasted it and turned up his nose, I decided to look for something else.

CHAPTER TWENTY-NINE

The temperature dropped again. Patricia, Galen, and Carlee fidgeted at the school entrance, rubbing what warmth they could through the sleeves of their puffy down jackets.

"Snow," Galen predicted, pointing at the heavy, gray sky.

"I hope not." I unlocked the door and lights woke as we walked past the motion detectors. I flipped the switches in the math department and the dreary mood seemed to lift as giggles and garbled words followed us down the hall.

Jane entered with the rest of the team and, as we arranged the furniture to resemble a courtroom, the students identified the major concepts for Patricia.

"This is the defense table," Brock said slowly, running

his hand across the tops of the desks we'd pulled together. "And the plaintiff sits there." He pointed across the narrow aisle.

Lorelei set up the makeshift witness stand next to the judge's bench. "Most of the action takes place here. As Maggie, you'll be sworn in by a mock clerk and if we adjust the seats, you should be able to see everyone."

Watching every word, Patricia paled.

Jane stood in front of her and smiled. "You're going to love it. We never know what's going to happen either, and if you can't understand something, just ask the counsel to please repeat what was said. With your ability to read lips, I don't think we need to tell anyone but the judges so they'll know how to direct the opposition. Do you want to try it?"

Patricia nodded ever so slightly and the students took up their positions, selecting favorite roles.

"I get to be the judge today," said Brock, strutting to my padded chair stationed at the front of the room.

Jane whispered, "I wonder where Harley is."

I shrugged.

Patricia arranged her chair so she could view every mouth, and each student turned imperceptibly to assist her. By the time the clerk called Maggie Murphy to the stand, she had assumed the persona of a young woman who'd had her heart torn in two.

"I'm looking for justice, Your Honor," she said, resolutely.

Not a pin dropped when she finished. Jane looked at me in disbelief. Then Lorelei rushed from behind the counsel table and embraced Patricia. She held her at arm's length and said, "You were great. How did you learn Maggie's part so quickly?"

Brenna and Ashley joined them.

As Patricia struggled to keep her balance amid the hugs and answer the barrage of questions, she said, "I've been studying Kindra's script since the first day I got back to Columbia. Ms. Wilk, do you think it'd be okay if I only played the part of Maggie?"

With all eyes on me and several heads nodding in approval, I said, "I don't see why not, until you want to try another part."

"Let's break out the goodies. It's time to celebrate!" said Carlee.

I opened a bag of Ida's sugar cookies and Jane shook her head. "Chicken," she said.

As the sugary crumbs and the last morsel of chocolate disappeared, the kids gave each other high fives and vanished. I trooped down the hall to collect a bucket of soapy water and towels to clean up the sticky mess and met Harley.

"Sorry I didn't make it on time. My real job got in the way," he said. "I didn't know if you'd still be here. Have the students gone?"

"Yup. They did a magnificent job but our instruction lacked your professional expertise."

He chuckled. "I'm sure you did fine."

"Patricia is wonderful as Maggie."

He looked a little leery.

"Truly. You'll love her performance."

With a solemn look on his face, he handed me a copy of an email. "This came today." It was our conference competition schedule. I scanned the list and looked up into bright eyes and a broad smile.

"We've already met some of the teams and we've done well. Thank you for the opportunity to work with these kids. They're phenomenal."

Jane's voice reverberated in the empty hall. "Katie, we could be finished by now. What's keeping you?"

The light in Harley's eyes dimmed a bit, maybe from the realization we had a chaperone, and I bit back a satisfied grin. Susie and Pete might be an item or might not, but it's nice to be appreciated.

* * *

Disappointed by my tardiness, Maverick dragged on our walk. "I'm here now, aren't I? When we get back, maybe we'll play catch." At the mention of one of his favorite activities, his head came up. His pace increased, and his tail began its steady tick tock until we returned and he saw CJ's truck in the driveway. We raced into my apartment, but it was empty, so Maverick and I went next door. Carlee greeted me with a determined look on her face.

"Ms. Wilk. C'mon in." Maverick and I joined CJ, my dad, Carlee, and Ida in her kitchen.

"Would you like some hot chocolate?" Ida asked.

"Mine is even warmer," Dad said, his eyes alight, raising his cup and tipping it toward the counter where I spied the bottle of one of his winter favorites—peppermint schnapps.

"You should have made Mrs. Clemashevski's seafood dip," Carlee said, chomping on a cracker and smacking her lips.

"She tried," Dad said.

All eyes turned toward me. I tried to hide behind the steam hovering over my mug but I felt my cheeks and ears turning red.

"And how did that go for you?" asked Ida.

"I thought, how hard could it be? I put together mayo, imitation crab meat, Swiss cheese, red onion, and that green stuff in the pantry."

Ida's eyebrows flew to her hairline and her mouth dropped open. "Swiss cheese? It's scallions, not red onions, and that green stuff in the pantry is *not* parsley."

"I'm sorry." I wanted to sink into the floor.

Dad began to laugh, a deep, rolling belly laugh, like the sound of a happy tympani, unexpected and cherished. Since moving in with me, every move he'd made was one of a house guest—careful and measured. This laugh was familiar and bawdy and honest and I loved it. The wave caught the rest of us and continued until Maverick woofed, announcing someone's arrival.

CHAPTER THIRTY

When I opened the door, Kindra backed away from Brenna and lost her balance, teetering on the top step. Brenna grabbed the collar of her friend's jacket and jerked. Kindra tumbled into the entryway to a collective gasp. She looked up apologetically.

"Happy holidays," I said cheerily and hauled them inside.

Kindra's eyes dropped to the floor. Brenna nudged her gently. "Go on. Maybe she can help."

As if she'd known they'd be coming, Carlee wandered in from the kitchen carrying a thermal pitcher and a plate of cookies. "Take your coats off and have a seat." She'd learned a lot from Ida. "Just in time for some hot chocolate and shortbread."

Dad carried two more mugs, and set them on an end table. Then he knelt in front of the fireplace and struck a match to the end of a fire-starter square. The kindling turned red and then the flames crackled, and he added a few larger logs. As the heat wormed its way into the room, Kindra and Brenna removed their coats, hung them on the coat rack, and made their way to the sofa. Dad and Ida drifted upstairs.

Carlee sat on the floor and curled her legs under her. She smiled and said, "Ida's getting ready to decorate for Christmas."

Carlee poured the hot chocolate milk. She spritzed real whipped cream on top, sprinkled cocoa powder, and then handed a steaming mug to each of us. I focused on the cream floating in the mug cradled in my hand, letting the heat dissipate, and waited for Kindra to speak. Carlee tugged an empty folder from beneath the tray and handed it to me.

Kindra finally looked up. "They've questioned my mom about Sophie Granger's death. Ms. Wilk, she didn't do it."

I blinked back surprise. *Of course, she didn't do it. They never do,* shouted a little know-it-all voice on my right shoulder. What could I say? *Just listen,* whispered the wiser voice on my left shoulder.

Maverick wandered over to Kindra. He slumped next to her and laid his head in her lap. His unwavering gaze pinned me to the chair, willing my attention. She stroked his ears and tears trickled down her cheeks. Brenna caught her other hand and squeezed.

"What do I do?" Kindra said.

"You work hard in school so your mom doesn't have

to worry about anything but herself. You support her. You listen to her."

Brenna looked disappointed, but fire burned in Carlee's eyes. Somehow, I'd let them down. They wanted my help, but I didn't know what to do. *Just listen,* I heard again.

"My mom's never had a fair shake. It's just not right. I have to help her."

"What do you mean?"

"She was a big city girl with fantastic dreams." Kindra's eyes gleamed. "She met my dad in college. They were both in engineering. And he was supposed to be real brainy." Kindra used air quotes and made a sour face. "They married when they were too young—because of me, and he moved her out here to the country. My maternal grandma was furious and cut all ties. I've never even met her. But my mom was determined to make her mark." She sniffed. "She's very good with tech stuff and set up a top-notch security system where my dad worked. She doesn't talk about it much, but I read about it; she caught a thief— my dad. Maybe he thought she'd fix it somehow and let him skate." She shook her head. "But other guys at work were pissed too. They told everybody she was a snitch."

Determination replaced some of the sadness. "My dad skipped before his trial and no one but his boss even acknowledges my mom." Sparks flew from her eyes. "I think they were all skimming and they're hypocrites. My mom jammed up their access to easy money and they still won't forgive her for it. She got a little reward and scrimped and saved and she bought a small milk operation. With all the bells and whistles she added, we've been able to operate in the black, going organic." Then the intensity in her eyes softened. "And she finally found someone and wasn't alone anymore—somebody she really liked."

"Ms. Wilk, you know about how the law works," said Brenna. "We were hoping you could squeeze some sense out of everything going on."

"They don't arrest someone on a whim. There must be some evidence. Do you have any idea what that might be?"

The doorbell rang again. Kindra jumped up, her hands swiping at her face. "I'll get it." She rushed to the door and pulled it open.

The photo in the paper didn't do him justice. Without the puffy eyes and red nose, Ransam Grainger might have been a good-looking man. All eyes turned toward me. I dragged myself off the chair.

"Come in." I sighed, resigned.

He wiped the end of his nose with the sleeve of his jacket. "Thank you for seeing me," he said.

I felt my eyebrows climb. Not one girl would look me in the eye.

I turned back to the door. "I'm not sure what I can do for you, Mr. Grainger."

"You know who I am?" He hung his head. "Yeah. I suppose everybody does now." I didn't say anything. "Kindra thought, your reputation at solving puzzles…"

I didn't catch the rest. In my early twenties, I had aspired to become the next brilliant cryptographer, maybe following in the shoes of Genevieve Grotjan. She helped break the code to "Purple," enabling the Signals Intelligence Service to decrypt important Japanese diplomatic messages during WWII. As that daydream dissolved, I drifted back to the conversation at hand, disappointment written on my face, but not for the obvious reasons.

"I'm sorry. I shouldn't have come," Mr. Grainger said.

"No, Mr. Grainger. It's not you. I was thinking of something else entirely. Sit down and tell me what you think I can do."

"Sophie and I have ... had been apart for a while," he said, sitting next to Kindra. "She is ... was a brilliant businesswoman. I adored her and admired her business acumen. For a long time, she alone kept us afloat financially.

"Then my ag-consulting business started to catch on, and she complained that I was boring—a workaholic. I loved her once. I'd like to believe that she loved me too. We just didn't have the same goals any longer. We occupied the same address, but she did her thing and I did mine. She spent hours away: at work, on the road, in the air, searching for something—happiness, I guess. Then last year she mellowed out, more content than I'd seen her in a long time. I'm pretty sure she found someone.

"Business bustled at her shop. They had more clients than ever. Sophie was the brains, navigating the social media platforms and using her vast series of connections. Serena Stewart was the brawn in their joint venture they called S & S Designs. They brought the best of both worlds to the table. They made grand plans which included an expansion and Serena went all in. So, when I met Debora, Kindra's mom, I allowed myself to be happy too.

"I'm not sure what happened. Sophie changed again, almost overnight. She decided to sell the business and our home. She owned both outright. And it seemed if she couldn't be happy, she was going to do her best to make all of the rest of us miserable."

Kindra scowled; her knee bobbed up and down.

Ida called from upstairs, "Hey, you young whippersnappers. I need help." Brenna and Carlee dragged

Kindra from the couch. They'd overheard enough, and Grainger looked grateful.

"What happened to Serena?"

"Sophie's new deal cut Serena out and she was devastated. They had nothing in writing. But I did find this in our home safe." He fished a sheet of linen paper out of his pocket and handed it to me. "This is company stationery. I already showed it to the police but they don't think it's important."

"What is it?" I asked as I read the list of seven names.

"Sophie rarely did anything without a specific purpose in mind. Serena, Debora, and I are all on it. It might not be anything, but it feels like some kind of hit list." He dropped his head.

The cuckoo clock chimed the quarter hour, filling the silence. I scanned the list: Debora, Ransam, Amelia, Ian, Annalise, Serena, and Natasha. A horizontal arrow pointed to an empty space on the next line. "Do you recognize any of the other names?"

He shook his head and continued, "I asked her for a divorce. She said that'd be over her dead body." He flinched. "I told her that I didn't want anything from her, but she wouldn't listen. Debora knew her. She'd set up the security system for S & S. She thought she could talk some sense into her."

"Did she talk to Sophie?" I said, sliding the list into the folder.

"Yes. Sophie insisted she stop seeing me. She called Debora…" He glanced around, eyes wide. "She called her names. But it didn't matter. I told her I didn't need her money. *We* didn't need her money. I just wanted to be free and I know deep down she wanted the same thing.

"Debora and I knew the divorce would be bitter. We decided to give her whatever she wanted."

Kindra and Brenna pounded down the stairs carrying a plastic tote. Fuming, Kindra responded to what she'd overheard. "Besides taking over Ransam's business, she wanted a piece of our farm. There was no way she was getting any of that." They dropped the tote to the floor.

Taking over part of a business, in which she had no interest, seemed harsh. "When did Debora visit with Mrs. Grainger?"

"They met for coffee…" Ransam lowered his head, interlacing his fingers, and continued, "…the day before you found her."

Was that the fight Kindra had witnessed?

"They have no doubt that Sophie was murdered," Ransam said.

CHAPTER THIRTY-ONE

I didn't make any promises, but I almost believed Ransam and Kindra. After they left, I carried the dishes to the kitchen, washed and put them away. I returned to my apartment and considered the meaning of the odd list of names Ransam had retrieved from the safe, and the ignition key found without prints. The authorities would be looking for a person with a possible motive to get rid of Sophie Grainger and couldn't rule out Debora.

Maverick pawed at the adjoining door and I trailed him, head down, contemplating Ransam's pressing request, so preoccupied I would've run into CJ if he hadn't grabbed my shoulders. "Sorry. I wasn't looking where I was going."

He winked as his fingers manipulated a tangle of blinking white lights slung over his shoulder, and rotated his broad torso, revealing a wonderland of decorating. Ida's fireplace danced. Soft strains of a string ensemble played carols in the surround sound. Electric candles wreathed in plastic ivy dotted with red berries flickered in the front windows. Dad stood off to one side, nibbling one of Ida's oversized gingerbread cookies, pondering the array of colors in the opened white cardboard ornament boxes on the floor lining the wall. Carlee sat on her haunches and presented a delicate creche figurine for Ida to inspect before gently standing it in the manger. Ida sat tall and regal in a gray wingback chair, directing the spectacle. I closed my eyes and breathed the pungent scent of burning oak, wrapping me in a blanket of lovely memories.

I heaved a sigh, responding to a sensory overload, and all I could think of was Christmas until Ida's imperious voice brought me back.

"Debora did not commit this murder. Did you get everything sorted out?"

I gave Carlee *the look*. "They beat it out of me," she confessed.

Five hopeful pairs of eyes cast their laser beams on my face. "Not exactly."

"What does that mean?" Ida asked.

Carlee's brow furrowed.

"Debora was very unhappy with Sophie, and it looks like Ronnie Christianson believes Debora had reason to see her gone, but Mr. Grainger is hoping I can perform some magic that will get her out of the hot seat. There might have been another man in his wife's life, but I do know there was another woman in his. And he indicated Sophie was also battling the terms of the dissolution of her business with her soon-to-be-ex-partner. With them to consider, and, including Ransam and Kindra on the list—"

I held up my hand as Brenna jumped in to defend Kindra. "I'm speculating. That makes at least four individuals who wanted to get rid of Sophie. In fact, it sounds like, lately, she rubbed everyone the wrong way."

Ida's doorbell chimed. She rocked forward and back, using her weight to leverage her body from the comfortable chair.

"I'll get it," I said.

Red and green blinked through the narrow rectangular cut-glass windows framing the heavy mahogany door. The lock clicked and the door fell open. A clear soprano voice sang, "We wish you a merry Christmas." The flashing Santa hat topped a cherubic face with bouncing blond curls and vivid green eyes. Her smile started at her toes and wriggled to the end of her cold, red nose. She motioned to a man hauling a fir tree over the tailgate of a huge, new, metallic red truck blocking the driveway.

Ida sidled next to me, putting her arm around my waist, clenching my ribs, and leaned in. "If it isn't Serena Stewart," she cooed. "You didn't forget." She blew air kisses.

The delivery could be serendipitous.

Glancing past us into the room, Serena observed. "How could you think otherwise, Ida Clemashevski? We've been delivering your Frasier fir for how many years now?"

"I can't count that high. Come in." Ida bustled. "You know where it goes, young man?" she said to the gray-haired giant lugging a ten-foot evergreen through the entry.

"Yes, Ida. It goes in the bay window so everyone passing by is able to admire it from the street in any direction," he said with a slight inflection and the tedium of someone who has repeated this line countless times before.

The giant balanced the tree with one hand securing the

compressed branches in the middle and the other grasping the base of the trunk already locked in a tree stand. When he righted the tree in the alcove in front of the windows, he loosened the twine and the branches sprang out in a fragrant pine-scented Christmas hug. Even without adornment, its beauty added to the meticulously decorated room, so stunning it could take its place among the homes in an interior design magazine.

"Serena, you've outdone yourself. Every year my tree is more splendid than the last. Thank you from the bottom of my heart. I wasn't certain you'd have the time or the desire to cut and deliver trees, but I'm very happy you are."

"I'll admit, my delivery list is a bit abbreviated this season. I had a number of cancellations. Some people aren't sure of the status of S & S and to be honest…" Her eyes glistened and she blinked rapidly. The giant accompanying her huffed. "…that is a question I have myself."

"Can you and your scrooge-for-a-dad stay for a bit? Have a cookie and a hot toddy?"

"We really shouldn't."

The giant pulled his stocking cap off and released his head of shoulder length salt-and-pepper hair. He squashed the cap in his frying-pan-sized hands, and said forcefully, "We'd love to, Ida." He stopped Serena's protest with a hard stare.

"Serena, Lars, please meet my friends, Carlee and CJ Bluestone." CJ clasped their hands. Carlee waved.

Ida pointed. "Brenna de Silva." Brenna nodded.

"I've delivered your trees since you were this high." Serena held her hand by her knees. "Tell your mom we have loads to choose from this year." Brenna blushed.

Ida hurried on. "And this is Harry Wilk and his

daughter, Katie." Dad waved and when I shook her hand, I noticed a questioning look in her eyes.

"Have we met?" she said.

"I don't think so." Maverick took that moment to lick her hand, begging for a scratch and Serena happily obliged, seeming to forget her question. I owed Maverick a T-bone steak for that diversion. My name came up when folks talked about Sophie Grainger. I was certain, given enough time, Serena would peg me as the one who discovered the body. And she probably wouldn't be too keen to find herself on my list of suspects.

"Katie, hang up their coats in the front closet and then you can help me in the kitchen."

CJ and the girls began to arrange the lights he'd untangled. Serena unwrapped layer upon layer of outerwear which I dutifully hung, and then I excused myself to collect more cookies and libations.

As Ida heated the water, I took down eight mugs. I squeezed two lemons and poured a shot of whiskey in five of them, then drizzled a tablespoon of honey in each. Ida poured the hot water on top of the mix. I stirred, releasing a divine scent which I topped with a sprinkle of nutmeg. I inhaled the start to the holidays.

"She didn't do it either," Ida hissed, sidling next to me. "I've known Serena for her whole life. It's not her."

I carried the tray, conveying the largesse of Ida's heart, to two possible suspects, trying to figure out how to get Serena Stewart to talk.

It turned out all Serena wanted to do was talk. She and Ida dropped onto the couch. Dad took up residence in one of the wingbacks, sorting glass balls. Lars grabbed two chairs from the dining room table and slid them across the floor, planting one in front of me and dropping into the other. We crowded around the coffee table, all reaching for a cookie and a beverage.

"Oh, Ida. I miss Sophie," Serena breathed. Lars snorted. Serena said sharply, "I do miss her. She could be a bearcat about money, but she kept our business in the black. She was a financial whiz. She kept the books and as long as everyone got paid, I was happy with the arrangement. She brought in design clients from every corner of the eleven-county area. Many of them didn't even know they needed our services until Sophie sold them on a plan."

"Were there unhappy clients?" I asked. Ida's eyes went wide. One eyebrow arched and the other made a huge, annoyed dip.

Serena let out a laugh. "A few, but she smoothed everything over. She was the brains and I loved bringing her plans to reality. She created remarkable plans with her design software, and I brought her computer-aided-dreams to life. What am I going to do now?" Ida wrapped her in a hug. "We never finalized the terms of our dissolution although Ransam always treated me like her partner. I think he would like me to buy him out, and I hope he puts my money where his mouth is."

"You have nothing in writing?" Dad asked. The cogs in his business mind whirred.

"I didn't think I needed anything. Sophie and I split everything from the beginning, the losses and the gains. And until recently, the gains far outpaced the losses."

"What changed?" I asked.

Lars grunted. "Sophie's unpredictable moodiness chased away customers they'd had for years. She'd never have survived this long without Serena." Leaning forward, he placed his elbows on his knees. Then he reached up and combed his fingers through his hair.

Serena laid a hand on her dad's arm, but his anger rose and his voice thickened. "It's true. She had no regard for friendship or love or loyalty or honesty. She even accused you of stealing."

Glass shattered.

"Sorry," said Dad. He lowered himself to his knees and gathered the shards of a bright red ornament.

In a soft voice, Serena said, "I didn't steal anything. I never even looked at the books. When she showed me the withdrawal slip, she said no one should have known the password. She screamed at me and asked me how I found it and what I did with all that money. I tried to calm her." Serena's voice took on an edge and she breathed sharply. The words came out furiously. "But the next day, she had her attorney serve me with papers to sever our partnership." Her voice softened again. "She died the next day."

The accusation hung in the air like the stench of spoiled seafood. Lars seethed. Serena looked at her folded hands.

"Was money missing?" I asked quietly.

"Oh, yes. Three hundred thirty thousand dollars is missing."

My cheeks puffed when I exhaled. That was a tremendous amount of money to misplace. "Did Ransam know the password?"

Lars spoke. "Possibly, but early on, Sophie treated him as if he were incapable of understanding the way business should be done, letting him know she was in charge. When his business started to take off, she told him he needed to keep his finances separate for tax purposes. She didn't expect him to do well and I think she really wanted to keep him away from her money."

The fire crackled. Maverick's tail thumped. CJ and Carlee looked at one another, hands poised to position an additional string of lights. Ida cleared her throat and said kindly, "We believe you, Serena."

I didn't know what I believed, but I couldn't rule out Serena. Nor would I rule out Lars. Instead of paring down my list, it grew.

I excused myself and helped Dad sweep the remaining pieces of the ornament into a dustpan and deposit it in the kitchen garbage. "I'm so darn clumsy," he complained, trailing me.

"Aren't we all," Ida said as she waltzed into the kitchen carrying the dirty dishes. "Serena and Lars have had enough chit chat and Carlee and CJ finished putting up the lights and are taking Brenna home. Do you have time to help me hang a few ornaments?"

"At your service, m'lady," Dad said as he made a grand gesture of bowing and nearly toppled.

After letting him pretend to escort Ida into her living room rather than the other way around, Dad and Ida sat in matching chairs, ordering me to crown her tree with glass trimmings in every shade of the rainbow and all different shapes. I got my exercise steps climbing up and down the ladder rungs as Ida pointed out the bare spots for the ornaments to fill.

Her artistic eye revealed itself in the clever planning of the tree décor. "A place for everything and everything in its place," she said as I positioned the last ornament. She dimmed the room lights and the tree glowed. I gazed in wonder at the swirling snowflakes dancing intricate patterns in the streetlights behind the windows, seeming to land on her tree. Dad handed me a warm cup of something noggy, a generous sprinkle of nutmeg peppering the froth. I sipped and inhaled the scent reminiscent of easy days long gone. Carols floated on the air. Warmth from the fire blanketed the room. It was perfect.

I took one cleansing breath but, before I exhaled, the front door burst open, banging against the solid frame.

CJ's eyes were on fire. Carlee walked behind him into the room, pale and small.

"Gather your pack, Katie. You and Maverick need to come quickly. We have a lost youth and the temperature is dropping."

I sprinted through my apartment and threw on warm clothes. I stuffed four bottles of water and two power bars into the outside pockets of my ready pack and headed out. A gust of cold wind slapped my cheeks. Snowflakes swirled as the wind tore the door out of my hand and lashed my hair around my face, bringing tears to my eyes. Ever-changing Minnesota weather always confounded me. I dashed after Maverick, sliding onto the front seat of CJ's truck. He bounced down the driveway and squealed down Maple Street, wipers slapping at the muck smacking the windshield.

I studied his face as the streetlights pulsed above us. "What happened?" I involuntarily shivered.

"The police raided a party hosted by a student home from college. Some of the underaged partygoers scattered. One of Carlee's friends is still missing."

Heat blew onto my feet. I eased back into the seat. "Kids do dumb things all the time."

"She ran Friday night." His knuckles turned white as

he clutched the steering wheel. I sat forward in response to his contagious sense of urgency and stared through the streams of snow afire in the glow of the headlights.

"And her quality of life may be dependent on more than simply the weather."

"What do you mean?" A harsh intensity had replaced his usually calm, composed demeanor. His hat shielded his eyes, but his rigid body sat bolt upright in the seat. He ripped at the hair tie and his straight black hair fell, shielding the set of his jaw.

"Young people have threatened her well-being."

"Why? What did she do?"

CJ's cold voice stabbed through the air between us. "She warned you."

CHAPTER THIRTY-TWO

Annalise?" I shuddered and rubbed my hands together. CJ nodded. "Trying to maintain her integrity cost her in the eyes of the group she thought she wanted to join."

I gripped the armrest and leaned forward in a vain attempt to urge the truck forward with more speed.

"You understand," CJ said with an admonition.

"Yes."

"Who knew about her warning?"

"Galen."

"That explains how Carlee knew. I don't believe Galen would have turned on her."

"Jane and I discussed the message so Drew probably knows as well. I suppose someone else might have overheard our conversation. I didn't think it needed to be kept completely private."

"Carlee and Brenna have tried to contact her and there's been no response. That is very unusual for her, even if she only sends an emoji."

We sloshed through forbidding miles and pulled into a familiar parking lot near the geographical marker on Duke Hill. Our headlights raked across the lot and landed on a recognizable, beat-up, tan Chevy Chevelle, which disgorged a parka-wrapped body. Although a wide fur edge hid his face, it could only be Westin. He marched through the headlight beams, disappearing into the gloom and reappearing next to the driver's window.

He hauled himself onto the running board as CJ's window slid down. "The prez went to her daughter's home for the holiday and Jimmy considers this a wild goose chase. He's calling the shots. It's just us, I'm afraid." With Hazel Sommers, the local SARTECH coordinator, out of town, assigning the canine teams fell to her second-in-command, Jimmy Hanson, and he never fully appreciated CJ's expertise. There was no love lost between us either. His son was caught stealing and he blamed me.

CJ gripped the steering wheel. His eyes bored into the sheets of snow. "You are still willing to assist?"

"Yup." Westin snorted and dropped to the ground. "Let's get this show on the road." Westin tramped through the snow to his car and opened the door. A black-and-white ball of fur bounced onto the snow and sat, looking up, tongue hanging out.

Maverick paced in the rear seat, eyes bright, panting. I snapped on his vest and he knew we needed his best. I pulled my face mask up. CJ handed me a pair of goggles. When I didn't take them right away, he shoved them closer and nodded. The strap encircled my head. I donned my stocking cap and cinched the ties on my hood. I pulled my gloves farther onto my hands. I'd have pulled them up to my elbows if I could. I slid off the seat and Maverick flew out after me. We joined CJ, Westin, and his collie, Riley, at the front of the truck. CJ's longing glance emphasized the loss of his own search-and-rescue canine.

"Renegade will be ready soon," I said, laying a hand on his forearm. Westin let loose with a mirthless chuckle as we briefly imagined the free-for-all when she joined Riley and Maverick.

"Carlee said students at the party noticed members of one gang harass her about her failed attempt at showing what she was made of."

"Sounds like hazing to me," said Westin. He pulled out a notebook and read, "She ran from the raid, got a ride from a friend, and asked to be dropped here." He closed the flap on his notebook and looked up.

"Carlee is worried about Annalise … very worried. I will do anything for my daughter." He finally found the daughter he never knew he had and lived the love. He pulled a bundle from a plastic bag and shoved it into my hands. "We need to hurry before the trail is any more compromised."

I clicked on a flashlight. "Maverick, this is it." I knelt and held the well-worn fleece lined denim jacket under Maverick's sensitive nose. He raised a ruckus, circling, barking, and high-stepping. "Maverick, find Annalise," I said as I passed the jacket to Westin and Riley.

Maverick and Riley took off, and CJ, Westin, and I rushed after them, skidding downhill on the slurry. The thin layer of new ice on the stream cracked into large chunks, and the water swirled around my boots. I slogged through, hoping the waterproof spray would do its magic. Maverick slowed only long enough to make certain that I followed.

To one side, Riley led Westin who hunched his shoulders and plowed into the wind as it howled. On the other side, CJ plodded with determination, oblivious to the strands of hair whipping around his face. My flashlight beams pierced the shimmering sheets of crystalline flakes before catching Maverick's black coat darting between the trees like a shadow. I hurried before snow filled in Maverick's paw prints. When he turned to look at me, his eyes reflected a sinister green-gold.

I wished I was back in Ida's living room, sitting by the fire, listening to beautiful music, composing a holiday missive, and decorating gingerbread cookies, maybe even eating a few. Then I thought about Annalise being caught outside, unprepared for the cold, and unable to place her trust in those she thought she knew best. I shuddered and ramped up my tracking speed, matching CJ's stride as nearly as I could. I found myself puffing and perspiring in spite of the temperature. I slid the eyewear onto my forehead and swiped the sweat dripping into my eyes before my lashes froze together. Over the wind I could hear Westin call, "Annalise. Annalise." I replaced the goggles and joined him. "Annalise."

CJ marched on.

Maverick and Riley ran forward, circled back, and sped forward again, playing leap frog with the terrain. We'd catch up and it would begin all over. Ninety minutes after we'd begun, I noticed the silence. Instead of being driven to the ground, the flakes began to drift. Slender moonbeams pierced the parting clouds and brilliant stars wrestled through the breaks, dotting the sky with sparkles reminiscent of sugar crystals on Ida's favorite cookies.

Maverick's barking broke the peace.

"He's found something," I said.

Riley and CJ bolted.

When Westin glanced my way, I caught the edge of his smile deep in the fur-lined hood. He shook his head and we took off running. The blanket of snow on the ground cushioned our steps, swallowing the sound. We followed a narrow path and skirted an area overgrown with evergreens and prickly brambles until the tracks disappeared.

Westin and I stopped to examine a stony patch leading to a wall of granite. No tracks. The snow had blown clear of the rock. We backtracked and scoured the ground for any indication of the way they'd gone. Westin held a hand to his mouth, signaling quiet, then motioned the direction I should take, pointing his leather-covered hands to the right. He moved in the opposite direction.

A sliver of moon took up residence as the clouds drifted out of sight and the wintery world shimmered.

I listened for the dogs, but only heard my bootsteps. I lost sight of Westin but knew if I'd whistle, he'd come running. I continued my search, calling, "Annalise. CJ. Maverick. Riley."

And then I heard it, a faint but piercing bark. I reached for my phone stowed in my pack, and turned sharply, a bright smile tugging at my icy lips. The weight of the backpack shifted and I felt the earth give beneath my feet. The brown and black and blue spun in front of me and I picked up speed as I hurtled into a void.

CHAPTER THIRTY-THREE

I enjoyed wherever I'd been. I knew if I opened my eyes the beach would fade, the piña colada would disappear, and, worst of all, Charles would vanish, and I missed him desperately. I didn't want to leave but a gripping need gnawed at the edges of my dream. I reluctantly pried opened one eye, then the other, and squinted up into three pinpricks of light, blurred by tears.

The freezing temperature whipped me into the present. The pack strapped to my back had wedged into some space behind me and held me in place, arched over a bump on the ground, poised like a sacrifice to Boreas, the Greek god of the north wind. I thrashed around, trying to grab onto anything. Where my phone should have been I found an empty pocket. I took off a mitten and fumbled for the clasp at my chest.

When I finally pinched the release, I popped out of the straps and rolled onto my side. Mentally, I took inventory of my various parts and they seemed to be in working order. I pulled my mitten back on, and clenched and unclenched my fists and wriggled my toes to get circulation going. My fingers burned. I guessed that was a good thing.

The stars didn't cast quite enough light and I felt blind. I stood and took a tentative step, tapping my toe, trying to feel through the ultra-thick lining of my boots, searching for roots or rocks that might trip me. My head connected with an outcropping. I squeezed my eyes shut and rubbed the tender spot shooting pain behind my right eye. I took another step, keeping one hand out in front of me, and touched a craggy wall. Groping behind me, I found more wall. My heart raced. I was surrounded by rock.

I tested the surface for handholds or indentations and found none, just a sheer rocky surface. I couldn't reach both sides of the shaft at the same time but I ran into fine cobwebs that tickled my face and, for my own piece of mind, I hoped Lorelei's comment about spiders hibernating was true.

I slumped to the cold ground and licked my lips. I had food, water, and wore multiple layers of winter clothing. It had stopped snowing. The wind had stilled. Every part of me was intact and I had people. CJ and Westin would find me. I just had to be patient.

The display on my watch lit up and I couldn't believe so little time had passed. I caught a bit of my surroundings in the momentary glow. One more tap and the dim light cast its eerie beam on an alien presence—a small animal skeleton, and I backed into the opposite wall.

I listened but only caught the whisper of the wind, the cracking of limbs, and the thump of my heart. I closed my eyes and prayed and almost missed the rhythmic swish. My mind scrolled through the list of the possible origins of the noise.

"Hello?" I called. "Yoo-hoo!" I shouted. "Anybody there?"

The rustling quickened.

"Can you hear me?"

"I hear you. Keep talking. I don't see you."

It wasn't CJ. It wasn't Westin—no sarcastic remarks. Then, who was it?

A head wrapped in a thick scarf wound around the fuzzy hood of an anorak peeked over the edge. "Katie? What are you doing down there?"

"Harley? What are you doing up there?"

"I asked you first," he said with a chuckle.

"Well, I sort of fell down the rabbit hole and I can't get out," I said, and I felt my lower lip protrude in a pout.

"I'll be right back."

"You can't leave me," I squeaked.

"And I can't think of a way to get you out of there without a rope or a ladder or help of some kind. I'll be right back."

"How far do you have to go?"

"Not far. Promise."

I watched the minutes scroll by. I called out softly, "Harley?" The slight breeze hummed over the top of the hole. I stamped my feet and slapped my hands around my arms to ward off the cold and the panic. What could be taking Harley so long? Where were CJ and Westin? Where was Riley? Where was Maverick? Had they found Annalise?

A happy bark answered my question and heralded the return of my conquering hero.

"Maverick!" I cried. "Here, boy." Ears flapped back and forth as he tipped his head one way and then the other at the top of the pit. He yipped, circled away, and returned. "That's my boy!" But how could he help me get out of here?

A few stars winked out as a human head popped over the rim. I shielded my eyes from the intensity of a flashlight. After the few seconds it took for me to become accustomed to the beam, it turned, shining onto CJ's stern face which melted into one of bemusement. "Do you have a rope in your pack?" he asked.

An exasperated sigh escaped from my quivering lips. "I didn't even think about what I carried that could get me out of this mess." I unzipped the pack and rooted around under the light, yanking out a nylon rope. I tied a bowline to one end and a bottle of water to the other end. I tossed the bottle to CJ who snatched it out of the air. I strapped on the backpack, stepped into the knot and cinched it, tugging to indicate my readiness.

"Hang on." He mumbled something unintelligible, and Maverick barked.

He disappeared from view and I lifted off the ground in spurts, starting and stopping. The fifteen feet took us all of sixty seconds to climb past the rocks and roots, and yet you couldn't pay me enough to sink back into that hole. I crawled over the edge and kissed the rocky ground, then crawled away from the abyss.

I wanted a hug, but giggled as Maverick rushed in and his tongue lashing pinned me to the ground. "I love you too, Maverick." He sat, and I crawled to my knees.

CJ coiled the rope. He made his way around me and shoved it back into my pack. I lost my balance. "What was that for?" I whined.

"A reminder."

His comment hit me between the eyes, and my words came in a rush. "Did you find Annalise? Is she all right?"

CJ nodded slowly. "Westin took her to the urgent care clinic. She has a bad sprain."

I blew out a breath.

CJ continued to nod. "She ran because she had already been caught drinking underage and feared a second violation. She hitched a ride here, became lost, and now she just wants to go home."

"I'm baaaack," a voice from beyond the light intoned, sluicing through the brambles on cross country skis, a rope slung over his shoulder. Harley stopped for a moment, assessed the view in front of him, then rushed in, pulled me off the ground and into a bear hug.

"Nothing broken?" Harley asked. He gave me the once over, then dragged me into another hug. "What were you doing?"

I almost toppled when he released me.

CJ's face, already in darkness, darkened even further. "We found a girl who will need some help. She has some demanding friends she needs to deal with."

"Searching again?" Harley asked, a bit of incredulity creeping into his tone. "And I can see how that went for you," he said, hinting I might be more of a liability than an asset.

I laughed, but it was bittersweet because Harley was right. My carelessness led CJ and Westin to split up to try and find me after we'd already spent a lot of time looking for Annalise.

Maverick nudged Harley. "You're right, doggy. I shouldn't judge. I was there when you found Drew." Maverick's tail had stopped wagging, and he raised his head, then sniffed the ground.

"My phone! Thanks Maverick. It must have fallen out of my pack." I hesitated. "Harley, what are you doing out here?" I ran my hand along the straps of my pack, and raised an eyebrow.

Harley answered, his head hung sheepishly, and pulled a small camouflaged box from his pocket. "When the snow stopped falling, it looked like a wonderland. I came out to hide another geocache."

CHAPTER THIRTY-FOUR

I dragged myself from sleep and splashed cold water on my face in a feeble attempt to get my eyes to open. I glanced in the mirror and what looked back at me could've cleared the crows from the corn fields for miles. Hair stood out in every direction and gray-blue bags hung beneath my eyes. I had a raspberry on my forehead and a purplish-black bruise on my cheek. My nose dripped and my lips were cracked. The comments I could expect from my oh-too-honest students might sting a bit, but Annalise was safe. It had been worth it.

As I completed the partial makeover, memories of the Thanksgiving holiday came crashing down around my ears. I hadn't slept well, bombarded all night long with memories of my weekend, the good and the bad. My mind spun, my head ached, and my back felt like it would go into spasm. I decided to work on organizing some of the items on my overly full plate or I'd never sleep again.

I pulled a pen and notebook from my desk drawer and began with the day before—Sunday. Holding a warm cup of orange tea, I penciled in 'help Ida decorate,' and then drew a thick black line through completed chore number one. I followed that with 'find Annalise.' I scratched off a second major accomplishment. Then I jotted down as many other tasks as I could think of, immediately checking off those I'd already finished like washing breakfast dishes and making my bed. I cheated whenever possible. I crossed off additional jobs such as practicing search-and-rescue techniques with Maverick, and filling my cookie jar, even though the cookies weren't my gingerbread men. I included routine responsibilities: mock trial practice, dinner with Dad, writing lesson plans, and walking Maverick. I read the *now* manageable list and pared down my worries.

Eventually, I carefully printed, 'prove Debora did not kill Sophie Grainger' which roughly translated into 'find who did murder Sophie Grainger.'

* * *

Although more than one student and faculty member managed a double take, the rude comments on my appearance didn't materialize—until the last five minutes of the day.

"You look like you barely survived a tornado. What happened to you?" asked Patricia as she signed the obvious word for twister.

The subdued students listened for my answer. "I got caught out in the cold. Thanks for caring." A few of the students glanced surreptitiously at Annalise's empty desk.

"No, really," Patricia said. "What happened?"

"I worked last night," I admitted reluctantly.

She gave a tsk while the rest of the class erupted in questions behind her. I shook my head, trying to quiet the pandemonium. Hands shot up in a more orderly manner, and Patricia turned to watch the exchange.

"Is it true your dog saved Annalise's life?" asked one.

"My dog Maverick and his friend Riley found Annalise. Riley is a certified search-and-rescue canine and Maverick is probationary."

I maneuvered the practical application of numbers into the conversation. "Certification warrants a seventy percent pass rate on a written exam. If there are seventy-five questions, how many correct answers do you need?"

"You have a pretty smart dog able to take an exam," Patricia said.

Someone yelled, "Fifty-two and a half."

"Yes, that's—"

"I heard Annalise was hypothermic and needed a transfusion," said a student clad in black. "I vant to suck your blood," she added gleefully.

"She'll be fine." I tried to change the subject. "If you have ninety minutes to complete a sixty-question exam, how much time can you spend on each question?"

"I heard she didn't want to get caught at a party and she ran out on her friends." The words forced the air from the room.

"But her friends asked us to look for her." It'd be better if I didn't acknowledge the gang.

A voice yelled, "One and one-half minutes per question."

"Correct," I said as I pulled out my teacher edition.

Before I could get into sales, markup, percentages,

and how you know if you've found a good deal, another voice called out, "If there were seventeen underage kids at a party that was raided and the cops caught seven, what percentage got away?"

* * *

Harley and Jane couldn't attend the final run-through before the first competition that would really count, so I took the playful barrage of colorful comments directed at my battered face as well as I could and my snide "ha-ha" retort made me feel better.

The kids performed with ease. They corrected and cajoled one another to keep on track. They didn't need much assistance from me so I made a diagram, mapping outrageous arguments and tenuous connections between Sophie and her possible assailants.

I jotted down probable motives and unintentional actions that might have led to Sophie's death. I brainstormed alternate ways for Sophie to have died. I added faulty starter to the list along with bad manners, souring personality, jealousy, and unhappiness. It still didn't look very promising for Debora.

According to Serena, Sophie developed computer aided design software to draw up plans for clients looking for more suitable accommodations and to improve interior designs, remodel, or retool existing spaces. Serena didn't know what had become of the software, but she hoped it would be sold with the business she expected to buy.

Lars revealed his vehement dislike and distrust of Sophie. He was protective of Serena and wouldn't let her suffer the whims of her partner, but that seemed like a flimsy motive for murder. And I trusted Ida's assessment.

Kindra harbored some resentment and revealed her dislike of Sophie when defending her mother. Yet under the gruff exterior, lurked the heart of a gentle soul. On the other hand, Patricia couldn't seem to care less.

Ransam Grainger still held an egregious excuse to want his wife dead. She held the family purse strings and, even though he said he was willing to give it all up for love, he might not need to anymore.

And what would his attorney, Stanley Mossa, do to secure a win in the divorce proceedings?

Sophie's treatment of Debora was just over-the-top nasty. The unfortunate timing of their meeting coincided with Sophie's final day. My pencil continued to circle Debora's name until the paper shredded beneath the graphite.

And what about the missing money?

"Whatcha doin', Ms. Wilk?" asked Lorelei. "You look pretty serious." She glanced at the pages in front of me and then at Brock. "There's always the boyfriend." She turned and announced, "Dress for success. Let's all look great tomorrow." She and her teammates marched out of the room.

I drew a line from Sophie to an empty circle but I couldn't assign a motive for her death or identify a boyfriend.

Needing a trustworthy, impartial, and astute sounding board, I dialed the number at the top of my favorites. He'd lived in Columbia his entire life. He'd certainly have an opinion about the Stewarts.

"Hello, this is Dr. Pete Erickson's phone. He's unavailable right now. How may I help you?" I hung up on the exuberant female voice.

CHAPTER THIRTY-FIVE

I rolled my head down and around on my shoulders, forcing the kinks from my neck in hope of waylaying the torturous headache brought on by mulling over all the combinations surrounding Sophie's death in addition to Nurse Susie's overenthusiastic answering of Pete's phone. My embarrassment multiplied when I realized she'd probably relished seeing my name on the display screen, knowing I hadn't the nerve to leave a message.

I missed Pete. I missed our talks and our time together. He'd been one of my first real friends in Columbia. Even though I didn't like it, because of his study schedule in telemedicine, the vision of two ships passing in the night fit our relationship.

But I could always talk to my dad.

Feeling more settled, I turned the heat on high and relaxed into the seat of my van. I thrummed my fingers on the steering wheel and organized my thoughts for our upcoming discussion.

When I rounded the corner of Maple Street, my foot jammed down on the brake. My heart leaped to my throat. Blue and white lights flashed on the ambulance parked at the end of the block in front of Ida's home and the two-block drive took forever.

I pulled to the curb. The door of my van held fast so I rammed my shoulder against the frame. The door squawked open. I slammed it but it didn't catch and I left it hanging ajar. I stumbled across the street.

Please, God. I repeated the words over and over, tripping up the stairs and crashing into my apartment. Ida stood at my kitchen table, dabbing her eyes with a tissue.

"No," I cried. I fell into Ida's open arms, hiccupping, my shoulders heaving. "Where is he? What happened?" Maverick circled underfoot, nudging my hand. "Not now," I screamed, instantly regretting my harsh words as I bent to rub his silky ears. "Sorry, boy. Just not right now."

As the words left my mouth, I heard clattering across the wooden floor in the living room. I shoved out of Ida's arms and chased the emergency medical team. The man pushing the gurney held an IV, dripping fluid into Dad's arm. The woman held some type of breathing apparatus over his nose and mouth.

"Dad!" I cried. "Where are you taking him? What happened?" Somewhere deep inside, I knew they were doing what was necessary, but I couldn't get my heart and head to work together.

"He's had a seizure. We're taking him to Columbia Memorial Hospital. You can meet us there," the female said. I read pity in her look.

As I followed them out the front door, Ida croaked, "Call me, please."

My van door still wouldn't latch. I held the door closed as I sped through the streets and cold air seeped in through the narrow opening around it. My fingers lost feeling and the door felt heavy enough to swing open of its own accord. A prayer burned across my lips in spite of the temperature.

There were no empty parking spaces in the lot closest to the hospital entry, so I pulled into the ramp and ran the two blocks, sprinting through the emergency doors. I attempted to keep the edginess out of my voice and said to the girl behind the desk, "Harry Wilk was just brought in by ambulance. Can you tell me where he is?"

"Family?" asked a no-nonsense teenaged admissions clerk without looking up. The Sponge Bob SquarePants' pattern on her smock did little to instill confidence.

"Daughter."

"In triage. We'll call you as soon as we have information on his condition. Please fill out these forms and take a seat." My eyes followed the glance she gave over her shoulder. Through a gap in the thick gray privacy curtain, I caught a glimpse of medical personnel surrounding a figure lying on a gurney before the door to triage closed. I didn't recognize any practitioner, but as I dialed my phone I thought, even if it included Susie, better the devil you know.

Just before the phone rang for the fourth time, my finger hovering over the button to end the call, a drowsy voice answered, "Yeah."

"Pete? It's Katie." My voice quavered.

"Katie? What time is it? What—"

"I'm sorry to call, but you're the best I know and…" My gasping sounded horrendous. As I snuffled, I rasped, "Pete, Dad's been admitted to the hospital. Could you—"

His voice catapulted over the phone line. "I'm on my way. Hold tight." Pete's dad had recently survived a severe heart attack. He understood my plight without additional words.

I clutched my phone. Waves of panic poured over me. I'd nearly lost Dad once before in the attack that still haunted me. We'd often biked the trails that ran around my hometown, but the last time, when Dad spotted the glint of a gun barrel, he and Charles formed a human shield. Sometimes I wished it had been me.

I dialed Elizabeth. She didn't answer. I didn't leave a message.

I collapsed into a hard, red plastic chair in the waiting area and dropped my head into my hands, willing a miracle. My fingers tangled in my hair. I squeezed my eyes and remembered Dad standing strong, a hearty laugh burbling from deep in his gut, or bellowing "O Holy Night" in his rich tenor. His beaming smile lifted my spirits every day. I locked away my tears, shielding my heart from a very bad dream. My lips moved, repeating the prayers that followed the beads on an imaginary rosary.

A cool hand smoothed my brow and brushed the strands of hair off my face. I opened my eyes and melted into kind chocolate eyes. Pete sat next to me and pulled me close, rocking me. I buried my face in his shoulder, blubbering.

"What am I going to do?"

He took both of my hands, locking them together, cupped in his. They tingled when his lips touched the tips.

He stood and disappeared behind the triage doors.

I rocked on the chair, my nerves wound tight, sorting what I needed to do: call Elizabeth again, give Ida an update, inform my principal, lay out my lesson plans. My fingers fumbled with the buttons on my phone and the blurry names scrolled before my eyes. Before I pressed call, Pete pushed through the doors, smiling.

"Your dad will be spending at least one night and you, my dear, will be going home to rest."

I started to protest.

"I won't hear any excuses. Your dad is suffering from dehydration and exhaustion and is hooked up to an IV. He will be fine, but they want to make sure everything is working properly before they release him."

My heart beat a slower rhythm, and in a lame attempt at humor, I said, "So I can't skip school tomorrow?"

"Nope. Your dad and I expect you to carry on after you make an appearance so he can tell you how well he really is."

"Truly? You wouldn't lie to me."

"He'll be fine. I'll be here all night, two floors away."

Pete stood and reached for my hand. I held tight as he led me back to a cubicle where Dad awaited transport to his own private room. "With his medical history, no one is taking chances. We'll do a very thorough work-up. Don't be surprised if he doesn't remember what he's said tonight. He may react differently tomorrow. He's on a bit of happy juice."

No words came.

Dad's hair stuck to his forehead, slick with sweat. A tube snaked its way around his head and over his ears, delivering a hiss of oxygen. His pale coloring matched the faded bedclothes, but his eyes defied the inactivity and they spoke volumes of discontentment. The IV stand rattled when he lifted the arm attached to it, reaching out to me.

I slid a chair next to the bed and took his hand. The strength of his grip squeezed an oomph from my lips.

"Sorry, darlin'. I wish you wouldn't leave me but they gave me something to make me sleep, and I'll be fine. Go home and talk to Ida. She's a wreck." He took a slow, deep breath and closed his eyes. He'd be fine. I sighed and my lips curled up. Then Dad exhaled. "You won't do me any good here. Your salary's gotta pay for my ambulance ride."

CHAPTER THIRTY-SIX

Ida stood in her front window, backlit by her sparkling Christmas tree, waiting. I pulled into the garage and parked, peeling my icy fingers from the errant door. I sat and took a deep breath, willing my chest to relax, and I dialed Elizabeth again. She answered on the second ring.

"What do you need, Katie?" she said quietly. "I just stepped out of a meeting."

"Dad's fine." I thought I should get to the bottom line. "But he will be spending the night in the hospital. He's being treated for extreme dehydration."

"How did you let that happen?" I couldn't answer. "Will he be all right?"

"Yes. My doctor friend is staying with him tonight."

"The coroner? A little premature, isn't it." A snort

escaped. "I'm sorry." She exhaled. "It's just so much." She and Dad had spent down their reserves while he was recovering but she'd finally attained her dream job for a cryogenic firm and it had extraordinary benefits. The demanding schedule, however, didn't allow her much time to care for Dad, so he'd come to live with me while she sorted everything out. "How long will he be in the hospital?"

"He'll be home tomorrow." I waited a moment, then asked, "Will you be coming for Christmas?"

She didn't answer right away. "I'm not sure. I need to be ready for anything at a moment's notice. And my kids will be coming home." She sounded excited. Austin lived a few miles away but Sandra lived in sunny California, and didn't make the trip too often.

"Give them my love."

"I'll get to Columbia soon."

"Bye," I said, but she'd already hung up.

I surveyed the hodgepodge of items sheltered from the elements in the cold storage, hoping for enlightenment, and amid Ida's eclectic collection I spotted a coiled bungee cord that would do nicely to hold my door in place, at least for a while.

I entered my apartment, shivered out of my coat, and followed my nose to the kitchen. Ida carried two cups of hot chocolate topped with whipped cream and confetti sprinkles and handed one to me. She nodded at the table set with two plates, two spoons, and two decorated titanic-sized gingerbread men.

"Can you talk about it?" she asked.

"He is extremely dehydrated, but he responded almost immediately to the IV fluids. I think, with everything going on during the holidays, it just got away from him, but they are checking everything just in case." I hung my head and heaved a sigh. "I've taken his improvement for granted. I just have to pay attention and remind him to take care of himself. Pete said he'll be fine. He's working tonight and he'll check on Dad."

Her left eyebrow rose.

"What?" A funny smile graced her lips and she shook her head. "What?" I asked again.

"Pete's not on call. Susie's looking for him. They had no coursework, so they registered for an additional two-day workshop which begins tomorrow at noon. He worked until six and was supposed to be on the road tonight." Her smile grew into a chuckle. "Susie was beside herself."

I groaned. "Do you think he'll make it on time?"

"He's just watching Harry and Harry is fine so Pete'll get his beauty rest and be off early in the morning, but I'll check with him tomorrow." Her brows furrowed and she asked, "Are you doing all right?"

"Yup. Except for my rusty van door. It won't close. Can I use one of the bungee cords from your garage?"

"Absolutely. Sometimes I'm just glad I keep everything."

The word everything could easily be replaced with junk, and she did keep a lot of it but, at the moment, I was fortunate she did.

Before I slipped out into the frigid night air, Ida said, "They make remote starters for older vehicles now. It usually warms up the engine and the interior with a few minutes lead time."

"Good to know."

When I returned from ice-land, I inhaled the scent of chocolate. She handed me another warm mug and I slurped greedily. "This is *really* good."

"It's the rum," she chuckled.

* * *

There wasn't enough rum to help me sleep though. I tossed and turned, reading the red numbers on the clock face too many times to count. I juggled my worry for Dad, my anxiety for our upcoming competition, and the possible identity of Sophie Grainger's murderer.

I rose early and dialed Pete's number.

"You shouldn't have told me you were on call, but I appreciate your staying. Dad couldn't have been in better hands."

Pete laughed at my feeble reprimand. "I never said I was on call, but that I was here all night, and I like your dad. They want to keep him for twenty-four hours, just to make sure the meds he's taking are the right dosage and that he understands what to watch for in the future. Call before you come to pick him up. I think he'll be raring to go."

I hung up, smiling and sighing. It was the small things after all. What a guy! I called the nurse's station on Dad's floor and was told he too had had a fitful night but was finally sleeping soundly. "Please tell him I will call again around noon."

Maverick and I circled the twelve blocks near our apartment, blowing puffy white clouds into the cold air. "We'd better make this good, Maverick. Today is packed."

I dressed for success, rounding out my black suit jacket with coordinating pants, a white cotton shirt pressed with sharp creases, steel gray pumps, silver stud earrings, and a clunky silver necklace that hadn't seen the light of day since I don't know when. I grabbed my messenger bag which, to me, looked more professional.

* * *

I wouldn't need my van, so I scheduled a remote starter install and an adjustment to the driver's door. The shop owner could fit me in and volunteered to pick up my van at school. I left the keys in the office with Mrs. McEntee.

Annalise was waiting for me when I returned to my office to collect the mock trial materials.

"How are you, Annalise?"

"I'm good but I'm going to live with my grandma for a while. I think I need to get out of here, get a fresh start, but before I leave, I wanted to thank you and your dog for coming after me."

"And I wanted to thank you for saving my backside."

A smile inched its way onto her lips. "I also want you to be careful. The group I decided not to join can be dangerous."

"You mean the gang?"

She nodded. "I never made it to the inner circle, but I heard things. They might have rented one of the storage units that blew up and—"

"The one where they found the fentanyl?"

She nodded again. "And they believe you saw them there."

My face scrunched, trying to remember. I didn't see anyone until Ronnie and Jake showed up.

"Don't get in their way, Ms. Wilk. Be careful." She turned to leave and looked back over her shoulder. "And thanks again."

"You're welcome. If you ever need anything…"

After Annalise left, I tried the hospital but didn't catch Dad in his room. The message I left for him at the nurses' station reminded him about our competition, and I promised that I'd call on my way home.

I'd scheduled the bus to leave one hour after lunch. Jane and I each carried a plastic tub crammed with writing utensils, easel pads, props, costume accessories, and an assortment of office items, and shoved them onto the front seats. Jane swiped the dust from her navy-blue skirt. The matching blazer hugged her slight frame. She wore a light gray silk shirt, and sky-high red heels. She'd pulled back her hair in a perfect chignon.

As the students clomped up the steps, they stopped and gawked. Jane and I gave each student a high five. Lorelei teased, "Who died?"

"Dressing for success," I retorted, ceremoniously tugging at the cuffs on my jacket. Everyone laughed. "Is that the kind of comment I should get when I pay attention to what I wear?"

Brock hollered from the back of the bus, "Where's Mr. Brown?"

"He'll meet us in Cold Spring. You can't expect him to ride the bus—"

"Like the rest of us plebeians." Jane finished my line. She whispered, "You do expect him to attend the competition today?" I shrugged.

The bus roared to life, and we all slipped into an edgy quiet for the entire ride, mentally preparing for battle. At registration, however, they recognized students we'd met at our earlier competitions. Their genuine camaraderie made our kids giddy with excitement. I greeted some of the other coaches as well.

Stanley Mossa herded his team down the hall, demanding they focus on the pages in front of them. Rollins smirked at my motley crew.

We'd arrived with plenty of time to locate our rooms and gather our thoughts before the competition. The kids were still tense, so Jane broke out a giant box of granola bars and small bottles of water. She withdrew four ties, ready to loop over a head and snug up to any neck. She whispered, "Drew helped with the Windsors."

Galen took advantage of the offering and exchanged his weirdly knotted Mickey Mouse tie for a ready-to-wear purple silk paisley. Carlee straightened his collar while Lorelei examined the rest of the troop, making last-minute adjustments.

"Y'all look fabulous," Jane gushed, her southern lilt emerging with her enthusiasm. "You're gonna crush 'em. Remember, never ask a question to which you don't know the answer. Be very, very respectful. It's a performance and you can out-perform even the most seasoned team. You already have."

We gathered in our circle, fists to the center. "You've done so well." I tried to imitate Jane. "Y'all rock." I failed, so I yelled, "Let's go get them."

"EsqChoir!" The fists flew to the air with a flurry of fingers.

Standing in front of the results board an hour later, Jane smiled. EsqChoir won its first round. We headed to our classroom to congratulate everyone when Allie came running.

"Ms. Wilk," she screamed. "There's something wrong with Patricia."

CHAPTER THIRTY-SEVEN

Patricia sat doubled over, curled on a chair, surrounded by her shattered teammates. She rocked forward and groaned so softly she appeared to be humming. Red splotches covered her face and tears coursed down her cheeks drawing dark lines of mascara. Big round eyes filled the drawn faces around her. Allie cried on Brock's shoulder. Lorelei chewed her thumb and paced. Even our even-keeled Zoe leaned against one wall and stared at her feet. Jane cradled her phone between her shoulder and her chin, waving her hands, directing the students to give us room, trying to connect with Debora.

Patricia flinched when I knelt next to her. I rubbed her arm, whispering, "What's wrong, Patricia? What can I do?" totally forgetting that she couldn't hear a word I said. I tapped her lightly so she would look right at me. "What's wrong?"

Her stilted words came out around hiccups of pain. "I need to go home."

"Do you need a doctor?"

She vigorously shook her head. "No." She pulled her knees into her chest and forced out the words. "Can you just take me home?" she sobbed. She looked so small and helpless. "I just want to go home."

Jane leaned over and whispered in my ear. "Her mom doesn't answer."

Harley had finally arrived and hovered in the doorway, peering over the students. I caught his eye and he hustled through the circle, kneeling next to me. "Can you take her home?" I asked.

"It would be better if *you* took her home." He fished out his keys and dangled them from his fingers. "Jane and I'll stay." He dropped the keys in my outstretched hand. "I have a code. Just lock the keys inside."

My team stirred uneasily. "Patricia isn't feeling well and I'm taking her home. Ms. Mackey's in charge and Mr. Brown will be here too. I expect you to do your best. Good luck."

When Jane drew close enough so the students wouldn't hear, I said, "Call Ransam Grainger if you can. He might know where Debora is and I'll call Pete. He'll know what to do."

"I'm in the north lot," Harley said and repeated reassuring platitudes to our decimated team. Jane managed to help Patricia stand and the two of us guided her down the endless hall toward the exit. As I reached for the entrance door, someone barreled into me from behind.

"Ms. Wilk, what happened?" Kindra cried. "What's

wrong with Patricia?"

Patricia looked at her sister and closed her eyes. She said through clenched teeth, barely audible, "I'm going home. I don't feel well. Do your job." Her pain seemed to ease as she chastised her sister. She opened her eyes, directing Kindra to look at Mossa and Rollins standing just around the corner, heads bent together conspiratorially, watching us. Kindra gave her sister's arm a pat and slipped down another hall.

Harley's vehicle chirped when I pressed the unlock button on the fob. Jane opened the door and eased Patricia into the passenger seat. I slid into the driver's seat. Jane gave a small salute and turned back to the school.

My phone pinged with Patricia's home address and Debora's cell number. I locked in the address and dialed the number. I left another a message.

I gently touched Patricia's elbow. She glanced at me and I said slowly, "What happened?"

She turned away from me and pulled her knees up.

Adjusting the seat seemed to require a PhD in flight simulator use with all the fancy electrickery on the dash and, for a moment, I panicked. Then Patricia's seat gently reclined. If she could do it, so could I. I thought she might try to sleep. I glanced at her once during our silent forty-five-mile drive and the steering wheel lurched, so I kept my eyes focused on the road.

When I pulled into the school parking lot, Patricia readjusted her seat and stretched.

I tapped her arm. "I can call Dr. Erickson. How are you feeling?"

"Never better," she answered with zest that belied her earlier malady.

"You're not sick anymore?"

The guilty look on her face set me on my ear. Her eyes blazed and she handed me an envelope she pulled from her backpack. She nodded as I slid my finger under the flap and withdrew a notecard.

'DEAF AND DUMB GO HAND IN HAND.'

The malicious words brought tears to my eyes. "Is this why you didn't want to stay?"

"I wasn't ready for it today, but I will be prepared next time," she said, glaring at me.

I signed, "Sorry." And added, slowly saying, "Your friends wouldn't do this."

She looked at me, her eyes squinting, her jaw clenched, and finally nodded. "Who else knew?"

"Anyone could have found out. It's not a secret." The thought drifted. Who would want to make Patricia feel so bad? "You do know that it's not true."

Her rueful laugh sounded so old. "Sorry I took you away from the meet."

"No problem. My dad's in the hospital and I'll be able to pick him up earlier than expected. Can you text your mom? Find out where she is. You shouldn't be home this early so if you can't get hold of her, you can come home with me and my dad and have dinner. If Mrs. Clemashevski made supper, you're in for a treat. If not, we're having pizza." Her eyebrows performed disbelieving calisthenics. She pressed the keys on her phone and shook her head.

"Let's go then," I said.

I tossed Harley's keys under the front mat and searched the lot for my van, finally remembering that it was undergoing a winter transplant and called the shop. The owner said my van was in transit. I just finished reciting my credit card number as it pulled in. Patricia and I headed to the hospital.

The exasperated look from the nurse pushing Dad's wheelchair should've prepared me for the vitriol to come. She helped load a sulky patient with too many hours in the hospital into the passenger seat of the van. Dad seethed. I sent Ida a quick message of warning.

"Dad, this is Patricia." She looked out one window and he examined the cars in the lot out another. "She's Kindra's sister. You know, the girl from the coffee shop?"

"Hello, Patricia," he said, brooding. With no response forth coming, he turned in his seat and said, acerbically, "Cat got your tongue?"

She continued to gaze out the window.

"Patricia is deaf."

Momentarily stunned, Dad sputtered before muttering an apology she also couldn't hear.

"You left me in the hospital," he grumbled.

"The doctor thought you might've had a TIA. Plus, you were dehydrated and you weren't even well enough to know you were dehydrated." I sat up straighter. "I'm sure you had superior care overnight, much better than I could have given you at home."

"Your boyfriend couldn't get enough of me and I'm not saying it kindly. He literally took samples of some bodily fluid every two hours. What's the matter with him anyway?"

"Pete … Dr. Erickson is just a friend." I flushed. "And you're lucky he was there."

One of us steamed enough that I had to turn on the defrosters.

We pulled into our driveway, heading to the garage, and Patricia laughed. "Is that your dog?"

I cleared the foggy glass and stared through the window. Then I scoped out the yard. I turned to look at

Patricia. Her contagious chuckle caught me, and I asked, "What dog?"

"He just jumped off the kitchen table."

"So that's why we have all the holes in the tablecloth," said Dad with a mischievous gleam in his eyes.

"Maverick," I hissed.

A savory stew simmered on the stove. Fragrant French bread smothered with a garlicky cheese sauce bubbled under the broiler. And when I pulled open the refrigerator door, a big bowl of greens dotted with tomatoes, onions, croutons, and white cheese took up the entire top shelf. I thoroughly washed the table, lifted plates out of the cupboard, and grabbed a handful of silverware while giving Maverick a stern look he ignored.

Ida stuck her head in, checking the time on her wrist, "It'll be ready in five minutes. I thought you'd appreciate supper."

Patricia had wandered in and said, "Smells good. I'm Patricia." She extended her hand and Ida took it. "They need a referee." I had incorrectly assumed she'd been unable to tell what was going on between Dad and me.

Ida answered while signing. "Yes. I believe they are stressed." The woman knew how to do everything.

Patricia giggled and grabbed Ida's fingers, correcting a sign.

"How?" I said, signing one of the few words I knew.

"I had a student and I practiced a little American Sign Language with him."

"You are i-n-c-r-e-d-i-b-l-e!" I finger-spelled each letter deliberately.

Dad hollered from the living room, "Where's the tattle-tale who turned me in to the EMT's? Can't trust anybody."

Ida turned to go.

"Dad!" I yelled back. "Get in here and apologize." Sometimes he wore my patience down to the bone.

Dad shuffled into the kitchen, looking sheepish. "I'm sorry, old woman." If my memory served me correctly, they were about the same age. He was pushing her buttons and she pushed right back.

"Not as sorry as I am, old man. You made it back!"

Silence hung in the air for just a moment. Then Patricia said, "I'm starving." Boy, could she read a crowd.

"Smart girl," Dad said. He offered his elbow and she took his arm. He patted her hand, then waved to Ida who latched on to Dad's other arm. Who escorted whom?

My phone vibrated on the counter. I grabbed it and pressed connect. Jane raised her voice to be heard over the ruckus on the bus. "We did it," she shrieked, sounding so much like Reese Witherspoon in *Legally Blonde* that I pictured Jane in a pink wool suit, screeching, and laughed out loud. "We hopped on the bus right after they announced that we won our bracket. They'll email you the results and the next pairings. We won! It's a double elimination, but we won our cases."

"Sounds like everyone's celebrating."

"And a judge asked where Patricia was. He didn't know her name but he asked for our first trial's actress playing the part of Maggie Murphy. Lorelei told him she'd become ill and had been taken home. Don't tell her, but she was awarded the rookie-of-the-day in our bracket and Lorelei has the prize. She'll get the prize at practice tomorrow."

Jane lowered her voice. "How's she doing? Patricia showed the note to Carlee and she teared up when she told me about it. Who would do such a juvenile thing?"

"I don't know but I don't think it was one of ours."

"I don't think so either. But tomorrow we should discuss expected behavior."

"I agree. Patricia was devastated at the time but I think she's over it and ready to take on the world."

"Harley might not make practice tomorrow. The case he has pending is requiring a little finessing, he said. But I'll be there."

"Thanks."

An ecstatic Kindra picked up Patricia after her team returned. "We rode in a coach bus. It was so cool. And we won, Ms. Wilk. We won our bracket!" She concentrated, her fingers dancing in synch with her speech as she chewed her lower lip. "I'm not supposed to be happy, but I'm glad EsqChoir won its bracket too." She smiled slyly. "We'll beat you if you make it that far, though."

Patricia dropped in to the passenger seat and gave her sister a harrumph. "No way!"

"Have you heard from your mom?" I asked.

Patricia pulled the door closed. Kindra said, "She's got an attorney. But she's worried. I wish she'd talk to Mr. Mossa." Drew said he had an unbelievable track record but I didn't trust the man.

CHAPTER THIRTY-EIGHT

I removed the list Ransam had given me from my messenger bag. Why these names?

Dad wandered over to my desk. "What do you have there, darlin'?" Although my head was beginning to ache, filled to the brim with the happenings of the day, I flattened the page against the tabletop, hoping Dad would have some insight. He clucked and tilted his head to the right and then to the left. "Well, it won't take you long to solve that puzzle. Meanwhile, I'm off to bed." I cleared my throat. He continued, "After I drink a gallon of water."

"Dad, I don't know what I'd do without you."

"I'm sorry I growled at you. Ida showed me the error of my ways. I wouldn't be here without the two of you." He winked at me and did a little jig and wriggled his brows.

"Meanwhile, I've got a phone call to make."

"Dad!" It came out as three separate syllables. I playfully batted his hand and he chuckled as he bustled off to his room. "Tell Elizabeth hello."

My eyes locked on the page again. Five of the names had a clear association with Sophie. Ransam and Debora remained a couple in spite of everything Sophie had done to derail them. She'd been vindictive and bitter. Maybe this was a hit list of a sort. Ida had Serena's back, claiming her hard work contributed equally to the success of S & S. But Lars gave quite a different picture of Sophie's impact on the health and welfare of the business. The lost funds added to my questions. Had Serena taken it? Had Sophie taken it and tried to blame Serena?

Among the other names, the only Natasha I'd heard of had died in a tragic accident but she had a daughter named Amelia. Although the phone directory did not yield an Amelia Cross, it did list a Frederick Sandburg. A glance at the clock told me it might not be too late. I dialed the number. It rang seven times and just as I was about to hang up, a male voice said tentatively, "Hello."

I hadn't thought my conversation through and it came out a bit stilted. "Hi. My name is Katie Wilk. I'm a teacher at Columbia High School."

"Un-huh?"

"You're Amelia Cross's brother, right?"

He must have been nodding; I heard a jostling sound.

"Mr. Sandburg?"

"She's my sister. What do you want her for?"

"I have a few questions—"

"Nope. No questions. We've done that already."

Afraid he'd hang up, I hurried my explanation. "It's

about Sophie Grainger."

A long pause and I thought he still might hang up. I took a shot in the dark. "I understand your sister knew her."

"Real sad about Sophie."

"I'm trying to get a hold of your sister. Could I get her number from you?"

"That'd be a big no."

I sighed and shrugged my shoulders. We should all be so lucky to have someone watching out for us.

"We've had a lot of unwanted publicity. But if you give me a number, I'll tell her and she might contact you," he said.

I rattled off my number and crossed my fingers as the call ended. Amelia Cross knew Sophie. That made four. It might be a stretch, but Natasha Sandburg may have met Sophie through her daughter.

While I waited for the return call, Maverick and I took a walk. A slightly different path elicited all types of new smells for Maverick and he stopped every ten feet to ferret out the scent-leaver. The cold encouraged me to move more quickly. "Let's go, Maverick," I said as I tugged him from one boulevard tree to the next. Rounding the third corner, I second-thought the length of our outing when I caught the flurry of bicyclists at the end of the block. Before being seen, I spun around, racing back the way we'd come. I wasn't about to wait around to find out if they had me in their sights again.

Better safe than sorry, and leery about what might yet come flying down the street, I fumbled for my phone. I fought Maverick for every foot as he engaged his guarding reflexes. But before I could make a call, it shrilled. One-handed, I aimed for the connect button and the phone danced off the tips of my fingers. A moan escaped from my chattering lips. I scooped up my phone in a handful of snow and tried to connect before the ringing stopped.

"Hello. Hello." Nothing.

The caller had blocked the number, and I had a sneaking suspicion it had been Amelia. Then the phone rang again.

"Hello!"

"Katie? It's Pete."

"Hi, Pete." And my heart tripped. I really did miss him. I panted.

"You sound busy."

"Just walking Maverick. How are you?"

"Good. Do you have time for supper on Friday?"

Friday, yes! I thought, when Maverick stopped abruptly and pivoted, growling at the night, pulling. I shoved the phone in my pocket and gripped the leash with both hands, retreating, dragging Maverick.

"Who are you? What do you want?" I yelled. I heard a clattering across the street and I still had a block to go. I steered clear of the first two dark houses, aiming for the chaotic lights set up in the third yard. The noise followed, rending the calm night apart. "Come on, Maverick." I pulled and he pulled back, and his rumble grew into a bark. Ida's porch lit up, four houses away. I still didn't see anyone but Maverick's low-pitched growl prompted me to increase our speed. Two more houses lit in answer to Maverick's barking and the clattering stopped.

My heart continued to thud until I reached the door. I fumbled for my key but the knob turned in my hand and I chastised myself for not locking the door. I slipped inside, closed the door, and slumped against it, eyes closed. I tried to breathe more rhythmically and slow my banging heart.

Heavy pounding threw my heart right back into flight mode. I pushed in the lock button with one hand, threw the deadbolt with the other, and backed away from the door.

The light flicked on behind me and Dad stood in his red plaid pajamas and moccasins, hair standing out every which way. "Are you going to answer the door?" he asked, as he scratched his scruffy face.

His presence bolstered my courage. I leaned forward, flipped the light switch to the porch. Through the flimsy curtains I saw a familiar silhouette.

"Pete?" I threw open the door. "What are you doing here?"

The look of concern on his face as he extracted a phone from his pocket made me reach for mine. I hadn't disconnected the call. He'd heard everything.

"Are you okay? I texted Ida to watch for you. What was all that?"

I explained the few times we'd been accosted by the bikers, but assured both Pete and Dad that it couldn't continue. Winter wouldn't allow for biking. They looked at me, disbelieving my naiveté.

"I'm sorry you felt you had to come to my rescue," I said, trying to make light of the incident.

"If you're certain the bikers were after you, you should report it."

"I have reported it, but the bikers haven't done anything more than circle me and I don't want it to get any worse."

Pete shook his head. Dad left the room.

"Hot chocolate?" I asked with a tiny grin, holding up a cookie jar as a secondary enticement. After warming the milk and adding cocoa and miniature marshmallows,

I joined him at the kitchen table with a small plate of Ida's krumkake.

"Can I take your coat?"

He waited what seemed like a very long time before he answered. "I can't stay long." He didn't remove his coat, but he did unbutton it and took a slurp around the floating sweet topping which left a white mustache.

I giggled. It felt good.

"About Friday," he said.

My short-lived elation fizzled as realization dawned. "We have a mock trial competition on Friday." My heart felt heavy. I thought I glimpsed disappointment, but I could've been wrong.

"That's keeping you busy."

"We won today." I couldn't contain my enthusiasm about the team and he listened patiently for five minutes. With the cocoa and cookies eaten, and the adrenaline depleted, I stifled a yawn. "How's your training going?"

"It's been fantastic." He grinned.

I yawned again.

"We'll catch up soon," Pete said. He rose and gave me a benign kiss on the forehead, taking his leave.

Drat.

I rinsed the dishes and willed the phone to ring again. I'd take a call from just about anyone. While I waited, I sat at my kitchen table and pulled out Ransam's list.

Annalise was an unusual name, but there could be more than one. I checked my contact information and dialed Brenna de Silva.

It rang six times before she answered warily. "Hello?"

"Brenna, it's Ms. Wilk."

She puffed out a sigh of relief. "You heard we won, right?"

"Yes, I did. Congratulations!"

"It was so cool, Ms. Wilk. We all thought we did well but the announcement confirmed what we already knew. We only yelled a little. Mr. Brown bought us all a hot dog and a soda for the road and, on the bus, Ms. Mackey told us Patricia was all right. We were so relieved. She has Maggie's part down cold. Even better than her sister, I think. What do you need, Ms. Wilk?"

"How's your friend, Annalise?"

Silence. I was getting a lot of that.

"We've been talking and she's very grateful to you and Maverick." She added, in a very quiet voice, "That could have been me."

"What do you mean, Brenna?"

"I was supposed to go to that party with Annalise but she wasn't talking to me. I thought she was mad at me, but now I'm not so sure. She might've been keeping me at a safe distance."

"Why would you take a chance like that?"

"I don't know. It sounded like the thing to do."

"You know you signed the eligibility agreement with the Minnesota State High School—'

"Sure, Ms. Wilk," she said. I could almost see her eyes roll. "I know and I'm sorry. Annalise might need some more tutoring. She won't ask, but she needs help getting on the right track."

"That I can do. When you see her, could you ask her if she knows Sophie Grainger."

"Is that the lady who died from carbon monoxide poisoning?"

"That's the one."

"I can answer that. That lady lived across the street."

CHAPTER THIRTY-NINE

After practice, for our celebration, Jane poured glasses of her famous strawberry lemonade and Ida sent three dozen almond snowball cookies which disappeared upon opening the box. While we finished nibbling and sipping, Jane shared the judges' comments and the students jotted notes to complete their preparation for the competition rounds to come.

When she shared the real reason Patricia took an early ride home from the meet, she faced complete silence and the emotions on my students' faces ranged from disbelief and sadness to anger converging on vigilantism. I had no doubt the nasty message was news to them. Jane concluded her discourse by reinforcing our need to be kind and respectful, even to someone who had no right to expect the honor.

Right before we called it a night, Lorelei gathered the team. "For doing a stellar job as Maggie Murphy, Patricia Halloran, you have been awarded the rookie-of-the-day. I am pleased to present this candied gavel," she said, and the team applauded. "And we can't wait to wipe up the court with our opponents. You'll be all right?"

Patricia's eyes circled the room. Her uncertainty met support, optimism, and encouragement. "I'm fine."

"Make sure you check with your teachers and get Friday's assignments." The recited words melted together and the students filed out, ignoring me.

Harley waltzed in as Jane wiped the residue from the desktops, smearing the powdered sugar that seemed to have drifted everywhere. He settled at my desk, studying the competition results to do his lawyerly strategizing from behind the silver rectangle. Then he groaned.

"What's wrong?"

"I just remembered that I have to get this packet to the jail. I can't read these now." The chair screeched when he stood and rammed against the wall behind him.

"Can I deliver it?" The words sort of popped out.

He thought for a moment. "Would you? I mean that would save me time I can put to good use here."

I sought an affirmation from Jane.

Jane said, "I'll lock up. You go."

I grabbed the packet.

"Katie." Harley held tight and retrieved his keys. "Take my car. It's in the west lot."

I snatched the keys out of the air, eager to ride in luxury again. A smile inched its way across my face. "Be right back."

I nabbed my coat and rushed out of the math area and

crashed into Patricia. I bent to help pick up her scattered books.

"You okay, Patricia?" I asked. She laughed at my attempt at signing.

"Could I catch a ride home?" she said.

I liked the sign for ride, and mirrored it. I nibbled by bottom lip. "I have to deliver this packet for Mr. Brown and you're on the way. I'm sure he won't mind."

"Thank goodness," she said and grinned.

When we stepped outside, I pulled my coat closer and wrapped my scarf around my neck. The shiny Range Rover stood out like an ornament in the lot under a street light as far away as possible from the entrance and any careless car-door-dingers. I pressed one of the buttons on the remote, expecting a chirp as the door locks disengaged. Instead, the SUV roared to life.

"What a ride!" I said. Patricia paid no attention to me talking to myself. I suppose people did it all the time. I'd work on it. Then I clicked another button on the remote.

Before Patricia slid into the passenger seat, she tipped her head back and stuck out her tongue to catch the first flakes drifting from the dark overhead.

Patricia hummed as she settled into the warming seat. While flipping switches and pushing buttons, I studied the instrument panel for the windshield wipers, heat regulator, gear controls, and lights, trying to figure out what I could possibly need on the short ride, while not appearing too nosy.

I ran my gloved hands over the pristine dash, mentally assigning a swipe with my scarf to return it to Harley's level of cleanliness. Ambient lighting changed to the color of merlot and warmed the glossy black interior.

"Wait. What? Whoa!" I wriggled in my seat and Patricia watched me, chuckling. One of the buttons I'd pressed activated a massage on my backside. We giggled and I touched my lips with the fingertips of my right hand and dropped it into my left, "Good?"

She responded in kind. "Good," she said.

Doing everything by the book, I swiped the blinker arm, pressed the button to drive, and eased out of the parking space. I swallowed hard, thinking maybe I should have let Harley deliver his packet.

I took the bypass, gliding along slightly below the speed limit. Even so, power vibrated around the heated steering wheel, thrumming up my arms.

The warm sounds of Christmas music floated into the beautiful space, gently increasing in volume. What a great sounding audio system! I wished Patricia could hear it. I glanced her way. She was flipping through a plastic wallet insert.

I reached to get her attention and the car's lane assist jerked the steering wheel. My hand snapped back into place and I brought us back to the center of our lane. The volume of the music increased gradually, surrounding us. The steering wheel lurched again and I fought a bit for control. The windshield wipers started up on their own, smearing the two or three flakes daring enough to challenge my path. Squinting, I might have seen a fourth flake, but what I thought was, *What a waste of energy.* I reached for the radio switch to turn off the music and the steering wheel veered to the left toward the median. I grabbed it with both hands and pulled us back into our lane. Patricia looked up.

My phone rang. I couldn't answer it but Patricia noticed the lighted face and she picked it up. She must have pressed connect and speaker phone because I heard Pete's voice sail into the air around me.

"Hello, Ka—"

"Pete, this thing is trying to drive itself."

He chuckled. "Seriously. I don't know what to make of the new cars. Are you test driving?"

"I borrowed Harley's Range Rover and, really, it's driving itself." My strident voice sounded like it belonged to a crazy person.

He said in a serious tone. "Turn it off, Katie."

Why didn't I think of that? I put the blinker on, taking my foot off the accelerator. I stepped on the brake and nothing happened. I stomped again. I pressed the ENGINE START/OFF button. Our speed increased. I jammed each of the other buttons: P, D, N, R, and S. Nothing in the vehicle changed. Patricia's left-hand sought purchase on the seat next to her.

"Can you turn down the music? Where are you, Katie?"

"On the bypass." The music played even louder and I yelled to be understood. "Nothing is working right!"

Pete's calming voice competed with the *fa-la-la-la-la* of "Deck the Halls." "Katie, where are you?"

A small green rectangle flashed by. "We just passed the second mile marker after the Main Street exit."

"Use your emergency brake." I nodded, assuming he heard my head bob. I jammed my foot down on the emergency brake and saw sparks on the side of the car. Patricia gasped.

Our speed slowed a bit with a squeal. I steered to the shoulder and heard a heavy clunk. Our speed picked up again. "It didn't work. We're coming up on the Johnson Avenue exit sign." We flew by a string of cars.

"Pete!" I yelled, honking my horn at the cars reckless enough to get in our way, slipping past the fog line, dipping dangerously toward the center.

"There's a snowbank—"

"There's no snowbank, Pete," I screamed through the increasing volume of the music.

"Listen to me." His harsh voice penetrated my wall of fear. "There is one big snow mound in the ice arena parking lot where the county hauled the snow it plowed. There should be enough to cushion your impact."

"We're going to crash into a snowbank?" I shrieked, uncomprehending. A loud melancholy howl came from Patricia as she felt the tension in the SUV soar to a peak.

"You've got to get off the bypass."

I roared up the exit and closed my eyes as we tore through the stop sign at the end of the ramp. For a fleeting moment, I recalled my desperation and grief after Charles died, but now more than ever, I wanted to live. Patricia's wail gave me the strength to hang on and I held both of our lives in my hands.

"The parking lot is going to be on your right. The snow mound is on the far end. Try—" His garbled instructions compounded my anxiety.

I pulled to the right, balancing on two wheels, and kept pulling the wheel to the right, sheering a road sign off at its base as we careened into the lot. "There's no snow. No snow." I scanned the lot for anything to plow into. *Please, God,* I prayed.

I recognized a landmark and knew where we were. Behind the neat landscaping of the arena lay a section of the waterfowl protection area Maverick and I often walked, a long, wide, stretch of grasses and reeds. Our headlights glinted off what remained of the snow mound, small clumps of frozen snow and dirt gripping the pavement. Had it still been there, we'd have plowed into a hill of ice. Instead, we ricocheted from side to side, as if in a pinball game, and the SUV caromed through the gauntlet of solid remains. I steered toward a slight rise. We became airborne for one peaceful moment. I glanced at Patricia. She braced herself, her hands against the dash. Her wide eyes took in the snow-covered marshland I hoped would slow us.

Pete bellowed, "There's a wide turn." *We're way ahead of you,* I thought. "And then head toward the snow mound. I'm on my way. I'm dispatching the EMT's. Katie—"

Our screaming drowned out anything else he wanted to say.

CHAPTER FORTY

My head pounded. My jaw pulsed. I swallowed to fight back the nausea and squinted to block the flashing lights.

"Over here." Mumbled words arrived at a dizzying clip.

Beams sliced across my face. I shielded my eyes and adjusted my position. My hand met a mass of fur. Not fur, curls. The damp curls clung to my hand and I forced myself to look. Patricia lay crumpled next to me on the seat. She was too still. I battled my aches and sat up straighter, struggling to release my belt so I could reach her. I wouldn't move her but my hands followed the contours of her shoulders and her head as I searched for injuries. "Patricia," I whispered.

The brightening lights bounced with enthusiasm. The

doors squealed when opened. Before I could protest, bodies crowded the space. "Be careful," I croaked.

Patricia thrashed and cried out. She bolted upright and shouted, "I'm deaf not dumb."

"Patricia," I cried as they assisted her out of the seat. Fingers probed my forehead and someone flashed an irksome light in my eyes. A face materialized from behind the light and when Pete came into focus, I understood Dad's annoyance. There were more important things he should be doing.

"Katie, look at me." I tried to hold it in but a moan escaped. "Don't move. I'll be right back."

A few items had fallen to the floor. I leaned forward and retrieved a comb and the plastic insert and slipped them into my pocket to return to Patricia later. I laid back against the headrest and closed my eyes to still the vertigo.

"Katie, what happened?" Pete asked when he returned. I absolutely didn't know the answer. "Can you walk?" I think I nodded. My pulse hammered. "Good. Let's get you out of there."

"Patricia." I forced her name past my lips.

"We're taking care of Patricia." With Pete's assistance, I took a trembling step out of the vehicle. The snow crunched and I broke through a layer of ice. Ice cold water poured over the tops of my boots. I shivered. My teeth chattered. My head pounded. Pete pulled me through the marsh to dry ground. "I need you to come with me to the hospital."

I mumbled something unintelligible because I had nothing worthwhile to say.

"She'll be okay." Pete assured me and I believed him. I sighed looking back at Harley's Range Rover, locked in the freezing marsh. It would not be okay.

Police lights flashed on the road behind Pete's car. "I'm going to check in with Ronnie. Stay." I leaned against his truck, supported by the big blue machine.

I didn't remember the ride but I knew I'd arrived when the irritating lights of the ER made my head spin, transporting me back to another hospital, racing next to a gurney, clacking rhythmically down a seemingly endless corridor.

My fingers followed the quilted pattern of my coat, trying to divine what happened, assessing the new assault on my head, face, neck, ankles, back, and wrists, as the ER nurse took vital statistics.

The curtain parted and Ronnie Christianson said, "Hello, Ms. Wilk. Dr. Erickson gave me his version of the accident. I'd like to hear yours."

Tears welled up in my eyes and my heart rate quickened. "I don't know what happened. It started easily enough, but the music came on by itself and the wipers started slapping back and forth and the brakes wouldn't engage. I couldn't slow down. I couldn't stop." I sniffled.

"Uh-huh," he said. "Where did you get the wheels?"

"Mr. Brown. He had a packet..." I gasped. "It needs to go to the jail."

Ronnie's eyebrows raised.

"You can ask him. He gave me his keys." I closed my eyes and groaned. "Is his Range Rover ruined?"

Ronnie shook his head. "It won't be a cheap fix."

"Ronnie ... Chief Christianson, it was like someone else was driving the car. The steering wheel stiffened and pulled to one side of the road and then the other. Patricia'll tell you." I hoped Patricia would be able to tell him. "Please,

I need to see her."

"First, we need you to take a breathalyzer test and draw blood."

"A breathalyzer test?" I almost shouted. Realization dawned and I inhaled sharply. "Sure."

Ronnie attached a clear plastic mouthpiece and handed me an instrument the size of my phone. "Blow." I blew extra hard.

His eyebrows climbed. "You're sober."

Duh. Of course! What did you think? were the less colorful words I wanted to say.

Pete read from a clipboard, and then removed the syringe and elastic band from the nurse standing next to him. He stepped forward.

"What are *you* testing for?" I asked, anger seeping in around the edges.

"Narcotics, but I won't find any." I rolled up my sleeve. After the needle stick, I looked away, concentrating on the clock on the wall. So much to do, so little time. "The results will come back in about three days."

I feebly answered the questions Ronnie put to me, silently encouraging him to speed up so that I could visit Patricia before they sealed her off from the rest of the world.

Pete evaluated my discharge status. "You are battered and bruised but, though the salient parts are in working order, I'd like you to spend the night."

"Dr. Erickson." Ida's voice boomed and she bustled past the flustered duty nurse. "I'll be taking Katie home now. She'll be carefully watched, I assure you." Resistance was futile and he gave in.

"I want to see Patricia," I said, pleading with Pete.

"Not right now. Our team is looking her over. She's being well cared for. We'll figure this out, Katie. Call me if you need anything," Pete said more to Ida than me. "She hit her head pretty hard. And you know what that means."

"Yes, I do," she retorted. She lowered her voice. "How is dear Patricia?" She asked the question to which I most wanted the answer.

"She'll be released as soon as her mother finishes chores, so until then, she can rest easy here."

"You believe me, don't you Pete?" He nodded slowly.

The hospital doors whooshed closed behind us and I took a cleansing breath. Hospitals never agreed with me.

Ida entwined her arm with mine and her short stride set a measured pace across the lot. Before we reached her purple Plymouth Barracuda, Jane's Fusion barreled into the lot. She slammed on the brakes, slid from her driving perch, and rushed me.

"Katie." She grabbed my arms and turned me from left to right so she could check both sides. "You look awful."

"And that's different how?" My attempt at levity fell flat and I wasn't able to say more for fear my tears would fall again. Her passenger door clanged, and when Harley stood in front of me, the tears flowed anyway.

"I'm so sorry. I don't know what happened. I could have killed us both. I don't know how I lost control of the car. Your Range Rover is behind the ice arena, stuck in the marsh."

"Both?"

"Patricia asked for a ride home. I should have asked, but her house was on the way."

He opened his arms and I walked right into them. I sobbed on his shoulder and he lightly brushed his hands through my hair, murmuring, "It's all right. You and Patricia are okay. There's nothing we can't fix." That made me cry even harder.

Jane and Harley followed us home. Jane and Ida waited on me, and we finished off a pot of chamomile tea and a half dozen cookies before the nightly news came on. Maverick nestled next to me with his head in my lap. I couldn't concentrate on the news, thinking about what could've happened and the effect it would have on Patricia.

One phone call changed all that. Patricia's mother called to thank me. Beyond my blubbering, she assured me that Patricia was fine and couldn't wait to show off her battle scars at the competition Friday. I used all my resources to convince Harley, Jane, and Ida that I should be there with her.

We toasted with Jane's smoky Don Lockwood, and the last thing I remembered was clinking glasses.

CHAPTER FORTY-ONE

None of my understanding students gave me any grief even though the bruise on my cheek and the knot on my forehead looked worse after the second day, but I felt better than I looked after skipping practice and taking a much needed break. Friday came quickly.

I scheduled the bus to leave at one thirty so I washed down the last of my peanut butter and honey sandwich quarters with milk. Then, I ticked off the items on my list: water bottles, pens, and legal pads, and added a small first aid kit. I tucked the case file into my messenger bag, switched my flats for dress shoes, and headed out, following a trickle of teammates.

Jane trotted beside me. "Harley and I can take care of this."

"If Patricia is going to be here, I have to be here too,"
I said.

She swallowed whatever argument she'd conjured up.

Sitting in the front seat, I welcomed each of my
students as they boarded the bus. I read confidence in
Lorelei's demeanor, trepidation in Brenna's, gaiety in
Carlee's, acquiescence in Zoe's, and fierce determination
in Galen's. When Patricia reached the front row, her smile
filled the doorway.

She looked like she'd been through a meat grinder. She
sported a butterfly bandage on her forehead, a blueish-
green circle around her left eye, and a puffy nose, and I
couldn't have been more thrilled to see anyone. "Ms. Wilk,
how are you?" I gave her a fist bump. She yelped and
retracted her hand. "Ow."

"I'm sorry…" I attempted to sign but my reflexes
reacted as though through molasses.

"Got you." Laughter burst like the grand finale
explosions of fireworks on the Fourth of July. "I'm good.
Really." She dragged her backpack and a garment bag
down the aisle, slapping hands and bumping the backs of
unaware heads.

Harley hopped out of a Chevy Bolt with COURTESY CAR
stenciled on the door, a cruel reminder of the state in which
I'd left his Range Rover. He bounded up the bus stairs, and
stood on the landing. "How's the awesomest team?"

The students responded with, "Super!" and "Great!"
and "Ready to rock."

"We're gonna take 'em down today. Let's go team!" He
tipped an imaginary hat. "We're so ready for this. I can't
wait." He swung around the front pole and spun into the
front seat across the aisle.

When the last student bounced up the stairs, the bus doors closed, and Jane said, "Who's on the docket for today?"

Harley pulled a handful of papers out of his briefcase detailing the matchups. He ran his finger down the page. "Our first challenger is a team called the AdvoCATS. They beat both opponents during the first round but we'll surely pound them into the ground," he said, pleased with himself. "Hey, I'm a poet. Now, excuse me, please, but I have a little work to do."

Jane and I nodded as Harley rifled through more pages. Jane whispered, "I'm nervous."

With my voice kept equally low, I asked, "Why?"

"It's just a feeling I have." She turned to look at me. "Are you sure you're okay? I don't know how you and Patricia can apparently be so unaffected by your frightening ride."

Harley overheard Jane. "Officer Christianson has been able to collect reports of incidents involving cars with similar electronics and found that there could be a glitch between the navigation system and cruise control. I've filed a grievance with the dealership. With the police on my side, I think I have a solid case."

I nodded and Harley went back to work. I whispered, "Jane …"

"What?"

"It really felt like someone else was driving the car." My heart rate picked up. She patted my arm.

Fingers tapped Jane on the shoulder from the seat behind us and I caught Jane furtively palming a scrap of paper, laughing as if told a joke, but the grin on Galen's face didn't quite reach his eyes. I remembered one of the few words Kindra had taught me, opened both my palms upward, and signed. "What?" I mouthed. Jane raised a finger in caution.

I slid closer to examine the penciled words on the paper. 'Patricia is really scared but trying not to show it.'

"Why?" I whispered.

Jane said, "There is, of course, the SUV that drove itself, the callous anonymous note, plus the fact that she and Kindra are competing at the same tournament, perhaps against each other. And her mom asked if the general public is allowed to watch so she may be there for support of either, neither, or both girls."

"Debora is coming? I know both of them have been overwhelmed by the attention their mother is getting. Maybe this small degree of normality will be good."

The threatening, gray-covered sky completely blocked the sunlight by the time the bus pulled into the school parking lot at Rocori. The students spilled out, tension building as they mentally prepared for the meet. Their murmuring voices sounded like bees in a hive with a pressing need to meet all their personal goals. With a bit of wait time, the girls broke into a Queen song, "We Are the Champions." The boys, not to be outdone, chanted and pounded the rhythm of "We Will, We Will, Rock You," mumbling the rest of the lyrics.

Harley collected the team packets designating the assigned rooms, the sides we would take, the resources available onsite, including the availability of a nurse, the food service with the classic hot-dog/walking-taco-salad menu, the hours and cost of purchasing a T-shirt or mug at the souvenir stand, and the estimated time for the announcement of the results.

The kids changed into their lawyering duds and sat

in pairs, working through any particularly vulnerable arguments. When the clock ticked down to start time, Lorelei grabbed Patricia and led her team out the door chanting, "EsqChoir, EsqChoir." Jane trailed them, shouting enthusiastically.

Harley and I followed Galen and Carlee and the rest of the students into another classroom. I watched an unease settle on the challenging plaintiff team as our students filed in, looking ready to take on the world; I would've burst my buttons if I'd worn any. Our students were polished and smiling, sure of themselves, and the outcome reflected their preparedness. Both our plaintiff and defense earned an affirmative judgement.

"We're in the quarterfinals and we can go home. The loser brackets have a comeback trial." Jane bubbled. "I'm so glad Patricia is back. She wowed them again with her picture-perfect performance." The word picture brought to mind the plastic sheath of photos I'd pocketed after our accident and I vowed to return it to Patricia.

But we were headed for another kind of crash.

On our way to the bus, Deborah stopped Patricia and signed and spoke for our benefit. "Great job, kiddo. You've been practicing the part of Maggie Murphy since the day you got back, and you know it backwards and forwards. It's paid off."

Patricia rolled her eyes, but smiled. "Thanks, Mom."

I thought I could cheer her up and retrieved the photos and her comb from my bag. I handed them to Patricia. Her eyes widened when she recognized the cover photo of her smiling mother, two much younger girls, and a growly man wearing a ballcap. She stuffed the photos under the cover of her notepad.

"What do you have there?" Debora asked, tilting her head.

"Nothing, Mom. I gotta go," Patricia said, and as she sidled between us, the wire spiral caught on Debora's sweater. The plastic sheath slipped from between the pages and fell to the floor.

Debora picked it up. Her brows furrowed. Her hands shook. She forced the words. "I thought I destroyed all the photos of Ian. I never wanted to see that bastard's face again." Her voice trembled.

Patricia signed a response at a frightening speed.

Ian. Ian? Ian, Debora, and Ransam completed a trio from Sophie Grainger's list. But what did that mean? I ignored my buzzing phone.

"Maybe you weren't ready to come back to Columbia." Debora threw the entire set of photos into a trash can. Patricia burst into tears and collided with Harley who backed out of the classroom, hands raised, giving her space.

"Excuse me," Debora said, exited with purpose, and trailed Patricia.

I followed them both, skirting a crowd moving like a herd of elephants, to the commons area. I craned my neck around the mob that had gathered and saw Kindra consoling Patricia as Ronnie Christianson slapped handcuffs on Debora. Patricia broke free and ran out the front doors.

CHAPTER FORTY-TWO

Patricia's friends were supportive, but subdued. After the quiet bus ride home, I welcomed the dancing lights at 3141 Maple Street, blinking a red, blue, green, and gold pattern from the fir tree in Ida's front window, probably linked to her sound system.

Noting no other lights at the relatively early hour, Ida and Dad must have found something Christmassy to do. The community calendar listed concerts, sing-a-longs, performances of *The Nutcracker* by the local ballet studio, a holiday play, and extended shopping hours. It would be just my luck to find them at the outdoor ice rink.

Ida had promised to bring carolers to the nursing home. Maybe they were singing. With so much happening between Thanksgiving and Christmas, I needed to keep better track of their activities. As I drove into the garage, I gently tapped my bruised forehead, trying to rearrange the thoughts that cluttered my mind.

Maverick raised his head, watching me stack my bag and books on the bench by the back door. Next to him lay a pair of shredded red and green socks I thought I recognized. "Oh, Maverick." He jerked to a standing position, panting, wagging his thick black tail, likely anticipating a walk. "Not yet, big guy. I have work to do, and maybe you can help me."

The kibble clattered into his bowl. While his food disappeared, I sat at my kitchen table and pulled out the list of names: Debora, Ransam, Amelia, Ian, Annalise, Serena, and Natasha. Maybe the sequence organized Sophie's list in revenge order. Maybe it listed those she wished to reconcile with at the holiday season. I couldn't get the names to connect. Maybe they didn't all connect.

Debora and Ransam filled the number one and two slots of Sophie's list. They had experienced her anger and distrust. Kindra didn't like her either, but trusted her mom. However, Ronnie Christianson had to have evidence to take Debora into custody. Pete's dad, Chief Erickson was a stickler for rules, and although he was temporarily on leave, his departmental expectations remained intact. Maybe Sophie was looking for a reason to get rid of Debora and get Ransam back.

Debora and Ian had ended their relationship and it seemed that he had been out of Debora's life, and out of the area for more than a dozen years.

Sophie had been preparing to sever ties with her partner and Serena would have lost everything. Lars was none too happy either. Serena had a good excuse for getting rid of

Sophie, but how? Who knew where the missing money had gone? And why wasn't Lars's name included on Sophie's list?

I hoped Amelia would call again. Maybe she could tell me more about her mother, Natasha, and I could somehow link one of them to Sophie or someone else on the list.

Annalise's improbable connection troubled me the most. Maybe the Annalise on Sophie's list didn't live in Columbia, but Brenna told me that Annalise lived across the street from Sophie, which made for a fairly big coincidence in a very small world. But she couldn't possibly have had anything to do with Sophie's death.

I double-checked the arrow that pointed to the empty space and shook my head.

Too much information and too many maybes. Back to reality. I pulled out my phone and noted the missed calls and the unheard voice messages. I'd set my phone to silent during the trials, and never bothered to turn it back on. I lifted the phone to my ear.

"This is Amelia Cross. If you'd still like to speak with me, you can contact me at this number. Freddie said you had some questions. I don't know what I can tell you, but…"

I pressed the blue hyperlink in the transcription of the message. It rang once.

"Yes?"

"Ms. Cross? This is Katie Wilk. I was wondering if I might talk to you about Sophie Grainger."

"What do you want, Ms. Wilk?"

"Call me Katie." How to begin. "I sat in on the first day of your trial and—"

Her voice took on an edge. "I have nothing to say."

"I'm not a reporter. I don't need any information about your lawsuit. I'm merely a poor conversationalist." I tried to laugh. "May I begin again?"

Amelia didn't hang up. Maverick barked.

"What kind of dog do you have?" she said with a gentler voice.

"A noisy Lab. Sorry."

"They're the best."

I shouldered my phone, dug a chewy treat out of the cupboard, and tossed it to him, mouthing the words, "Thank you, Maverick."

"I am wondering if you knew Sophie Grainger."

"Why?"

"I am looking into her death. Your name came up."

"Why are you looking into her death? Did you know her? Why ask me about her suicide?"

"She didn't take her own life. Debora Halloran has been arrested in connection with her murder."

"Murder? What are you talking about? Why would Debora kill Sophie?"

"Do you know Debora?" The line went silent. "Ms. Cross? I have her daughters in my math class. And neither believes their mother is responsible."

Amelia Cross said, "The year before Natasha died, she talked a lot about how out-of-touch she felt. She'd stayed busy with her influencing business but was looking for something more meaningful to do. She was remodeling her home, making it a smart showcase."

I waited for a second. "Smart?"

"She wanted to control household electronics audibly and would have succeeded. She taught electrical engineering for a few years before she met my dad. I was eleven and

Freddie was seven. Dad said he wanted to raise a family where he grew up and Natasha was on board so they moved us here. She was a great stepmom. After George, my dad, died I hoped she'd find something else to give her purpose. Through her blog, she received the latest technology and she was always on the lookout for the next best thing."

Amelia exhaled. "She was a big idea woman. S & S Designs was helping her put together a new plan. She was hoping for more."

More what?

"She framed her only patent."

"What did she patent?"

"She and a student built an electronic device to govern house lights or something. I never understood it, but she was quite proud."

"Who was the coauthor?"

"Ian Halloran."

I gulped. Ian, Natasha, and Amelia. What could they mean to Sophie?

"Have you ever met Debora or Ian?"

"I've seen Debora around, but Ian Halloran was already long gone by the time I was old enough to pay attention. Why would Debora kill Sophie?"

I left the unsavory gossip for someone else to share. Instead of answering, I asked, "Do you know Annalise?"

"Who?"

"Never mind."

"I have to go to work. Good luck, Ms. Wilk."

"Bye," I said, but she'd already hung up. I starred the names on the list and added lines to show their tenuous connections.

The second voicemail came from Harley.

"Good job today, don't you think?" My lips stretched into a smile big enough to make my cheeks hurt. "Do you have time to get together tonight and strategize? I'm calling Jane next. I hate to say this, but if we make it to the finals, it'll be Mossa's team against us. We have to be ready. From what the kids say, I'm sure Mossa has an arsenal of conniving tricks. We have to figure out what surprises he might have up his sleeves and be prepared to combat his devious behavior. I'll try to stop by. If you're like me, you probably turned off your ringer and you won't get this message until I'm at your door." I snickered.

Dad left a text message. Hi, doll. Ida and I are rabble-rousing tonight at Sterling Manor. If you get home in time, come join us. We'll save your favorite carol for last. Then we're going to dinner. I ran song titles through my head. *Did I have a favorite?* Dad would know. I checked the log time. He'd left the message at five thirty. The third voicemail reminder called to me.

The message opened with forced, heavy breathing and a muffled voice said, "Forget or you're screwed."

Alone at night, the ominous voice made my hand shake. My heart thumped. My chest felt like it had been caught by a boa constrictor. *Forget what? What could I have seen?*

The phone rang. I didn't hold tight and it hit the carpet with a thud. I picked it up, reading Dr P on the screen display and pressed connect.

"Hello," I squeaked.

"Katie? You're back."

I swallowed hard. "Yes," I said, lowering my voice.

"Are you busy? Could I swing by after work? I have a … a fruitcake to deliver."

A fruitcake? "I'm home."

My heart did a happy dance, but just a little one.

"See you in about two hours."

I pulled up an app of holiday music and a bass voice reverberated the phrase, "You're a mean one, Mr. Grinch." I opened my phone to call Dad, when Maverick dropped his treat and hauled himself to a standing position, barking.

CHAPTER FORTY-THREE

My kitchen felt like a beacon, drawing unsolicited attention from the unseen eyes of the black void outside. I flipped the switch to illuminate the porch, equalizing our positions. The visitor's hair reflected shiny gold highlights. Maverick continued to bark. The face remained in shadow until I slid the curtain to one side and Harley's smile beamed. I put my hand on Maverick's head to quiet him.

I turned the deadbolt and opened the door. "Happy holidays."

I relieved him of an elongated tray mounded with red- and green-iced sugar cookies and removed the clear-wrap as he stood a bottle of red wine on the kitchen counter. He threw his black anorak over the back of a kitchen chair, but kept the woolen scarf draped around his neck. He rubbed his hands together. "Celebrate-good-times-come-on," he sang, his eyes glittering impishly.

I collected my scattered pages from the tabletop and slid them into a folder.

"What do you have there?" he asked, crunching on a cookie.

"Just some notes." I didn't want to weigh down his happy mood.

"You're a great one for list making. Shall we partake of this vintage?" He grabbed the wine and held the bottle as if it were an exhibit. I nodded.

"You were quick getting here."

"Did you get my message?" I nodded. "Jane said she'd be by shortly. Where are your wine glasses?"

"Top shelf in the cupboard to the right of the sink."

A buzz came from his pocket. "Hold on." He took out his phone. "Hello." I snatched a cookie and nibbled. I'd have to get the recipe or lessons or both. "Sorry, but we'll see you early tomorrow. Goodnight, Jane."

"She's not coming," I said, aggrieved. I stood next to Harley, licking telltale crumbs from my lips.

He shook his head. "Are you still up for making plans for our competition?" I mumbled an assent.

He grabbed the glasses and the bottle and followed me to the living room. I swiped another cookie as we sat down and Maverick plopped himself between us. He rested his head on my knee.

"I know you want a bite, but don't try anything. Too much sugar just isn't a good idea, Maverick." I should take my own advice.

"The bus leaves at six forty-five for a nine o'clock start in Little Falls and tomorrow we're going to knock the socks off the competition." He uncoiled his scarf and threw it on the couch.

Just before he cut into the foil at the top of the bottle, he said, with a mischievous grin lighting his face, "I've got an idea. How about I take you to search for my second night-geocache instead? It's easy." I started to protest. "It might take a half hour. A celebratory find? The kids are ready. We really don't have anything else to do this evening. It'll take forty-five minutes, tops, including drive time, and I saw your crock pot in the cupboard. We can come back for mulled wine and more cookies," he sang, hitting me where my sweet tooth was.

I took a moment to dust the last crumbs off my fingers, figuring Pete's arrival time in my head before I said, "I'm game. But I've never made *mulled* wine."

He dabbed at his phone. "Here's an easy recipe. I saw oranges on your kitchen counter. Do you have cinnamon sticks, cloves, and cider?"

"It's December in Minnesota. Ida keeps my spice rack well stocked." I said, making my way to the kitchen. Harley hauled out the crockpot and I took down the spice jars. He juggled three oranges like they were baseballs. When he completed his act, he took a bow. I handed him a cutting board and paring knife. He tested its heft and proceeded to slice an orange into paper-thin wedges. I emptied my cider jug and plugged in the crockpot. "How much cinnamon and cloves?"

"It says add the amounts to taste. Mix the wine, cinnamon, cloves, cider, and a sliced orange and turn the crockpot on low."

I sprinkled hefty amounts, turned the knob, and closed my eyes, inhaling the delicate fragrance.

"It's thirty-one degrees outside and they are predicting a small accumulation of snow and below zero temperatures by early morning, but the sky is clear and the moon and stars are radiant right now. This'll be great."

I raced upstairs, pulled a sweater over my shirt, and yanked on thicker socks. I whirled around the newel post, slowing to a more reasonable pace when I spotted Harley leaning confidently against the banister at the bottom of the stairs.

He held my down jacket for me. I shoved my arms into the sleeves, shooting out a wool plaid hat with furry flaps. I tied the flaps together on top of my head, feeling like a real Paul Bunyan-ette. I batted at my pockets for a pair of mittens, and Harley's hands suddenly landed on my shoulders. He turned me around. The intense look in his eyes made my stomach lurch. "You're looking better."

Maverick jostled between us. I pulled my eyes away and found lacey straps dangling from Maverick's jaws. I grabbed the bra and smashed it in with the mittens.

"Wait. I almost forgot." I slipped under his arms, dashed to the kitchen, and I jotted a note to Pete, telling him to let himself inside if we hadn't yet returned from our geocache outing and have some mulled wine while he waited. I stooped to pick up a page of my scribbles that had fallen to the floor and shoved it in the folder with the rest of my notes. I grabbed a flashlight and clicked it on, swept the perimeter of my kitchen, and clicked it off.

Maverick's tail whumped. "I'm not sure he should come with us," Harley said. "It's woodsy where we're headed, and he'll likely find an assortment of strange things to hunt for like he did on our last hike. I'd hate to have him get lost."

Maverick tilted his head at Harley and then back at me,

judging our next move. "He'll be fine. I'll keep him on his leash this time." I scratched behind Maverick's ears and he wagged his wicked tail. "What's the name of this cache?"

"The Wheels of Justice."

I pulled up the app and typed in the name, reading the cache description, complete with caveats. I looked up, smiling. "It'll be another 'First to Find'."

"I'm putting on the finishing touches tonight." His eyes lit up like a tot at Christmas.

"You rated it two for difficulty and three for terrain. Is it hard to get to?"

"I'll be right there to keep you on the straight and narrow."

"I'd like to do as much as I can without help."

Harley nodded, patting at his neck. "My scarf?"

"On the couch." I pointed through the doorway, and Harley disappeared.

Maverick barked and raced through the kitchen before I even heard the knock.

I threw open the door, thinking Pete had gotten off early, but found a half dozen students piled onto the landing and crowded down the steps, singing "Rudolph the Red-Nosed Reindeer," bundled in coats, boots, scarves, gloves, and muffs, and decorated for the holidays with red-and-white Santa hats. Twinkle-lights blinked in wreaths hanging around their necks, and cartoonlike clouds formed around the words on the carolers' lips. They put on a great show, and they didn't sing half-bad either. It made my heart dance to see Patricia in the mix, smiling and laughing, ringing jingle bells.

When they looked past me, more than one set of eyebrows raised in reaction to the plate of cookies on the counter. I passed the plate in payment for their good cheer. The hands reached in and, before I could name Santa's reindeer, all that remained of the confectionary was a memory of my sugar-fix.

"Thanks, Ms. Wilk," I heard from more than one student and, before I could correct them, they were rushing down the stairs, waving. "See ya," they called as they marched across the yard. Patricia signed, "Happy holidays," words we'd practiced, and followed her friends.

I penciled Pete's name on the envelope and stuffed it into the door handle.

"Who was that?" Harley said, stepping behind me on the landing.

"Didn't you hear them? Carolers," I said. What a night!

"Can we take your van?" Harley said, stepping behind me. "My loaner's a mess and I'm afraid what Maverick might find." Harley's hand went into his pocket and searched. "My gloves." He pointed inside.

"The door's open," I said, and shivered.

"Go warm up your van."

"Watch this," I said, and pressed the starter fob on my keyring. My van belched and then growled. If I gave it time, it might even warm up.

"That's great. I'll be right back," he said.

I trotted to my vehicle, and opened the door. Maverick jumped in back. I slid into the driver's seat, huffing into my hands. The heater blew tepid air but took the chill out.

As I waited, I dug around in the ready-pack I'd kept behind my seat. I never knew when Maverick and I'd be called to help find someone. I pulled out a slim hiking belt equipped with a hand warmer packet, a handyman tool, a compass, a four-ounce collapsible water bottle with an imprint of the Columbia Cougar, an old glow stick, a toothbrush, dental floss, two sticks of beef jerky, a pen, and, of course, two small squares of chocolate. Maverick devoured the stick of jerky I held out to him. I secured the belt around my waist and zipped my warm, bulky jacket over it, scratching behind Maverick's ears.

Harley closed my apartment door and skipped down the steps, hopping in next to me. "Do you have a good flashlight, extra batteries, and is your phone charged?" I nodded, but checked the battery life of my phone anyway. "Drive toward the state park."

I tuned my radio to a winter music channel and we sang along with "Jolly Old St. Nicholas," "Grandma Got Run Over by a Reindeer," and "Jingle Bell Rock" at a significant volume with as much gusto as we could generate. I still wasn't sure which holiday song was my personal favorite.

We'd driven for maybe fifteen minutes when Harley guided us onto a field access road. We parked, and hopped out. I snapped the leash on Maverick and shadowed Harley. The wind had picked up and I pulled my jacket close.

Harley rubbed his hands together, anticipating a fair and impartial evaluation of his latest hide. I straightened my outerwear and refreshed the geocaching app on my phone. On a straight shot, we had a trek of less than two-tenths of a mile to the cache, but the description warned that walking through the unmapped terrain at night could be hazardous if not done with extreme care. My flashlight beam lit the first reflective marker of a cache which, during the day, would have been impossible to locate.

Although Harley knew where we were, I set a waypoint to remind me how to return to my vehicle. As the interior lights of the van faded, Harley flipped on a lantern.

"We're out in the middle of nowhere. How did you

find this place?" I shouted into the wind.

"The land belongs to a friend of mine. Ready?" he yelled, bouncing on his feet. I nodded and took the lead.

I stopped after about twenty feet when the field butted up against a wall of trees. I examined the face of my phone, changing to compass mode to determine our direction. The straight line on the screen would take us through an impossible tangle of wild flora. Harley's beam of light panned the wall of prairie grasses, prickly brambles, and sumac. About fifteen feet to the right, a distinct shadow broke the line of dry, yellowing shrubbery and looked like a way in.

Harley exchanged his lantern for my flashlight. I nodded my head, and led the way to a narrow path of trampled plants, pressed into the ground by footsteps, and what appeared to be tire treads.

We stepped into a wonderland where the shrieking wind ceased as if we'd slammed a door to the outside world. The tops of the tall trees swayed and shook glittery flakes onto our shoulders and the surfaces around us. Even the gnarled branches glistened. We stood as figures in a snow globe, transfixed by the fantastic soundlessness and singular beauty. Even Maverick stood still.

The temperature, however, brought me back to reality and I shuddered, swinging the lantern which shimmered off a marker eight feet off the ground, pointing down. We unearthed a box covered in camouflage tape couched in the gnarled base of the tree. I was almost disappointed we'd located the cache so quickly, but instead we found another set of coordinates.

I bubbled, "This is a multi-cache?" Harley nodded. "How many segments?" He held up two fingers.

We followed the semblance of a path, single file,

meandering dozens of feet back and forth, taking us around fallen branches, huge boulders, and tree stumps, past a deep, forbidding unknown, adding who knew how much yardage and time to our trek.

I searched for the FireTacks as often as I checked our direction on my phone and we doggedly made our way closer to the objective. My enthusiasm ramped up. Puzzles drew me like a magnet.

I let my pleasant thoughts wander. I promised Charles I'd live a good life and I constantly worked on processing that puzzle too.

The path turned back on itself and I caught a glimpse of Harley, an ominous silhouette against the midnight-blue velvet surrounding us. I gasped.

"What's wrong?" His voice came out of the darkness.

I shuddered again. "The wind caught me," I lied.

I licked a final sweet cookie crumb from my lips and thought how lucky I was. Then I frowned, thinking of Kindra and Patricia, and wondered who killed Sophie. What message had she tried to leave? Debora had installed the security system for S & S Designs, but life for her and Ransam could be better without Sophie. Amelia's mom, Natasha, had known an Ian. Annalise lived across the street and might have witnessed something. Serena's partnership and business were in jeopardy. I visualized the names from Sophie's list, spelling them: Debora, Ransam, Amelia, Ian, Annalise, Serena, and Natasha, and a pattern emerged. Each of the final two letters of one name began the next name. Debora, r-a, Ransam, a-m, Amelia, i-a, Ian, a-n, Annalise, s-e, Serena, n-a, Natasha, h-a.

CHAPTER FORTY-FOUR

I tripped. Harley righted me. "Thanks," I said.

I sought puzzles, codes, and mysteries everywhere and had developed a slightly suspicious mind. I felt a twinge of guilt at the direction my thoughts had taken before again setting my sights on finding the elusive geocache.

I concentrated on moving forward safely. With so much going on, I couldn't seem to weave the right threads together. Two threads, Patricia and Kindra, led back to Debora who in turn took me to Ransam. Ransam's thread linked directly with Sophie's. Serena and her dad looped in there too. Stanley and Oliver twisted into a coarse rope, tying together the students in mock trial and they, in turn, lassoed the rest of the school. Maybe the cold had frozen my brain cells. I'd woven a tangle of knots. I stumbled again, but righted myself and checked my phone. "Less than one-hundred feet remaining."

Harley said, "Yup."

As I adjusted to my surroundings, I isolated the noises invading the dark night. Twigs snapped, branches cracked, and brittle leaves crunched beneath each footfall. Something tiny scurried just outside the range of the lantern. Maverick's head went up and one paw hung in the air. The wind whistled in the treetops. I sniffled. My cold nose reminded me we still had a slight distance to go and my steps slogged. Maverick jerked the leash and I stumbled again.

Harley chuckled. "Are you going to make it?"

"Yes," I said, sucking in a breath. "I'm not used to wearing all this winter gear and it's weighing me down."

"Do you want me to lead? We'll get there faster."

I relinquished the point, returning his lantern, and three steps later we stomped into a small clearing. The brilliant pinpoints of stars scattered across the sky shined like crystals. A moonbeam peeked through the knobby tree limbs. My flashlight died and I tripped again. Harley stopped and turned around. "We're almost there."

With light from the lantern, the snow surrounding us appeared blue. I pulled out my phone and turned on its light. "Harley, we're so lucky you decided to practice out here in the—" What did Mrs. Clemashevski call Columbia? "—cultural Siberia of west-central Minnesota."

"It's not so bad. I met you." His honeyed voice made my heart knock against my chest.

"Where did you move from?"

"Vermont."

"Dorene Dvorak—you know her right?" He hummed.

"Before I met her, I thought all lawyers were political science or criminal justice majors, but Dorene majored in music. What was your major?"

He continued walking. I tramped after him, cautiously watching where I put each booted foot and collided with Harley when he stopped short and turned around, my hands landing on his chest. A deep chuckle rippled from within. "We're very close," he breathed.

Yes, we were. A curious chill wrapped around my torso and neck and my ears felt cold. I stepped back. Harley was smart and good looking and funny. He understood law. He gave his time and talent to our mock trial team. My students benefitted from his expertise and he still had time for a bit of fun. But there was something …

I touched my phone and a pale green-gold light coalesced on the screen, illuminating eerie dancing shadows on Harley's face as if he'd wiggled a flashlight under his chin. "We're less than fifteen feet away."

The compass arrow pointed straight ahead. My eagerness to find the cache and solve the puzzle took flight and I barreled past Harley to the remains of a wide ancient tree. It called to me, a monster signal with something to hide. I extended my hands, scraping the deep crevices and bulbous nodules in the bark, feeling for a hiding place. I searched the base, brushing aside dried grasses and unearthing crumbly leaves, but the path finder still indicated another three feet. I flashed my phone light into the scraggly dead branches above us, alighting on a pattern of FireTacks in the shape of an X pressed into the trunk. I circled the base, hurdling the overgrown roots, sweeping the tall frosty foliage aside to reveal an opening carved into the trunk. I thrust my phone into the hollow space and the distance reduced to zero.

The gap in the trunk started about a foot off the ground, expanding from six inches to twenty-four inches at shoulder level. We hadn't brought any TOTT, tools of the trade, with which to reach inside, but I thought I might just be able to squeeze through the narrow opening into the hidey-hole.

"This is it," I said. I directed the beam of my phone inside to chase away any critters but couldn't seem to get the angle right, fumbling with Maverick's leash.

"Here, let me," Harley said.

"Sit, Maverick." I coiled the leash, and patted his head. He rocked back and forth, feeding off my excitement. He shook like he was wet and his tags rattled. "Yeah, it's cold, buddy." When he settled, I dropped the leash. "Stay, Maverick." He shifted his weight from one paw to the other, yawned, and then licked his lips.

CJ once told me that meant something important but I couldn't remember what.

I handed Harley my phone while I unwrapped my scarf and whipped off my hat, piling them on a heap next to the tree so they wouldn't snag on the jagged bark. Harley held my phone above me and lit the cavern which must have been close to four feet in diameter. I stepped over the lip of the opening, squirmed through the crevice, and plunged inside, sprawling gracelessly.

Giggling, I climbed to a standing position, running my hands up and down the inner wall of the cavity. The primeval tree held many secrets, but not for much longer. The old wooden surface shredded beneath my mittens. "Can you shine that light in here? I can't see a thing and I want to make sure I'm alone. What size is the cache? Did you include any other description or attributes?" Impatient to make the find, I persisted in asking questions Harley didn't answer. "How long do you think this tree has been here? It's falling apart."

I knelt, exploring the ground at my feet, groping for some kind of container, and shoved a cylinder into the unlit recesses just out of reach.

The light behind me disappeared.

"Illumination, please. I can't see a thing," I sang.

Fear accelerated my imaginings which often played tricks on me, but not this time. My heart raced. My mind did a somersault. When it came to affairs of the heart, I avoided the obvious and my heart leapt to my throat. The arrow at the end of Sophie's list of names could have pointed to a name that should begin with h-a. Why would Harley's name be on the list? I see-sawed back and forth, trying to justify its presence or eliminate his name from the strange string of letters while waiting for the light to come back on. There were lots of names that began with h-a: Harvey, Harrison, Hayes, Harlan, Hamilton. Even Harry began with h-a. And maybe that wasn't the solution to the puzzle.

"A little light please," I said, glancing through the fissure. Then I recognized the set of Harley's jaw and his silhouette and recognized the man in Patricia's photo. But if Harley was Ian, Patricia and Kindra were his daughters. Had they been together much? Had they been together at all? Debora certainly would have recognized her ex-husband, wouldn't she? Maybe he'd changed after all those years, altered his appearance somehow.

"Harley?" I tried to stand; my balance was compromised by disorientation in the dark. I looked up and the moon caught the gleam in Harley's eyes, two glassy orbs in a blank face. I reached through the aperture, grabbing the edges.

The silky voice said, "My major was engineering."

Cold seeped into my toes and nose. I prepared to haul myself out when a grate slammed on my fingertips. I screamed, "Harley!"

A rough-hewn lattice had dropped into place and cut off my exit. Maverick pawed at the grate and chipped away some wood. "Harley, this isn't funny. Let me out of here."

"I'm not laughing," he muttered. "Idiot dog." Maverick yelped, and I heard his tags rattle as he tore through the brush.

"What did you do to him?" I screamed.

I cringed at the sound of his oily voice. "Everyone in Columbia has heard of your uncanny ability to solve crimes. When you called me to volunteer as an attorney-coach, I thought you'd recognized me from my fight with Sophie at the coffee shop. I needed to find out if you were testing me." He sneered. "After that first meeting, I was fairly certain you had no idea who I was. But being on site presented me with the perfect opportunity to keep my eyes on you and observe my girls."

"That's just plain creepy." I hadn't meant those words to be spoken aloud. "And your ex-wife?" I added. Harley snorted. "Your new look must be pretty good. She never took a second glance at you."

He dropped something and it crunched beneath his foot. He said, "I've lost sixty-five pounds and had my nose straightened." He let that sink in. "She knew me with a mustache and beard. Clean-shaven, cheek inserts, blue contacts, and blond hair plugs hide a multitude of sins. Debbie never saw me with much hair. I let the earring hole on my lobe close for a more professional look and seriously upgraded my wardrobe.

"But when I saw you hiding in the gallery at the trial, I knew you were putting the pieces together, zeroing in on me." He retrieved the shattered pieces of my phone and shoved them one by one through the wooden slats into my hands. Then he drew a chain in front of the door and snapped a lock through the links.

"I had jury duty," I said, awash in disbelief. "And had you ever thought that I might have been doing research for our case?"

"But you weren't, were you? You ask too many questions." I'd heard that before.

"You give me too much credit." I fumbled with the shattered pieces of my phone and they fell to the ground. I'd kept all the answers just outside of my train of consciousness. I didn't want to believe the worst in people. I rattled the cage door.

"What do you think you know?"

"Natasha recognized you," I said as I thought of the little inconsistencies I hadn't wanted to believe.

Harley shook his head.

"Then she recognized your work."

"I sold one of my control panels to a hot company she kept track of. She followed up with them because we'd worked together on a similar prototype. The trail led back to me. First, she praised my work. The next time we met, she lauded our work together and wanted a small cut. I was fine with that arrangement. She'd given me a good bit of guidance early on, possible improvements to make what I implemented, and assistance in gaining a copyright. But then she tried to jam me up, insisting we should be equal partners, working together, or she'd reveal my presence to law enforcement. Don't feel too bad, though. I got her kids a huge settlement to even the score. Simonet Electronics never knew what hit them."

"What did you do?"

"I sent Natasha a celebratory bottle of her favorite bubbly. I knew she couldn't resist. She sat in her hot tub every night, summer and winter, so I was pretty sure I'd catch her in. I followed her movements on her phone and closed the cover remotely. She operated her innovations by virtual assistant.

"George," he said in a gravely voice. "Close spa cover.

"Everything worked according to my plan."

"What could she have possibly known about you that would warrant her dying? Even if she knew about the theft—"

"You've heard about my dubious past." He sniggered deviously. "I suppose Debbie was more than willing to air that piece of dirty laundry."

"Your crime could no longer be prosecuted. You're well past the statute of limitations."

"But I enjoy my life as an attorney." Bells and whistles clanged. "People come to me with their problems and pay me well to fix them. I'd hate to lose that source of income and the respect that goes with it. And I'm good at it."

"Why would you lose your life as…" Oh, boy.

"I apprenticed with Harley Brown in Vermont where you can sit for the bar without a law degree. He was a good guy. When he passed on, I didn't have to take the exam. I appropriated his name and his license to practice. He didn't need it anymore. I moved home and everything fell into place."

I didn't want Harley to stay but I didn't want him to leave either. I kept talking. "I didn't see you fighting with anyone at the coffee shop."

He stepped away from the tree. "Natasha sent a cryptic message to Sophie and Sophie showed it to me. Natasha thought it might encourage me, but it put Sophie on guard and she discovered the missing money before I could implement my frame against the security company, Debbie's company."

"You were Sophie's new boyfriend." I inhaled. "You stole the money."

"It's easy to reroute money if you know all the details and superior Sophie was so willing to share all her expertise with someone she wanted to spend her future with. Both Serena and Debbie looked good for the theft. It was a great plan, but Sophie was getting too close. I'd installed a tracker on her phone too."

"Too?" The thought numbed my mind.

"That's how I found you."

He'd followed me. There'd been no coincidental or happenstance meetings. "How did you put a tracker on my phone?"

"I only needed seconds." Acting the good Samaritan and lending Harley my phone had provided him with ample opportunity. He'd been monitoring me.

"You didn't really place a tracker on my backpack when we searched for Drew?"

"I most certainly did. I'm constantly perfecting the technology and writing comparisons on my new influencing site, which, I've discovered, can be quite a lucrative endeavor. Too bad you won't be able to check it out."

"You wormed your way into her good graces and your expertise enabled you to take the money. After Natasha was murdered, Sophie figured out the message, didn't she? You had an alibi for the day of her death, but starting her car remotely wouldn't be out of your wheelhouse." Struck by a lightning bolt, I cried, "You drove your Range Rover remotely. Did you mean to kill Patricia too? Or just me?"

"My daughter wasn't supposed to be there." He struggled to hide the fleeting look of triumph in his eyes before he put on a penitent demeanor. "That was purely an exercise hacking telematics with an unfortunate outcome. I never expected you to survive the crash, but I'm glad you saved Patricia.

"I caught a lucky break when the officers working on the case suspected Debora for Sophie's murder."

A thought came to me. Pete should have read my note by now. He knew how to access geocaches. He'd find me.

"Why did we come here?"

"I almost got two for one and would have left you the last time, but CJ found you."

"Two?"

"A kid next door to Sophie saw us together and might have been able to identify me. I was hoping she might get lost for good, but her association with that gang made her an unreliable witness anyway, so I wasn't worried."

I found it difficult to swallow. He would have let Annalise die.

"This is a great place. This is where I had my first kill." A snort escaped. "You should see your face. I shot my first deer from where you're standing. It was a four-point buck." He pointed to his left hand. "By the way, if you are awaiting your knight in shining armor…" He dangled the envelope

I'd left for Pete between his thumb and forefinger. "No one knows where you are. I've already removed the cache from the server. They may never find you." He stooped to pick up my scarf and cap and his voice became deadly serious. "I'm not making any mistakes this time. With you and Debbie out of the way, everything will be all right," he said, and the sound of his steps, retreating through the brush, faded.

"Harley. Harley!" I didn't really want Harley to return, so I switched to a name I loved.

CHAPTER FORTY-FIVE

Maverick," I called again and again, my words snatched by the wind. I dropped to the frozen ground, breathing musty air tainted with decay, and pent up tears swelled. A narrow moonbeam slashed through the dark interior. My icy lashes stuck together as more tears leaked from my eyes. How would Dad take my disappearance? Ida always had my back. Pete and I never had time to figure anything out. Was Maverick okay? Could they find a substitute to teach my kids?

I didn't think anyone would suspect Harley of being anything other than what he seemed. My heart beat against my chest and my anger grew.

I swiped the tears from my cheeks and gritted my teeth. As I braced myself to stand, my hand brushed against the tube Harley had hidden in the geocache. I grabbed it. It looked like one of the items Natasha had reviewed on her webpage. I tried to stuff it in my pocket. I pulled out the bra, held it away, dropped it, and shoved in the cylinder. As I struggled to my feet, my belt jangled with its minimal inventory. I unzipped my jacket.

My first instinct was to crack the glow stick but I didn't want to waste it. My fingers slid over the handyman. I eased it from the pocket and opened the first blade. A bottle opener had its time and place and now the blade fit snugly between the slits. I scraped up and down and bits and pieces of the deteriorating hunting blind fell away revealing ribs of a metal cage. I tore at the remaining camouflage and stretched my hand into the opening. The chain dangled just off the tips of my fingers. Contorting my arm, I hooked one of the links on the bottle opener and pulled it as close as I could. On a dare, Charles and I had practiced opening combination padlocks just by the feel. We got pretty good. And I had nothing better to do. I confidently turned the face of the lock toward me and then let it drop. It needed a key. Panic set in. My second instinct was to surrender.

I shivered and pulled my hood over my head. I blew on my hands covered in mittens with more fashion sense than usefulness.

The rising moon cut a wider swath of pale silver that glinted off the edge of the cylinder in my pocket. Natasha praised this puzzle on her site, extoling its virtues as a method of giving a secret gift using special words to release the ends of the tube, and touting it as an excellent example of engineering done by one of the most ingenious inventors of his time. Because she advertised its use as a part of a romantic message-in-a-bottle, she commended the company's use of an appropriate phrase which could be altered by re-pinning the lock. I held the heavy Leonardo Da Vinci hollow cryptex in my hand, hoping Harley hadn't paid attention to the instructions on her influencing site. If he had, I was finished. As it was, I had nothing to lose.

I rolled the canister in my hand, tipping it to study the superficial indentations. In the faint light, I caught the shallow definition of one or two letters. The frozen rings wouldn't turn on the spindle so I tucked the glacial container under my sweater and grunted as it leeched what little heat remained from my core.

In the minutes it took to warm the cylinder, a cloud passed over the moon and my light source disappeared. I could barely see my hands and, no longer able to differentiate the letters in the code, hoped now was the right time to light the glow stick. I sat on the ground, undid my belt, and let it drop. Arranging the items in a circle around me as if I was blind, which, for the first time I truly understood, I took stock.

I reached for the glow stick and tried to bend it. It slid between my icy fingers and I couldn't crack the contents. I tried again. It remained dark. I wedged one half between my boot and my tree-cell wall and yanked on the other half. The snap was gratifying. As the contents slowly combined, the stick illuminated the interior with a dim sickly-green. I grabbed the cylinder, and could just make out the letters but still couldn't get a good grip on the rings. I indulged, opening the hand warmer packet and shaking the contents. The heat took some of the numbness out of my fingers, so I wrapped it around the cylinder for a minute, then pocketed the precious packet.

One by one, I rotated the rings, aligning the letters

between two raised arrows, intermittently angling the tube to deepen the shadows. When the final ring turned into place, I heaved a sigh and pulled the ends as if opening a Christmas cracker.

It didn't budge. My head dropped to my chest. My sluggish brain demanded rest in the mind-numbing cold. My heart rate decreased. I slumped against the inside of the trunk of the tree and, closing my eyes, I slipped to the ground.

I love you. The clipped British accent I imagined was music to my ears—Charles.

I love you too. But the cryptex doesn't work.

Try again. You can't give in.

Why not? My students will be fine, great even with a new teacher. Pete and Susie have their thing going and Dad has Elizabeth. Ida's apartment will be rented in no time, and Jane has found the love of her life. I miss you.

Try again.

I'd given Charles a promise that I'd live a good life, but my life had run amok.

I love you. I love you. I love you.

The voice persisted, getting edgier, more urgent. I peeled open my eyelids. The words morphed into barks. I shook my head, dislodging the icicles taking residence there. Maverick attacked the cage again, drawing his doggy nails against the metal with a chalk-on-blackboard screech. I unfolded my stiff torso and hauled myself to a standing position.

I removed a worthless mitten and wriggled my fingers through the slats. "It's okay, boy. It's okay." He licked all of me he could reach with the earnestness only a dog-mom could love.

Encouraged by Maverick's insistence, I reexamined the letters on the cryptex which read, ILOVEV. I'd misspelled the easiest message ever. I rotated the last ring and felt a subtle easing of the metal discs. I inhaled, grabbed both ends, and separated the two caps.

At first it held fast. I pulled harder. When it came loose, something dropped out of the inner compartment. My fingers fumbled along the ground. The contact I made was electric. I closed my fingers around a key and prayed. The cryptex wasn't called 'a lock on your heart' for nothing.

Maneuvering the handyman tool over the links, I drew the chain bearing the lock closer to the key. My pulse raced. The heart-shaped lock connected with the metal rib on my prison door with a startling clang.

I angled the lock to insert the key but dropped the handyman and its weight yanked the chain and the lock out of reach. I couldn't even cry.

I curled my fingers around the bars, closed my eyes, and my head fell forward. *I failed again.*

Even Maverick licking my fingers couldn't bring me out of my slump. He pawed at my hands and I couldn't move. He knocked against the door and I didn't budge. When he whimpered, I opened my eyes and then opened them wider.

Maverick held the lock in his mouth close enough for me to hook one of the links with my pinkie and secure the lock against the metal frame as I inserted the key. It turned. The lock snapped open. I slid the key into my pocket and, one finger at a time, pulled the links nearer until I could knock the lock off the chain which I drew through the rings securing the entry. I pushed. Nothing happened. I rammed my shoulder into the grate. It still didn't move. I sagged against the door barring my exit.

I closed my eyes. Harley thought of himself as an engineering marvel. He hunted here. He had to be able to close himself away from the rest of the world and still get himself out.

I ran my hands around the edge of the cage door and up and down the interior. I stopped each time my fingers located a bump, a nodule, an indentation, or anything I could press, flip, pull, or turn, hunting for a secret release. The green light of the aging glow stick faded, but the moon had reappeared.

Just before completing the sweep of the interior, my forefinger slid into a depression in one of the tree roots. I pushed and a button popped out the other side. I twisted it through three hundred sixty degrees and nothing happened. I slowed the rotation, turning in tiny increments, and at the same time yanked on the knob. After a few attempts, I felt a slight give, so I closed my eyes and counted to three before the next attempt.

CHAPTER FORTY-SIX

The click ricocheted in the silent space. I pulled and shoved and put my shoulder to the door. It slid up and out of the way with the whoosh of Ida's manual garage door. I scrambled out of the hole to a wildly happy dog. If I could have, I would have wagged my tail too, but instead I knelt and hugged Maverick until his slobbery kisses froze on my face.

Then I remembered CJ's instructions—your dog may be stressed if he licks his lips, shakes like he's wet, or yawns. "You knew there was trouble, didn't you? Thank you," I whispered and opened the bottle of water. I took a long swig, then poured some into my cupped hand for Maverick to lap up. "Let's go get him, boy!"

But first we'd have to find our way out. No longer able

to access my waypoint directions, I hobbled after Maverick through the brambles and branches, bushwhacking to an empty parking lot. Why was I not surprised!

"Let's go, my friend." We followed the road, frosted with moonlight.

My dad's old adage—cold hands, warm heart—didn't make me feel any better. Even though I juggled the weakening hand warmer back and forth, my teeth chattered, and I stumbled on numb feet. The cold air snaked under my hood and around my neck and ears and I snuffled, but Maverick trudged forward. We plodded on until the hazy golden glow of a yard light came into view and we picked up the pace down a long driveway.

My appreciation for the pristine farm buildings waned when I heard cows mooing and snorting and swishing in answer to my call. With only hours to the start of our competition, I just couldn't seem to catch a break.

Maverick barked, then he jumped at my face with a tongue lashing. "I'm sorry, boy," I agonized.

Maverick continued his antics until I too heard the truck rumble down the gravel road. The headlights cleaved the early morning dark and I waved.

The truck slammed into park next to the barn and the driver jumped from the cab. "What the hell are you doing out here? Ms. Wilk? Is that you?"

"Ransam?"

I quickly filled him in, and the incredulous look on his face almost made me think I'd imagined everything until I got to Ian's, or Harley's, veiled threat against Debora, and Ransam bolted to his truck.

"They released her on bond to be able to watch the mock trial today. Let me call my backup. Our cows have a very rigid milking schedule," he said, his phone to his ear.

"Go. Go!"

Within seconds, Ransam, Maverick, and I were in his truck sailing toward Columbia. He tossed me his phone after he'd tried to call Debora several times and couldn't get through. I tried Kindra, but she didn't answer either. Checking the time, I smacked my head. Mossa's team was already on his coach bus, riding in style, and if he saw her answering her phone, he'd confiscate it. I thought about texting Jane, but Harley could be sitting next to her. My finger hovered over another number.

This is Ms. Wilk. Are you on the bus?

Yes. Y RU using RGs phone.

Is Mr. Brown with you?

No. We couldn't wait 4 either of U.

The phone rang in my hand from Patricia's number.

"Where are you, Katie?" Jane cried.

"It's a long story, but Jane, Harley is not who he says he is."

"Have you lost your mind?"

"When you couldn't join us last night—"

"Join you for what?" She sounded truly puzzled. Another lie.

"He left me to freeze to death, Jane."

I could almost hear the wheels churning. "What do you want me to do?"

"I've got spotty cell coverage. Can you call Ronnie Christianson? Tell him … tell him Harley Brown is an alias and he's really—" The truck hit a pothole and the phone flew out of my hand. I released the seatbelt and clambered to the rear of the cab, upending papers, used coffee cups, tools, and a host of agricultural paraphernalia.

Ransam caught my unnerved look as I tumbled into

the front seat, holding his phone with a cracked screen.

"Where're we going?" he asked with a fierce determination.

I thought for a moment and said, "Little Falls." Ransam's face hardened. He skidded and pulled a U-turn. The truck charged ahead. "The first trial is scheduled for nine. He'll try to be there." The truck surged and I clung to the seatbelt.

Too soon, we slowed to a crawl, encountering a caravan of semis hauling livestock. Ransam pounded on the steering wheel, honking his horn and passing as soon as he was able. The trees and grass and fields and farms blurred and we completed the eighty-mile trek in just over an hour.

I'd visited Lindbergh State Park and the childhood home of Charles Lindbergh as a kid but my limited recollection of the location of the courthouse frustrated Ransam. We scoured the low-rise skyline for taller buildings and beat a path to a cream-colored brick clocktower.

Ransam cranked the wheel and parked with his backend hanging out between two school buses.

"Stay, Maverick," I said. We sprinted through the double doors.

After we passed through the metal detector and entered the atrium, I grabbed Ransam's arm, stunned, fearing for the safety of so many students, teachers, parents, and enthusiasts milling about. I didn't know what Harley would do. I followed Ransam's finger pointing up the wide staircase.

Stanley Mossa looked over the railing from the second floor and scowled. When I caught his eye, the scowl turned to a sneer, and he herded his students away from view.

We skirted the line and Ransam bounded up the stairs after them, calling for Kindra. I searched the faces and saw Debora marching down an alternate hall. I trailed her through a narrow doorway.

She strode up behind a tall man, and poked his shoulder. "You son of a—" He turned slowly, with a look of calm understanding. "Oh! I'm sorry. I- I thought you were someone else."

I didn't duck fast enough. Harley saw me and grasped the closest arm, dragging Patricia after him. Debora cried out a warning as her original instincts were confirmed, nearly drowning out the wailing sirens.

The narrow corridor funneled the sounds away from me—thudding, a crash, and a scream. I peered around the corner as Patricia disappeared through a shattered door. I raced after them.

Picking my way through the splintered wood, I followed the pounding footsteps. Full light from the large glass panes cast darting shadows as I crept up the clock tower stairs.

Struggling grunts and painstaking footfalls continued until the commotion grew below me, echoing off the walls, and I could no longer differentiate those sounds from Harley and Patricia. I quaked, thinking about what he'd do when cornered.

"Harley?" I gripped the handrail and tiptoed onto the last landing. "Harley, let her go."

Patricia cried out.

Working with law enforcement, Charles and I had learned some of the rules of engagement: talk, use his name, use her name. "Harley, she's done nothing to you. Let Patricia go," I called out, marshalling what little bravery I could. Each tentative step took me closer to the top and my heart pounded in my ears. I covered my head with my arm as I breeched the rectangular trapdoor at the top into the outside world.

Harley gripped Patricia's shoulders. He yelled and she cowered, looking away.

The arctic wind whistled through the open archways. He hadn't heard me, but when Patricia saw me and recognition dawned, some of her fear fell away and Harley knew he wasn't alone. He wrenched her around to use as a shield.

"You," he roared over the wind. I stepped onto the landing and he shook his head.

"Let Patricia go, Harley."

"She's my ticket out of here."

"You don't really want to use her that way."

He scoffed as he pulled her closer. I glanced over the ledge. It was a long way down and I never liked heights. I turned and caught trust in Patricia's eyes. She was ready. For what?

"You know, I was a goner, Harley, but I had help getting out of your treehouse."

He cocked his head.

"You were right. We shouldn't have brought the dog," I said.

He smirked. I edged closer and he yanked Patricia.

"Stay where you are."

Keep him talking. "Your hunting blind trap was brilliant but I watched Natasha's review, and I knew the cryptex held a key to the lock that came with it. She gave away the premiere code, which still worked, by the way."

His eyes glittered with fury. "I fastened the lock out of reach."

"Not for Maverick."

Goosebumps crawled up my neck when he cackled.

I didn't know if it would work but I motioned to Patricia. She lifted her chin and fierce determination billowed off her. Harley should have trembled. Then I gave her the signs for three, two, and one. I hoped Father Steve taught me correctly.

Patricia relaxed and Harley lunged to get better control on her limp figure. Then she reared up and knocked the back of her head into Harley's face. He cried out. She stomped on his instep, turned, kicked at his groin, and broke free. As she ran into my arms, Harley rose and bellowed like a bear. She tripped and we fell. He took two long strides toward us but was blocked when a black streak exploded through the opening, standing on four paws, hackles raised, teeth bared, snarling and barking. Maverick!

Ronnie appeared, panting, his face full of questions. Maverick backed off. The nasty snarl lessened to a menacing growl.

"That dog attacked me," Harley said in a rush.

Who did he think would believe that! Panicked, I studied Ronnie's reaction. "He's lying."

"I was just trying to make amends with my daughter—I haven't seen her in years." His hand beckoned Patricia. "I gotcha. Come here."

She buried her head in my shoulder.

"He's really Ian Halloran," I said, running my hand over her head.

Ronnie squinted and answered, "I guess you can call yourself anything you want these days."

Patricia shuddered and mewled quietly into my shoulder.

"Is she all right?" Ronnie asked.

"She will be. Her mom is here," I whispered.

"We know." His partner, Jake, popped his head through the opening.

"Harley might've been seen arguing with Sophie Grainger the day before she died."

"Is that so?" Ronnie said, his attention riveted on Harley.

"You idiot, you're a witness! You know exactly where I was at the time Sophie died," Harley exclaimed vehemently. "Traffic court."

Ronnie relaxed.

"He used a remote starter," I said.

Ronnie's face registered understanding and he bristled. "Ian Halloran slash Harley Brown, you're under arrest for the alleged abduction of a minor and you're considered a person of interest in the murder of Sophie Grainger. Anything you say…"

Before he finished speaking, Harley lunged at Patricia and me. Jake tackled him, and threw him to the floor where Officer Christianson snapped on handcuffs. Jake glanced at me, a smile on his face. Then they dragged Harley down the stairs.

I hugged Patricia and lifted her face so she could read my lips. "Are you all right?"

She nodded.

I hugged her again and we followed Maverick as he raced down the steps. Debora, Ransam, and Kindra waited on the first landing. They grabbed Patricia and covered her in kisses.

"She was great! She kicked Harley's…" My face reddened. I probably shouldn't be quite so happy.

Debora cradled Patricia's jaw, looking into her eyes.

"I'm so sorry, honey. Let's go home."

"But I want to compete," she said.

Jane rushed up the stairs and wrapped her arms around me. "I can't wait to hear about it, but right now, our kids are worried and chomping at the bit. They're delaying the event for an hour but we have to get down there or they'll disqualify us, and Katie, we really have a shot at this."

The rest of the morning passed in a flurry. Our team put on a brave front after having watched their coach being hauled away in shackles, and, surprisingly, exuded more confidence than in any other head-to-head round. Jane organized and cheered, cajoled and explained, filled out the paperwork, and provided healthy snacks while I attempted to put one foot in front of the other and not topple over. Exhausted as I was, I couldn't help thinking about possible alternate outcomes unrelated to our mock trial.

We had a few minor hiccups, but who wouldn't. Once the kids got rolling, they seemed to drag Jane and me along for the ride. When we completed the round, the students awaited results in the largest courtroom. Their supporters lined the walls and filled the atrium. A bubble of teammates protected Patricia from prying eyes, but her look of discomfort faded when Kindra broke away from Mossa's team and joined her.

Once our host caught the attention of his audience, the microphone crackled over the speaker system, and he explained the rules, restating the objectives of the co-curricular activity. Before the natives got restless again, he held aloft the pages with the results, naming the top four competitors who would be going on to the semifinals.

Mentioned first, although supposedly not reflecting rank, Stanley Mossa gloated as he marched to the podium to collect his team's evaluations.

The host announced three more teams and, except for Lorelei, who gnawed on her nails, our students acted fairly nonchalant until they heard the last team name; Team EsqChoir made the semifinals and their excitement exploded. Kindra hugged Patricia whose smile reached from ear to ear. Even Oscar clapped. Mossa's gloat soured.

We congregated in our assigned room.

"Spill," said Jane. Our team earned what few answers I could give. I finished my story while petting Maverick. "Ransam hadn't locked the doors of his truck and a rebellious animal lover released Maverick before he could tear up the interior of the cab. Jane said no one could stop him once he'd entered the building. Harley never knew what hit him."

"Yes!" Galen cheered. "I knew it."

CHAPTER FORTY-SEVEN

Jane's phone beeped from a blocked caller. She read, "Review ALL rules."

"What does it mean?"

Jane plopped into a chair and opened the mock trial file. "Let's get to work."

She finally read, "All semifinal and final teams must supply a licensed attorney to serve as a referee or be summarily disqualified." Jane stared at me with huge, round eyes. "They'll make an exception, won't they?"

I stared back. "Mossa won't let them."

"What'll we do?"

I felt the tension at my back and turned to find all eyes glued on me. I rotated in the seat and knelt. "Hey, gang. Ms. Mackey found a rule that requires we have an attorney with us."

Their rumble was justified.

"But we'll figure it out." I turned back and found Jane jabbing frantically at her phone.

"Dorene?" Jane said and told her what we'd need. When she hung up, she shrugged and said, "She'll do the best she can."

We all trudged to the welcome table, easing through the metal detector. The patient greeter listened to our story and replied, "We got a call this morning from one of the other teams and we're going to have to hold you to providing an attorney/judge. You have…" She glanced at her watch. "You have forty-five minutes."

We drew our team positions and Jane and I split up into our assigned rooms. The clock ticked by. After fifteen minutes, I drew a deep breath and said to my students, "You deserve better."

Lorelei and Patricia hugged. Brock shuffled his feet. I marched out and ran into Mossa. "Heard about your difficulty. Too bad. We wanted to take you to the cleaners." I recoiled as I skirted past.

Fifteen more minutes passed and the greeter gave a hopeful smile. I shook my head. She pulled a page from the bottom of her pile, grabbed a pen, and set them in front of me as a very well put-together blonde strode to the table. She shrugged out of her long down coat and draped it over her arm. Then, she tugged at her navy-blue suit jacket and announced, "Shauna Eileen Kennedy, Team EsqChoir, reporting for duty."

The greeter smiled broadly and placed a folder on top of the growing pile in her arms. Ms. Kennedy whispered, "Dorene sent me."

The trial flew by. I beamed with pride; both our defense

and plaintiff teams ramped up their performances. Team EsqChoir could be selected for the finals.

During the break, Jane and I hunted down Ms. Kennedy.

"Thank you so much for being here, Ms. Kennedy," I said, sliding into the chair at her table.

"Shauna," she insisted. "It's been great. When I was in law school, I coached a high school team and this brings back good memories. By the way, you should hear the rave reviews your kids are getting. You've done well."

I reddened, thinking about how much misplaced faith we'd put in Harley.

"I heard about your coach," she said, laying her hand on my sleeve. Her briefcase buzzed. "Excuse me." She opened it, retrieved her phone, and stepped away from the table.

"We owe Dorene big time," Jane said. "We couldn't have done it without her."

Shauna returned to our table frowning. "I'm so sorry. My boss called and I have a client I have to meet with immediately. I can't stay."

"We probably won't make it anyway." Jane sighed, then she wrinkled her nose. At the end of her gaze stood Mossa in the doorway, looking pleased with himself. He saluted before leaving the room just as the gong sounded, calling us to the atrium for results.

Our kids had already heard from Oscar that our new attorney had to leave. *Wonder how that happened,* I fumed. Somehow, Mossa had undermined us at every opportunity. And sure enough, our scores pitted us against his team in the finals, but the third-place Little Falls team was asked to remain, because, lo and behold, they'd also heard our attorney was called away. We were given until three fifty-five to secure new representation.

Dejected, our students paced, marking time until our departure.

At three thirty, a hand waved at me through the crowd. Ida brushed snow from her bright red hair and barreled through the metal detector. Dad followed.

"You shouldn't have come—"

Ida's hand fluttered. "We know all about it. Hang in there."

At three forty, Mossa crossed to the welcome table where it seemed his request was denied. He returned to a chair near his team, sat, and crossed his legs, dangling his Gucci-clad foot.

At three forty-seven the doors flew open and Dorene Dvorak marched in, shaking hands with the host. The entire space erupted in applause and I took a breath not realizing I'd been holding it.

We were in.

The team with the higher overall score got to choose which side they'd like to present. Mossa opted for defense, pitting Oscar against Patricia.

"Let them try to do their worst," Patricia said, defiantly, emphasizing each word with a sign.

My students gawked at the formal surroundings as the officer led us through the venerable building to the main courtroom. They stared with reverence at the judge's desk, the rich warm wainscoting, the jury box, the witness stand, the gallery, and the colorful pattern fashioned on the defense table by the sun streaming through the glass windows. Onlookers and supporters filled every seat. Maverick curled around my feet. Debora, Ransam, Dad, and Ida sat next to Jane and me, right behind the plaintiff table, and that was fortuitous.

When Oscar began his cross-examination, he initially allowed Patricia to read his lips, but all too soon, he periodically looked down to read from notes he knew by heart, or he circled the table cutting off the view of his lips, waiting for her misstep. Incredibly, Patricia never dropped the ball, never missed a beat. Oscar noticed Debora's hands moving at the same time I did, and stepped into the line of translation as he asked the next question. He turned and gave Debora a look of pity. He smirked and glanced up behind her, and his predatory façade melted.

Oscar turned back to Patricia and plied her with a carefully articulated question. I looked over my shoulder. Westin leaned against the doorjamb, grinning. Both teams performed the remainder of the case like seasoned professionals and Lorelei gave her best-ever closing statement.

The student-jury found for the defense.

Dorene gave me a thumbs up. Jane grabbed my hand.

In my book, the teams tied. These high school students rivaled the best court scenes television law could provide.

The judges retired to deliberate. No one spoke. The tick of the antique clock seemed to slow.

Somewhere a door slammed.

The building seemed to breathe.

When the door to the judges' chamber opened, the panel of judges filed out and they took their places on the bench. The head judge shuffled some pages, adjusted her bifocals, and announced, "Unfortunately, we have a disqualification." A murmur started. Her gavel struck the plate. "Order, please." The crowd quieted immediately and she said, "The team taking second place is Writ Ten." My heart sank and Jane moaned. Mossa somehow nailed us anyway. She continued, "And the golden gavel for first-place goes to EsqChoir."

Mossa stormed out of the courtroom.

Our orderly, quiet, and reserved students blew the roof off the building as soon as the trophy landed in Patricia's hands. Hugs and handshakes went around the room. Ida grabbed my cheeks, bussing them. Dad whooped. Maverick looked from one of us to another. Jane laughed.

Westin approached reticently. He extended his hand. I shook it and he asked, "You haven't seen Oscar, have you?"

"Not since—"

Kindra dashed into the mix, holding a leather jacket. "Oscar's gone."

CHAPTER FORTY-EIGHT

Westin heard. "Gone where? Why?"

Kindra looked sheepish. "Most of us didn't know but, for years, Mr. Mossa's been getting the cases weeks ahead of time. And he has copies of the scoring rubrics. Oscar reported our team's irregularities to the judges, and now he's missing."

"We have to find him." Westin grabbed the jacket.

Maverick and I raced after Westin.

"He's not as tough as he pretends." The words came in spasms as Westin craned his neck, looking.

"Where would he go?"

Westin stopped in his tracks. "His dad drowned. We have to find him."

We ran, Maverick bounding ahead, and when we

crossed First Street, the Mississippi River water thundered from the dam three blocks away, drawing Westin.

Maverick veered south.

"Westin!" I bellowed, and we both turned to follow my dog.

Fat white flakes frosted the James Green Park sign, the frozen ground, the evergreen trees, the wooden benches, the marquee, and the two figures on the foot bridge. Maverick sat, guarding Oscar, accepting the gentle petting. Westin bent at the waist, hands on his knees, gasping. As his intake slowed, he stood, inhaled, and walked onto the bridge.

Oscar accepted the jacket Westin offered, and then collapsed into his arms. Westin reacted slowly, and then crushed him fiercely. I heard him over Oscar's sobs. "My boy, my boy."

"Here, Maverick," I cued, and we walked down the path toward the landing overlooking the raging waters of the dam. When Westin and Oscar joined us, Oscar said, "Everyone'll hate me," and added, tentatively, "Dad."

"Actually," Westin said wisely, "they'll hate themselves but you'll take flak for their discomfort. They all got taken in." Oscar nodded. "I'll give you a ride home."

Oscar searched Westin's eyes. "I think I'd rather face the music now."

We walked back to the courthouse, Oscar and Westin trailing. When we were near enough, Brock and Galen began a slow clapping, and, little-by-little, other hands added to the din until everyone, the attorney judges, the greeters, the students, the custodial staff, the parents, and even Oscar's teammates, cheered.

Jane sidled to me. She stuck two fingers in her mouth and an ear-splitting whistle shrieked from her tiny frame.

Maverick wagged proudly.

"The head judge said we won without Oscar's admission," Jane said.

Reveling in our victory, taking photos, and making phone calls, ours was the last bus to leave the courthouse, exiting the town through a sprinkling of multicolored Christmas lights popping on. Amid the happy energy on the bus, Jane said, "You've got to explain everything all over again."

Jane's arm hung over my shoulder the rest of the way to Columbia.

* * *

I thought the cars filling the lot belonged to the fans of our basketball team playing in the gym until the occupants spilled out and surrounded our bus, four and five deep, waving pompoms and banners and hooting. I choked up. Maverick, Ida, and Dad led the procession. Red and green lights blinked from Drew's crutches. Westin had his arm around Oscar. Parents and students cheered; Kindra and Debora yelled the loudest. CJ and his perfect puppy stood rigidly, fatherly pride scratching at the surface. I got a nod from Mr. Ganka who stood behind the crowd next to a jubilant Mrs. McEntee. Pete Erickson winked, but never quite smiled.

The hint of a melody and the words of my favorite holiday song drifted like snowflakes. The treetops, the sidewalks, the car hoods, and the bushes in the landscaping glistened, reflecting pinpoints of starlight and we listened for those sleigh bells in the snow. We'd have a white Christmas.

The tune in my head stopped abruptly when Susie slid her arm into Pete's and flashed her glittering left hand. My heart sank. Even from this distance I couldn't miss the scintillation on her ring finger.

Ida stepped into my line of sight and applauded with more enthusiasm. Maverick added a bark, and Jane raised my arm in victory. I surveyed my growing family and smiled.

Then I caught movement beyond the group. At the far end of the parking lot sat a rider astride a bike equipped with fat-tires for cycling through snow. He raised his right hand and pointed two fingers at his visor and then aimed his fingers at me. I had to figure out what I had seen and stop the harassment, but that would have to happen another day.

SMOKY DON LOCKWOOD

1 oz bourbon

1 oz scotch

2 tsp maple syrup

1 dash Angostura bitters

2 dashes chocolate bitters

Dash of orange juice

Garnish with an orange peel and use a cocktail smoker.

* * *

What's next for Katie and Maverick?

The biggest fundraiser in town turns into a battleground between two rival senior citizens. After 40 years of not speaking, Grace Loehr and Ida Clemashevski have buried the hatchet. But when they both bid on the same unusual art piece at the Holiday Gala, the claws come out again. The temperamental artist is murdered, and the suspects abound, but then Grace is found dead. Are the deaths related? Katie Wilk is four months into a new job teaching high school math when her landlady is arrested for the crimes, but the only way to show proof of her innocence is to find the guilty party and it doesn't look good.

Watch for Book 4 in this acclaimed series, coming soon!

* * *

Thank you for taking the time to read *Tinsel, Trials, & Traitors*. If you enjoyed it please tell your friends, and I would be so grateful if you would consider posting a review. Word of mouth is an author's best friend, and very much appreciated. Thank you,

Mary Seifert

**Get a collection of free recipes from Mary—
Visit her website to find out how!**
MarySeifertAuthor.com/
Facebook: facebook.com/MarySeifertAuthor
Twitter: twitter.com/mary_seifert
Instagram: instagram.com/maryseifert/
Follow Mary on BookBub and Goodreads too!

Made in the USA
Columbia, SC
24 July 2022